The Poltergeist's Ship
Afterlife Calls

K.C.Adams

Copyright © 2024 K.C. Adams

All rights reserved.

This book or any part of it must not be reproduced or used in anyway without written permission of the publisher, except for brief quotations used in a book review.

First published in 2024.

Cover design by 100 Covers.

1
Edie

Exam results day. The day every teenager dreads.

Two years of studying had taken me to the college steps. Momentum kept me walking. I didn't want to know what my results were. If I didn't know, I couldn't fail.

I had no idea if I'd failed or not, but I was terrified that I had. While I'd really tried during exam season, concentration and retention hadn't been my friends. I'd been finding it hard to remember things lately but I was too afraid to tell Mum, or college, or anyone else. What if they thought something was wrong with me?

I walked into the big, personality-lacking hall where my peers were collecting their results. The sun glared through the windows, as if shining a light on those who'd done well and shaming those who hadn't.

I was acting like I'd already failed even though my results weren't in my hands yet. Hope for the best, expect the worst, right?

A few people looked up as I entered the room, but when they saw it was just me, they returned to their conversations. Some people were smiling and giggling, while others were in the corner, crying. Which group would I be in?

I pulled the sleeves of my hoody over my hands and wrapped my arms around myself.

Tessa's friends, Melanie and Laura, were standing just to the left of the door with Josh. Melanie caught my eye and smiled.

It had been eight months' since Tessa's death, but sometimes, it still felt like there was a hole in the room where she should've been. She was so loud, so well-known, it was a hard space to fill even for those of us who disliked her.

My hands shaking, I went to the desk, gave the receptionist my name, and collected my envelope.

Everyone else was there with friends. I didn't have any. It was just me. Ever since Dominic had betrayed me.

Melanie and Laura were civil to me, but I didn't class them as friends. This wasn't a moment I was comfortable sharing with them.

Josh must've noticed me looking over. He met my eye and nodded. I nodded back then averted my gaze. His expression was unreadable, so I had no idea if he'd gotten the results he'd wanted or even opened his envelope yet.

We were talking civilly and had been for a few months, but things were still awkward between us. Sometimes I'd see Josh look at me like he used to, other times he couldn't look at me at all, or had a quizzical expression. He'd said the demons that had tortured him had made him question reality, so I figured that was why. I wished I could help him but I was worried anything I did would make things worse, so I just had to give him time.

The Poltergeist's Ship

Even though I hadn't wanted to, my parents and college had made me apply to a couple of universities. It would keep my options open, they said. Not if I didn't get the grades to get in, it wouldn't.

The walls in the open, spacious hall seemed to be closing in on me. The laughter of everyone around me sounded more menacing than any ghost or demon or necromancer I'd dealt with. They made Goodfellow seem positively tame.

My heart pounded so hard I felt like I was cycling through Sherwood Forest.

I had to open the stupid envelope and get the waiting over with or I'd just feel worse. So, with shaking, sweaty hands, I did.

My heart fell. Barely even a pass. In any subject. There was no way I was getting into any university with those grades.

Tears pooled in my eyes. I looked over at Josh again. He was smiling. He must've gotten the grades he needed. How I felt must've been obvious, because he gave me a weak smile. I turned away and headed for the door.

Mrs Mitchell, my English teacher, noticed me as I was leaving. 'Edie, have you got a minute?'

Practically hyperventilating, I begrudgingly stopped. It was a good job I hadn't applied much make-up as I wasn't sure how long it would've lasted.

'Are you all right?' Teachers saw the grades before we did. She knew how badly I'd done.

I pursed my lips, unable to think of something to say that wasn't rude or sarcastic.

'Your coursework was fine, it was just the exams that let you down. You can always resit them in January.'

I flapped my arms in the air. '*January*? That's ages away!'

'It gives you time to go back over each course really get your head around them. I'd be happy to help if you like.'

Great. I was a pity case.

'Thanks. Could you excuse me, please?'

'You know where to find me when you're ready.' She made it sound like she already knew that I was going to ask for her help and resit the exams. How did she know that? She didn't know me.

What was the point, anyway? I didn't need them to help Mum in the family business. I could be her apprentice regardless. Why waste my time and energy studying something I was clearly terrible at? Why prove that I was a failure at studying as well as my social life and necromancy?

Even if I did go to university, I'd never get to experience normal student life. I'd seen ghosts everywhere. And none of them would know me, which meant I'd have to explain myself again. And again. And again.

At least in my hometown the ghosts knew us so they knew when to approach and when not to. And we didn't have to explain anything.

If I studied somewhere too far away, I might end up surrounded by ghosts who didn't get it or wouldn't listen. Then what would I tell my new friends?

I was better off not going to uni.

But then, why did my grades bother me so much?

The Poltergeist's Ship

When I finally got out into the searing summer sun, my power walk turned into a run.

2

Niamh

Going on a cruise had always been on my bucket list. Edie and I had booked the tickets before I'd met Ben and everything had gone crazy.

Since Tessa crossed over eight months ago, things had been quiet, which I was grateful for. It had given Edie time to focus on her studies, although results day was still anxiety-inducing. I tried not to pressure her but I was panicking too. And that panic was hard to conceal.

But she liked to process things alone, the same as Javi and me, so I was really trying to respect that as she worked out what to do next.

She'd applied to a couple of unis to appease Javi, her college tutors, and me, but she didn't want to go. Not anymore. She wanted to stay and be my apprentice, insisting she could learn about both my trades – handiwork and ghost hunting. That meant I'd have to pay her, but then, I technically paid her anyway, just without the tax breaks. So why not?

Spectre watched from his spot on top of my wardrobe as I folded some more clothes and put them into my purple suitcase. He knew something was off, he just couldn't work out what. Tilly was watching me

The Poltergeist's Ship

from her spot beside my suitcase. Her brown eyes glared at me with typical westitude.

I felt bad leaving them for a week, but Ben and Fadil had promised they'd pop in to see how Spectre was even though he didn't need feeding because he was a ghost cat. Being a ghost cat also meant most people couldn't see him and he couldn't leave the house. It didn't mean he didn't get lonely.

We still didn't know anything about his past, and it wasn't like he could tell us, so we did our best to make him comfortable. He'd warmed to Edie and often snuggled up against her as she was the only person who could touch him. I wasn't sure if he could feel how warm she was or any of that, but they seemed to find each other's presences comforting and that was all that mattered.

Tilly was going to stay with Ben and Fadil for a week, which I knew she'd love. She'd probably also gain half her body weight in dog treats, but so long as they looked after her and she was happy, that was all I cared about.

The front door slammed. I jumped.

Edie thundered up the stairs, catapulting herself into her bedroom. Fiddlesticks.

She hadn't said anything to me, Tilly, or Spectre. All those things combined were very bad signs.

Tentatively, I went into the hallway. Spectre floated in, watching. Tilly pawed her bedroom door. I knocked on it. 'Edie?'

She snivelled. 'Not right now, Mum. Please.'

I sighed, wiping a tear from my eye. I hated her being in pain, but I couldn't change it. She had to open up to me when she was ready. 'All right, I'll walk Tilly.'

She didn't reply, but I figured she wouldn't complain as she clearly wanted to be alone. Spectre walked out of my room and stared at me.

I picked up Tilly, then jerked my head in the direction of Edie's room. Spectre studied me for a moment, then walked through the wall to his favourite person.

*

An hour later, when Tilly and I got home from our walk, Edie was in the kitchen, listening to music through her headphones and perusing the cupboards. Spectre rubbed himself against her legs. I doubted it made much of a difference with him being a ghost, but old habits and all that.

Edie picked out a chocolate bar, then turned around, jumping when she saw us. Spectre stopped following her and walked over to Tilly. She paused her music. 'Sorry.'

'It's OK,' I said, unfastening Tilly's lead. She and Spectre ran off to chase each other around the house.

Sighing, Edie sat at the table and dug into her chocolate bar. Instead of prompting her to talk, I remembered my old parenting books and waited for her to speak first, occupying myself by washing up. It ate at me, not saying anything. But I knew that if I asked her about it, she could shut down even more.

The Poltergeist's Ship

I filled the sink with water and pulled on my rubber gloves. The running water was the only sound to break up the tension as I waited for Edie to speak. After scrubbing dried-on cereal from a bowl, I slammed it onto the drying rack. Maybe I shouldn't take my tension out on the crockery. It was expensive to replace.

'I failed, Mum.' She pushed the envelope with her printed results over to me.

I removed my washing up gloves and took the papers out. They weren't even close to what she'd been predicted, but they weren't as bad as she was making out, either. 'That's not failure.'

She lowered her headphones and let them hang around her neck. 'It won't get me into uni, either.'

'I thought you didn't want to go.'

'I don't, necessarily. But everyone goes on and on about getting great grades, and look at me!' She waved her arms – and the half-eaten chocolate bar – in the air. 'All the teachers told me how great I'd do and I didn't even come close.'

I pulled out the chair opposite her and sat down. She was being so hard on herself and it wasn't her fault. 'School isn't always the best marker of intelligence. Plenty of people who get good grades never do anything with them.'

'And those who get bad grades?'

'They can see them as a marker of their permanent and unchangeable intelligence, or they can use them as motivation to better themselves, whether that's via resitting exams or going on to do something else.'

Edie stared into her lap. 'I just don't know if I'm ready for that.'

I reached over the table and squeezed her hand. 'You've been through a lot. You saved the town from two murderous psychopaths just a few weeks apart. Having to process that on top of revision is hard. Most people couldn't manage that. You don't give yourself nearly enough credit. And at least you have the cruise to look forwards to.'

Edie flinched.

'What?'

She squirmed in her seat. What else? 'I just...I don't know if I can do it. Not now. All those people floating around for a week? All that noise and stimulation? It was meant to be a way to celebrate, not commiserate.'

'It might cheer you up,' I suggested. I hoped. The tickets had been booked for over a year. There was no way we could cancel them now.

She pursed her lips. 'I'm not sure anything will right now. I just need time.'

'It might give you some time to relax,' I said, trying to win her over but having a sinking feeling her mind was made up.

'Why don't you go with Ben instead?'

'And leave you on your own for a week? When you're this upset?'

She'd never been on her own overnight before, let alone for a week. How would she cope? How would *I* cope?

She sighed, resting her elbows on the table and her head in her hands. 'I kind of think it's what I need.

The Poltergeist's Ship

Don't you think I'm old enough? That I can handle myself?'

No. No I did not. Not because I didn't trust her, but because I didn't trust anyone else.

'Maggie and Fadil would still be around. It's not like I'd be completely alone.'

I tapped my fingers against the kitchen side. Maggie had always taken good care of Edie, and I knew Fadil would do what he could for her even though he hadn't been feeling well himself lately.

It wasn't the same as me being there, but Maggie was basically Edie's second mum. And she was far more responsible than me most of the time. She'd even handled being tortured by a demon better than anyone could've imagined, tackling therapy with an openness and honesty that few people did. I swear she'd come out even stronger than before. My best friend was a truly incredible person.

'You and Ben have never been on holiday together before, and after everything you've been through, you've earned it,' said Edie.

I eyed her warily. She was laying it on a bit thick. 'Ben might be too busy setting up the bookshop. With the opening next month he's still got a lot to do.'

'But I could help with all that. Do the stuff that he doesn't enjoy or some of the stuff you've been teaching me to do. Painting the walls; building furniture; putting books on the shelves. How hard could it be?'

I squirmed, feeling a bit like she was dumbing down what Ben *and* I did.

'I could finish the website and get the online orders ready to go for him.'

She seemed to think she could cram a lot into a week, but she was also more enthusiastic about this than the cruise. I didn't want to break her spirit. Any more than it was already broken by her exam results. I at least had to let her run with this and see where it went.

'All right. See what Ben says. And check if Maggie can help you, too. She might be too busy with Abigail given it's the summer holidays.' Maybe one of them would have a reason to say no, because I sure didn't.

Edie jumped out of her chair and hugged me. 'That's perfect! I can help babysit, too!'

She and Abigail did get along well. Maybe Abigail's childhood naivety and confidence would give Edie the mood boost she needed.

It was the most excited I'd seen her in weeks, if not months. Maybe leaving her on her own wouldn't be so bad after all. Could it be exactly what she needed?

3
Edie

'Hey Ben, how's it going?' I said as I walked into his shop. Even though it'd been months since he'd put in his offer, there'd been so many hold ups with paperwork and building work, it still wasn't open.

It was so, so close, though.

His goal was to open it mid-to-late September, as everyone went back to school, college, and university. It was right on the high street, near the local college, making it the perfect place to get student and parent footfall.

To lure people in, he was going to offer an opening sale on textbooks. Hopefully they'd then stay to buy another book and some coffee. And tell all their friends about how great Ben's Books was.

Fingers crossed it worked. He deserved success.

He also deserved a holiday.

Mum had barely seen him lately, except on the days when she was helping him with the bookshop. If he wasn't redecorating, he was ordering inventory, or assembling flat-pack furniture, or treating yet another problem that'd come up with the bookshop. It seemed like every other day he had another plaster on his hand from yet another paper cut or DIY accident.

Ben walked in from the back room, which he'd been painting. That was going to be the stock room.

And the room where ghosts hung out. It sort of already was. Some of the ghosts had been scaring residents near their previous haunt because they were bored. This was the perfect alternative. There was more going on in town. They were also regularly around people who could see them and therefore able to help them if they needed it.

A few ghosts poked their heads out behind Ben. When they saw it was me, they smiled and waved.

Gwendoline, a nineteen-year-old from the collapsed mine, had become the authority figure. She kept everyone in check and helped them adjust to the afterlife. She was a patient, matriarchal figure whom everyone loved. And her experience as a witch was always useful.

The newest ghost was a blonde guy called Shane. He was in his early thirties and had died in a bike accident before he could propose to his girlfriend and change his workaholic ways. He was conflicted between wanting the closure of talking to her and the terror of confronting failures he could no longer make up for.

Whenever he seemed close to talking to her, he'd change his mind and find a way to make himself useful to us, such as discussing paint colours or running paranormal errands.

I didn't know the rest of the ghosts by name yet, but I was always nice to them. They'd been through a lot. Most of them had tragic pasts. It never hurt to show them a little kindness. Maybe my kindness would mean one less ghost turning into a poltergeist because of how much they hated the world.

I waved back, then they floated around the empty, half-decorated bookshop, mumbling about Ben's choice of colours, which were laid out on a spot on the back wall. Some liked the green and walnut colour scheme, like Gwendoline, while others like Shane found it too dark and thought Ben should've gone with white. Ew. I didn't necessarily like the green either, but white was so boring.

Ben ignored their discussion and walked over to me. He wiped his hands on his formerly white overalls then pushed his glasses up his nose. 'Hey Edie, how's it going?'

'You know,' I shrugged, perching on a stool beside a table opposite the front door. It was one of the first things Ben had put up so that we had a makeshift desk. The plan was to replace it with a couple of counters where we could put the till, a laptop, and the coffee machine. For now, the coffee machine rested on another small table with a fridge underneath it.

'Results bothering you?' he asked.

'Did Mum tell you?'

Had she been talking about me behind my back? Did that bother me, since they'd been together almost a year? It wasn't like he'd ever replace Dad, but I did like him with Mum...

'No. It's written all over your face.'

Oh.

I slouched on the stool. It was hard not to hide my disappointment. I could've done better. I *should've* done better. Everything that'd happened wasn't an excuse.

'If I was really that intelligent, wouldn't I have been able to do well in my exams regardless of everything that's happened?' I swung my legs, staring at them as they moved back and forth.

Ben leaned against the wall beside me. 'If only it were that simple. Trauma can impact memory, concentration, motivation.'

'Trauma? Who mentioned trauma?'

What was he talking about?

'What you went through with Dominic was pretty traumatic, don't you think? Plus everything with Josh, Tessa, Goodfellow, your family. Have you ever had time to fully process that?'

I wrapped my arms around myself and stared into my lap. It had never even occurred to me that I needed to process everything that'd happened, or that it would have long-term effects on my life.

Ben continued: 'Trauma isn't just about abuse or war zones. It's about feeling trapped. Unable to escape. Ignoring your own needs. A lack of boundaries.'

I frowned at him. 'You seem to know a lot about this.'

He shrugged. 'Where do you think Fadil got his psychology books from?' I hadn't considered that. 'You shouldn't be so hard on yourself.'

Meh. He was right.

But still: meh.

'I wouldn't even know how to process any of what's happened.' I ran my hands over my hair. Suddenly the ponytail I'd tied it into felt tight. I could feel it pulling on my roots, like pinpricks all over my scalp. I took the bobble out, but then my hair was scratchy on my neck and shoulders. I tied it into a bun. That'd have to do.

'So maybe don't start there. Just start by being kind to yourself,' said Ben.

This felt like my opening…

'What I could really do with is some alone time. But the cruise Mum wants to go on leaves in a few days.'

'Maybe a change of scenery will be just what you need.'

Wow they really were a couple.

'I just feel like Mum will hover and want to do stuff together, when what I really want is to flit between hibernation and productivity. Something to keep my mind busy.'

Ben frowned. 'You don't want to go?'

I shook my head. 'When we booked it I did. It looks amazing. There's loads to see and do. But so much has changed since then that I really just want to stay at home.' I drummed my fingers against the table. 'What if you went with her?' My voice quivered as I said it, so before he could reject my proposal I continued: 'It'd be the perfect romantic getaway before the shop opens. It might be your last chance to have a proper holiday for a while.'

'There's no way I could leave this place for a week. There's too much to do before the opening. I'm sorry, Edie.'

Restlessness filling my body, I began to pace up and down the empty bookshop in front of the glass window. It was smeared so that people couldn't see in yet. 'You could leave it to me. It would give me something productive to do while still avoiding the noise and crowds of a cruise. I've been helping Mum do up Mrs Brightman's house. I've grown up around DIY and business management. I know what I'm doing. Besides, most of what's left is mostly painting and building shelves, right? With a bit of website setup? If I'm going to prove to Mum I'm really an adult now, I need to prove myself. Fadil and Maggie will be here as backup if anything happens, which I'm sure it won't. Plus, it's easier for Fadil using my powers. We don't have to move the spell and I don't have to worry about them being too much.'

Ben studied me for a moment. 'You've put a lot of thought into this.'

'A little. But I have a point, don't I? Running a business is stressful, especially in the first couple of years. Wouldn't it be nice to have a break before everything kicks off?'

4
Niamh

'Are you sure she'll be all right on her own?' I said, rubbing my clammy hands on my jeans.

We'd managed to swap Edie's name for Ben's on the ticket. Maggie was now driving us to the airport, leaving Edie to have a lie-in and Josh to babysit his little sister.

We were flying to Barcelona, boarding the ship from there, then cruising around Europe for a week. We'd only been in the car for five minutes and we weren't even out of Nottinghamshire yet, but I was already nervous about leaving Edie.

'She's got to be on her own some day,' said Maggie from the driver's seat. Sometimes I really hated her common-sense parenting techniques. My paranoia had no comebacks for them.

'And if anyone can look after herself, it's someone who can literally drain someone's life essence,' added Ben. Not helpful. He was meant to be on my side. Which was the side that didn't want to leave Edie home alone for a week even though I knew she was ready for it and it was what she needed. *I* wasn't ready for it.

'We don't know that she can do that anymore. Not now that Fadil is using her powers as a magical translation service,' I said.

'She handled herself pretty well against Goodfellow.'

'That was a team effort! Led by a ten-year-old ghost,' I reminded Ben.

Ben pursed his lips. Normally I wanted to kiss them. Right now…not so much. 'Technically he was older than all of us, just trapped in a child's form.'

I threw my arms in the air, accidentally hitting the roof of the car. 'Semantics!'

Maggie met Ben's eye in the rearview mirror and the two of them laughed. My paranoid parenting was not funny!

'And anyway. It's not the paranormal stuff that bothers me,' I clarified. 'Things have been quiet since Tessa's death and Edie seems to have better control of her powers.'

Ben nodded. 'She's progressed well with her spell casting, even with Fadil using some of her powers.'

'Would she be powerful enough to defend herself if she needed to and I wasn't there, though?' That was what really worried me. 'And what about human murderers or rapists?'

'She can defend herself better than you can defend her, from humans and paranormals. Even with her powers lacking,' said Ben. 'Sorry,' he added when I glared at him. He was right. Again. Ugh.

Whether I liked it or not, my daughter was more powerful than I was. She always would be. Even with our 4000-year-old friend borrowing some of her powers so that he could speak English.

The Poltergeist's Ship

'I thought you said it wasn't the paranormal stuff that was bothering you, anyway?' said Maggie. She glanced over at me.

'It's not. Mostly. It's the exam stuff.'

Maggie reached over and patted my knee. 'She needs time to adjust. It's a grieving period when you leave college and you have to enter the real world. And on top of that, she hasn't lived up to the expectations of being a star student. You hovering over her probably won't help with her feelings of guilt and shame.'

'I don't hover!'

She patted my knee again. I was going to smack that hand away if she did it one more time.

'Some people just prefer to process things on their own,' said Ben from the backseat. 'Edie strikes me as one of those people.'

Maggie nodded, chancing a look at me. 'You are, too.'

I glared at her. She'd better not say the next line I knew she was thinking.

'Like mother, like—'

'Do *not* finish that sentence,' I said through gritted teeth.

'All right, sorry,' said Maggie, biting her lip to suppress a laugh as we got stuck in a queue at a roundabout. The car's engine automatically switched off and the gentle, soothing hum stopped. I hadn't noticed how much I'd been appreciating it until then.

'She'll have me, Fadil, Abigail, Josh, Tilly, and Spectre. And I'm sure Harry would step in if we really needed him.'

Silence fell over the car. The three of us exchanged glances. Then, we started laughing.

'All right, all right,' said Maggie as we moved again. 'He's not going to win any awards for moral support right now. But let's face it: even if she's never been home alone before, Edie can take care of herself.'

I sighed, slumping into the leather seat.

'She did a pretty good job of looking after herself when she was living with Dominic,' said Ben.

I turned around to scowl at him. 'He convinced her to use her powers to heal him so that he could become all-powerful. I'd hardly call being brainwashed by a psychopath a "pretty good job of looking after herself."'

'Stop scowling, you'll get more wrinkles,' said Maggie.

I turned back around and gave her the same look I'd just given Ben. She stuck her middle finger up at me. Charming.

'What I mean,' said Ben, 'is that in terms of basic life skills like how to feed herself or wash her clothes, she did fine. There's no magic that can help her adjust to being an adult. She has to learn that herself.'

'And most people adjust better when they go away to uni because they're forced into it, supported by their peers,' added Maggie.

'I didn't go to uni,' I reminded her.

'I know. But you were independent from when you left the womb. You had to be.' She was right. My mother was a raging narcissist and even when she returned from the Other Side to 'help' us, she still spoke in riddles.

The Poltergeist's Ship

Before Christmas, I'd called her up on the games she liked to play and the lies she'd told about our family heritage. We hadn't spoken since. I hadn't summoned her, and she hadn't appeared unannounced. Even though she could've if she'd wanted to.

As far as I knew, Edie hadn't spoken to her either. They'd never been close anyway.

When Javi showed up, he didn't mention her, which I was grateful for. I'd had to start forcing images of him colluding with my mother to the back of my mind because it made me less comfortable talking to one of my favourite people, which I hated. I loved Javi and always would. But I *hated* that he'd been taught how to be a ghostly necromancer by my mother on the Other Side. It would never not infuriate me.

All things considered, I'd done my best to be the opposite kind of parent to Edie. Had I gone too far and mollycoddled her instead? Was that why I was so worried about leaving her?

'You didn't mollycoddle her, if that's what you're thinking,' said Maggie.

'How did you know that's what I was thinking?'

She shrugged. 'Seemed a logical path from discussing your parents to discussing your parenting style and how you tried to go in a totally different direction.' Of course she'd made that connection. She knew me too well. I suppose that was part of knowing someone for most of your life and speaking to them daily. Supernatural comas not included. 'You'll never feel comfortable leaving her on her own. But likewise, she'll never get used to it if she isn't given the opportunity.'

I crossed my arms over my grey top. 'I hate you both and your logic.'

'No you don't,' said Ben.

I was pretty sure I did.

5
Edie

Mum had only been gone a few hours and the house already felt empty without her. I guessed her presence loomed over me more than I'd realised.

Was I going to regret being home alone? Mum or Maggie or Dominic had always been on the other side of a wall. Now all I had was a fluffy white dog and a ghost cat. They were cute and all, but they weren't exactly talkative.

Mum, Ben, and Maggie had left around seven. I'd tried to get back to sleep after waving them off, but it hadn't happened. Not even with Tilly and Spectre cuddles. So I'd gotten up, eaten breakfast, walked Tilly, then headed to the bookshop.

Ben had trusted the rest of its makeover to me. He had a clear vision of what he wanted, so I had no creative freedom, but Mum had reminded me that when you worked for clients you never got that anyway. We weren't paid to be interior designers.

Updating Mrs Brightman's house had been a luxury – we could do it however we wanted, since I was pretty sure Mum's plan was to move in there and sell our current place.

I wasn't sure what that meant for Spectre – I didn't want to leave him – but I was going to find a way to bring him with me wherever I went. It wasn't fair for him to live in a house with people who couldn't even see him, let alone touch him. And it wasn't like we could help him cross over since he couldn't tell us why he'd stayed. Maybe one day he'd cross over with me.

Ben and I had warded Mrs Brightman's house so that we didn't get any unexpected visitors. And I got a useful lesson in warding buildings from ghosts.

I was enjoying leaning more into my witchcraft heritage and trying to forget about my necromancy one. Witchcraft had done me a lot less damage than necromancy so far.

Fadil had access to a constant stream of my powers to enable him to embrace modern life, although I couldn't travel too far away or it'd stop working. It seemed I could travel farther than Mum had been able to, which was good, and apparently a testament to how much stronger my powers were than hers. Anywhere I went I could always take Fadil with me anyway. He liked exploring. We'd originally planned to have him borrow Ben's powers while I'd been away, but with me staying we hadn't needed to worry about transferring the spell.

While I could use my necromancy to heal people, it hurt me at the same time. When I'd used my powers to help Dominic, my moods had been skittish and I'd thought some pretty worrying things. I hadn't felt like me, but I hadn't been able to stop myself, either. It felt like a taste of my possible future, if I wasn't careful.

The Poltergeist's Ship

Fadil borrowing some of my power lessened the lure of using necromancy regularly. And now, I barely noticed the pull as I hadn't used that side of myself in months.

Witchcraft wasn't as addictive or damaging. It was only addictive because I enjoyed how good I was at it.

Ben had explained that I couldn't use my power for personal gain, like doing the washing up. It didn't count as personal gain if I was using it to unlock a door and help a ghost, though, much like what I'd done when I'd made up my first spell to free a trapped ghost and reunite her with her girlfriend.

That had been right before Dominic had told me how Dad had really died and upped his emotional manipulation. Sigh.

We still didn't know how powerful Dominic had really been – or what the extent of his powers were – but it didn't matter anymore. His sarcophagus was now in Leeds, on display in a museum.

I hadn't told anyone, but I'd been tracking it. It wasn't like I'd know if someone let him out the same way he'd let Fadil out, but as Gran had told me, necromancers were rare. It had taken four thousand years for one to find Fadil. Or at least, one who knew how to free him.

Technically Fadil had been entombed for most of that time, but even after his sarcophagus had been excavated and transported to the UK, he hadn't found one who could break the curse until two centuries later. So the odds of Dominic breaking free – in our lifetimes at least – were slim.

What really bothered me was that we wouldn't know if Dominic was free until he came after us. And I had no doubt that that was what he'd do if he ever did get out.

I had to stop worrying about that, though. It'd been eight months. If I spent too long worrying about where he was, I'd never be able to live my life and find some level of normalcy. And I was determined to have at least a little bit.

I took my keys from my pocket to unlock the bookshop. The lock wouldn't turn how it was supposed to. The door was already open.

Had someone broken in?

Surely it wasn't breaking and entering if someone had a key?

Tentatively, I walked through the front door and closed it behind me. The shop was warded. I could use my powers to protect myself. Why was I so paranoid?

Because people could be just as dangerous as the paranormal.

Fadil didn't have a key and it was too early for him anyway. He didn't like mornings and tried to avoid them as much as possible, especially lately as he seemed to be in pain a lot. He said mornings were the worst.

The hairs on the back of my neck stood up as I looked around the empty shop. There were no shelves up yet, so it was easy to see all the way around. I couldn't see, or sense, anyone in the room.

The back room. Where the ghosts hung out. Most of the time they kept to themselves, but it was nice knowing we could help each other without worrying about anyone seeing us talking to ghosts.

I could feel the faint buzz of their life essences from where I stood, but not enough to identify who was there. Separating out life essences from the same beings wasn't a skill I was very good at yet.

But I could tell when there were different beings in a location.

There was a life essence in the back room that didn't belong to a ghost, but wasn't quite alive, either.

Realising there was only one person that could belong to, I smiled to myself, shaking my head at how on edge I'd been.

Fadil walked out of the back room carrying two empty mugs. He narrowed his brown, yellowing eyes at me. 'Why do you look like a cat on the prowl?'

I laughed, picturing Spectre doing just that around the house. 'I forgot you could use Ben's key.'

'You thought I was breaking into my place of employment?'

As embarrassment washed over me, so, too, did the redness on my face and neck. Stupid natural gingerness. No amount of dark brown hair dye would ever stop my skin from going tomato red when I was mortified.

Fadil chuckled, turning on the coffee machine. It had been one of Ben's first purchases. Something about saving me money on my coffee addiction. No idea what he was talking about. I just really liked caffeine.

'You're not normally awake this early,' I said.

'Couldn't sleep, got bored, decided to get a head start,' he said with a shrug. Did they set off OK?' he asked as he placed our mugs under the machine.

'Yeah, just after seven.' To save time, Ben had stayed over at ours. He did most of the time, to be honest. I didn't mind, but I felt bad for Fadil being on his own so much.

Although he seemed fine with it. I think he liked it. He had spent four thousand years with nobody to talk to but himself. He was basically the complete opposite of me when it came to being alone.

'Good.' The coffee machine finished and he handed me my mug.

I picked it up and chugged the bitter liquid. That was better. I'd stopped making my own at home because this was far superior. If I carried on I was going to have to start paying Ben for how much I drank. I'd bankrupt him from drinking too much otherwise.

'Did anyone ever tell you how addicted to caffeine you are?'

'It's purely medicinal,' I said. 'It slows my brain down enough so that I can concentrate.'

During exams not included. Nothing could save me from those, apparently.

He chuckled, picking up his own mug. 'Sure it is.'

I leaned against the wall and looked out across the bookshop. 'Any new ghosts?'

'No, just the usuals. Most of them have gone for a wander around town. They like this time of day, when everyone is off to school or work. It's prime eavesdropping time.'

'Damn right it's prime eavesdropping time. Laters.' Shane floated in from the back and past us into the busy street. Did he stick around just because he liked eavesdropping? It did seem to be one of his favourite pastimes.

'Whatever rocks their boats,' I said. It wasn't like there'd be any ramifications for invisible people listening in on conversations.

Fadil walked over and stood beside me. 'How are you?'

I rocked on my heels, staring at the polished wooden floor. Mum and I had done it last week and I loved how it'd turned out.

'You're allowed to be upset, you know.'

'I'm not upset. I'm pissed. At Dominic for manipulating me and putting me behind, at myself for not trying harder—'

'Stop right there!' said Fadil. He seemed so annoyed at me I thought he was going to spill his coffee. 'You *did* try. I saw you try! I *helped* you try! You're still processing some pretty horrible trauma. That messes with you more than you think.'

Trauma. He was the second person to call it that. I was still wrapping my head around the idea that what Dominic had done to me was traumatic. It wasn't what most people would consider a form of trauma, nor was it covered in any of the helpful literature.

Then again, most people couldn't bring someone back from the dead.

Fadil put his mug on the table and stretched his arms out in front of him. 'My arms are really sore and stiff today. It must be from painting in the back yesterday.'

'Shouldn't we focus on painting in here first? Where people can see?'

He raised his arms above his head. 'The paint colour we needed wasn't in stock, so we just went with what we had. Ben has a very particular view and no other colour options or aesthetics are acceptable. The colour for in here is being delivered later, if the website tracking is accurate.'

'So then we should be able to get started later or tomorrow. That gives us plenty of time.'

Someone knocked at the door. We turned to see Maggie standing there, smiling and waving. Ever since she'd started talking to us again, it had been almost like she'd never stopped.

Every so often, she'd get a look in her eye if we said or did something, but it disappeared as quickly as it'd appeared, so it was impossible to know if I'd imagined it or not. It was the same look Josh sometimes had.

I opened the door and greeted her with a hug.

'Just dropped them off at the airport,' she said as she walked in and closed the door behind her.

That could've been me. But it wasn't what I needed, being stuck on a ship, unable to escape, only having a small room to separate myself from everyone. I wasn't ready.

'How's it going here?' asked Maggie.

'Pretty good,' I said. 'Starting painting in here later or tomorrow.'

Maggie looked around the space, smiling and nodding. 'I think this could turn out to be something really great. I can't remember the last time the town had a bookshop.'

'Really?' said Fadil.

Maggie nodded. 'It's such a shame. Books are so important.'

'Well, hopefully the rest of the town agrees and comes out to support it,' I said.

'I think the school and university crowds will help. I'm sure Manju could recommend some books the children are reading, or place some orders through here for the school,' said Maggie.

'Hopefully she does. That kind of bulk order would really help,' said Fadil. Manju was the first person he'd met after being woken up as she was the headteacher at the school where his sarcophagus had been on display. Thankfully, she knew our family's history, which meant she also knew to ring Mum when she'd found a 4000-year-old sort-of mummy wandering the corridors.

Maggie smiled.

The three of us stood awkwardly in the shop. Somehow, despite the large window, the room felt smaller. I guessed because I wanted to ask her something. But I also didn't want to ask. A part of me already knew the answer but needed confirmation.

Ever since I'd seen Josh on results day, I'd been desperate to know how he'd done. But I couldn't bring myself to ask him because then I'd have to talk about my own results.

'How'd Josh do? On his exams?' A lump formed in my throat. Josh and I had spent most of our lives working to this point. Now it was finally over. And our lives would never be the same.

Maggie beamed. 'He got everything he needed to study graphic design in Edinburgh.'

The lump got bigger. Of course he had. Even after missing ten days because he'd been in a coma and tortured by demons, twisting his ankle because of me – fine, Dominic using me – and his girlfriend being murdered, *he'd* managed to get decent grades. If anything, he'd suffered more. But I was the failure. 'Well, congrats to him,' I said, trying to hide my envy and not sound sarcastic. I was fairly sure I sounded sarcastic.

It wasn't just envy, though. His good grades meant that he'd be leaving before we'd repaired what was left of our fractured friendship.

I'd hoped one day we could go back to how it was, even if that was just as friends. But with him leaving, I wasn't sure that could ever happen. He'd be a totally different person by the time he came home for Christmas. Why would he need someone like me?

6
Niamh

Orcas. One of the most intelligent, yet evil, creatures of the sea. That was what our passenger group had been named after. Did the person who'd come up with the group names know we were named after evil dolphins?

Once our group was called, we could finally board. Until then, we were stuck in the waiting area, staring at the gargantuan feat of engineering on the other side of the window.

Hanging around in the airport-style lounge just increased my restlessness. The lines between nerves about Edie being on her own for the first time, and going on holiday for the first time in years, were blurring. I had no idea which was making me fidget more.

There were considerably more ghosts around than I would've liked. I suppose I'd been naive to expect the cruise to be entirely ghost-free. Statistically, there were going to be at least a handful on a cruise ship with seven thousand guests and hundreds of crew members.

Thankfully, all the ghosts seemed preoccupied with whomever they were haunting. Hopefully if they got bored they'd interact with each other, not come to us.

It wasn't often there was such a high concentration of ghosts in a small space, but I supposed the waiting area did contain a lot of people, the ship was right in front of us, and there were other ships docked nearby, too.

As long as they ignored us and left us to enjoy our holiday, I was happy.

Ben stood next to me, staring up at the ship we were going to spend our next week aboard. I'd known cruise ships were big, but knowing it and seeing it were two different things. From where we stood, we couldn't see the start or end of it. Or the top of it. I'd never felt so small. 'It's like a floating city!'

'Yeah, it's pretty cool,' said Ben. He unfastened the water bottle attached to his rucksack and took a sip, then offered me some. It was practically full. I had a couple of gulps then handed it back to him.

It was hot and humid in Barcelona, so I was grateful for the air conditioning unit nearby. Was it going to be this hot on the ship? Would that have air conditioning?

Who was I kidding? Everywhere had air conditioning outside of the UK.

We'd already gotten rid of our suitcases, so we just had our rucksacks with us and a small handbag for me, where I stored our passports, visas, and money.

'Supposedly they have everything you need on there,' he added.

'*Everything?*' I said sceptically.

'And everything the crew needs. Ships even have morgues on them, just in case someone dies in the middle of the ocean. Sometimes it's right next to the food freezer, too.'

I cringed. Of course Ben would know that. 'Why did you have to tell me that right before boarding?'

He chuckled, placing his hand on the small of my back, just below the bottom of my rucksack. 'You were brought back from the dead and a couple of freezers make you uncomfortable?'

I glared at him. Had he not noticed we were surrounded by hundreds of other people? What was he saying? 'Say that a little louder, someone might hear you.'

'No one's listening. Look around.'

The people around us were all wrapped up in their own conversations, talking in various European languages. It created a mesh of rhythms, making it impossible to tell what anyone was talking about. Maybe Ben was right.

Still, I didn't need the reminder that my daughter's psychopathic frenemy had stabbed me. I shuddered, Dominic's face forming in my mind. I really hated that guy. Even though we were safe from him, I still felt physically repulsed whenever I thought of him.

'Sorry,' said Ben, pulling me out of my thoughts. 'I shouldn't have brought that up in such a callous way.'

'It's fine. If you don't laugh, you'll cry, right? And it's not like our lives will ever be normal, will they?'

Ben tilted his head to get a different view of the ship. 'No, probably not.'

Starfishes were called, then lobsters. The number of people in the waiting area dwindled, leaving some seats near our window spot free. We grabbed them, placing our bags at our feet to give our backs a break.

'How many ghosts do you think there are?' I asked Ben.

He glanced around the room. 'Ten percent, maybe?'

Would I ever be able to escape them? Even when I'd tried while married to my second husband I'd still been able to see them, I'd just ignored them. It was so much harder to ignore them now.

'They won't care about us,' Ben reassured me.

'I hope you're right. We're not here to help anyone. Not this week,' I said.

Ghosts weren't used to running into people who could see them. Some thought they were imagining things, others waited until you were somewhere private, then there were the ones that demanded attention in public. That kind were awkward, to say the least.

If only we could ward our room. But that was kind of frowned on when it wasn't your property.

'We can just ignore them,' said Ben. 'If we act like we can't see them, they won't bother with us. There's no rule saying we have to engage with them just because we can see them. Everyone deserves a holiday.'

The person over the tannoy finally called for orcas to board. So we gathered our bags and headed to the queue. I definitely had more of a spring in my step than usual. It surprised even me. Ben smiled, watching me.

'Yeah, you're right. I got pretty good at ignoring them for a few years when I was with Dan,' I said.

Ben grunted.

'What was that for?'

The Poltergeist's Ship

He put his arm around my waist, his grip tight. 'I dislike how he treated you when he found out what you could do.'

'Hear, hear!' said Javi's voice in my ear.

I turned around, trying to smack him, but there was nothing there. So I ended up waving my arms in the air like an idiot. I mean, I would've looked like that anyway since I couldn't actually hit Javi. But it was a nice idea.

The couple joining the queue behind us eyed me warily. 'Sorry. Fly.' I turned away before they could reply, my cheeks no doubt crimson.

'Smooth,' said Ben.

'Shut up,' I said. 'Go away, Javi,' I added through gritted teeth.

Ben chuckled to himself. I was pretty sure I heard Javi laugh, too. I really hated how well the two of them got along sometimes.

*

After impatiently queuing – well, on my part, Ben was always patient – we could finally board the ship.

The walkway opened out into the atrium, a set of glass stairs and a large balcony giving it an airy feeling. Just above we could see hints of trees from the upstairs park area.

Performers filled the atrium, twirling ribbons and doing acrobatics. I could barely get out of bed without feeling stiff, let alone contort myself into some of the positions they were in. It looked uncomfortable. But I had respect for those skills. Being able to do even half of that took work.

I walked over to the ribbon twirler and watched her. She was intricate; delicate; flexible. 'I always liked the idea of ribbon twirling.'

'Why? So you could use one to strangle people if they annoyed you?' said Ben.

'You know me so well.' I grinned, squeezing his shoulder. 'It's the ultimate weapon because everyone assumes a ribbon twirler is harmless.'

'And what you're actually saying is that they're secret assassins?'

'I'm merely saying that they could be.'

The ribbon twirler winked.

'See?' I said to Ben.

He shook his head, walking in the direction of the nearest bar. 'Shall we get a drink? I avoided drinking much so that I didn't need to pee on the plane but now I'm regretting it.'

'Aeroplane toilets are horrible. I don't blame you.'

The grey and white bar was clean and modern, with white tiles around the bar and an animal print grey carpet around the seating area.

'*Hola!*' said the bartender. I lost the rest because it was in Spanish. The one time Javi interrupting would've been useful. Our bemused expressions must've explained that we were painfully English, because he switched languages: 'What would you like to drink?'

'Just water for me, please,' said Ben, ever the sensible one.

'Can I get water and tea, please?' I asked.

The Poltergeist's Ship

'Of course.'

We grabbed our drinks then sat down, watching others board – some with their spectral friends – as we dug in.

A woman in uniform wandered into my line of vision, a big smile on her face. It was framed by long brown hair that fell to her shoulders. She had on a light blue shirt and dark blue pencil skirt. Judging from her outfit and how many people she was speaking to, she looked like the captain.

'*Hola!*' she said, walking over to us. She tucked her long, dark hair over her shoulders. 'Welcome aboard the Seraphina!' She spoke with a soft Italian accent.

'Thank you,' I said.

She lowered her wire-framed glasses from the top of her head and put them on. 'I'm Captain Sofia Ricci. If there's anything any of us can help you with, don't hesitate to ask, all right?'

'We will, thanks,' said Ben.

She nodded, smiled, then walked over to the bartender to talk to him.

'It's nice to not have to worry about carrying money around once you're here,' said Ben, sipping his water.

'It's good if you're lazy,' I agreed, stirring my tea. 'Have you downloaded the app yet? I think that's how we track what's going on and how much we spend.'

'Spend? I thought it was all included.'

'It's for stuff like excursions, spa treatments, and the speciality restaurants that aren't included,' I explained.

'Oh ok. What's it called?'

I showed him the app and he downloaded it, flicking through what it said was coming up. 'So we go from

Barcelona to Palma de Mallorca, then we're at sea, then Florence, Rome, Naples, another day at sea, then we return to Barcelona?'

'That's the plan, yeah. I mean, sometimes things like the weather or someone falling overboard can mean we don't make a stop. But the weather is forecast to be good, and what are the odds of someone falling overboard?' I said, leaning back in my weirdly shaped white chair. The high back almost forced me to sit upright, but in a comfy way rather than an aggressive one.

'Fadil's research seemed to suggest it was pretty rare. But then, so are Victorian serial killers in the 21st century, so…'

'So many things wrong with that sentence,' I said, shaking my head. Only Ben could've said something like that. And only Fadil would've researched cruise ships when he wasn't even coming.

Ben smiled. 'Even so. I think you're right. The odds of something happening onboard are pretty slim. Let's enjoy the break before the bookshop opens.'

'Hear, hear.' I raised my cup of tea and he clinked it with his water.

7
Edie

'Are you all right to carry on here if I go take Tilly for a walk?' I asked Fadil. We'd just finished building the first bookcase. I stood back and admired our hard work. It looked good, if I didn't mind saying so myself.

'Can I start putting the books on? I can take some photos to use on the website.'

'Go for it.'

'Cool. I think I'll get lunch first. Want me to grab you anything?'

'No thanks. I'll probably take Tilly to that dog-friendly cafe she loves on the way home,' I said.

'All right. See you in a bit.'

I put on my headphones then walked home, pleased at how productive mine and Fadil's first day on our own had been. We could definitely have the place ready for Ben when he got back.

Tilly greeted me with her usual excitement when I got in. I clipped her lead on then took her out since she'd been on her own all morning. She didn't seem to mind – she'd been watching TV with Spectre – but I knew she'd probably need the toilet and want some attention.

To tire her out, I walked her the long way to the cafe. We went around Titchfield Park, which was full of other dog walkers and families on their lunchtime walks. But it wasn't noisy; no one was really playing sports like they sometimes did, probably because it was too muddy from the recent rain.

A cool breeze through took the edge of the heat, as had some light rain while Fadil and I had been building furniture.

At the back of the park was the graveyard where we'd faced off with Goodfellow. I didn't walk around it much anymore – since I couldn't go in there without thinking about everything he'd done – but nothing could make me feel any worse than I already did, and I wanted to walk farther, so I took her through the graveyard.

Tilly was unaware of what'd happened in there, so trotted down the path like she always had, stopping to sniff the occasional patch of grass. The bright sun bore down on us from high in the sky, making me glad I'd put on a pair of shorts and some factor 50. It wasn't too hot, but it was definitely bright enough that my skin would burn if I stayed out too long.

I was reading one of the World War II graves when Tilly, who was behind me, tugged on her lead. I turned around to see her rolling. In what looked an awful lot like poo.

*

It hadn't been just any poo Tilly had rolled in. It'd been fox poo.

So much for taking her to a cafe for lunch.

I called Fadil on the walk home. 'Could you grab me a sandwich or something please? Looks like I won't be going to the cafe after all.'

'What happened?' I could hear the concern in his voice.

'Guess who rolled in her favourite perfume.'

Tilly continued to walk alongside me, looking smug. I could smell her as we walked. It was gross. Every time someone walked towards us, I crossed the road so that they didn't have to inhale it. I sure didn't want to. There was no way I was going to inflict it on anyone else.

'The dog smells like fox poo. Got it. Do you need me to grab any shampoo or anything?' offered Fadil.

'No thanks, we're prepared.' This was not Tilly's first poo roll. And I doubted it'd be her last. 'I'm not sure if that's unfortunate or lucky.'

'Unfortunate you have to do it but lucky you have shampoo,' said Fadil. 'I'll get cake too. Think you'll need it.'

'Thanks. Might need a gas mask too. Can you get me some bleach as well please? I want to blitz the bathroom when I'm done blitzing the dog.'

'I'll see what I can get. Be there as soon as I can.'

'Cheers.'

*

The dog bath was…smelly. And brown. And it took a lot of mental strength not to throw up all over Tilly and her brown sludge. At least we had some rubber gloves I could wear while bathing her.

Once I was done, Tilly ran all over the house, rubbing up against the furniture to dry herself. So the house was going to smell like bleach and wet dog. Great.

Fadil opened the front door. 'Is it safe?'

Wet Tilly catapulted down the stairs, almost crashing into him.

'Ah, I see you're clean,' he said to her. 'Nice job,' he said to me.

'Thanks.' I plodded down the stairs as he came inside and closed the door behind him.

'So how bad was it? Or shouldn't I ask?'

'Not the worst, but not my favourite thing to wash off her fur, either.' I shuddered. 'I cannot wait to clean the bathroom. And I never thought I'd say that. Being an adult sucks.'

Bag in hand, he followed me into the kitchen. Tilly was close behind, hoping she'd get treats. 'It's not so bad. At least you have fewer people telling you what to do and you don't have to worry about exa—' He cut himself off, realising what he was about to say. 'Sorry.'

'You're right, though. If I hadn't failed I wouldn't have to worry about exams.'

'Are you going to resit them?'

'It's not compulsory, and if I don't want to go to uni it's not a huge deal, but I know I can do so much better. It bugs me.'

Fadil heaved the shopping bag on to the kitchen table. 'You know we'll all support you whatever you do.'

'But will Mum?'

'What do you mean? Why wouldn't she?'

I pulled out a chair and sank into it. Tilly stared up at Fadil as he unpacked the contents of the bag. She could clearly smell the food in it. Fadil passed me a paper bag. Inside was a takeaway container of mushroom stroganoff and a brownie, from the cafe I'd wanted to take Tilly to for lunch. Until she'd decided she wanted to roll in Westie No 5. The classic westie perfume.

'Thanks.'

He handed me some cutlery. 'It's not for you,' he added to Tilly.

'She thinks everything is for her.' I stirred the stroganoff, inhaling the smell of sweet mushrooms.

'Well in this case it's not deserved. Even if I did get her some treats from there as well.' He put them on the counter, near where we stashed her other treats. 'She can have them when she's been good.'

'So never, then?'

Fadil bent down and rubbed behind Tilly's wet ears. 'You don't mean that, you're just annoyed at her.'

I sighed. 'Yeah. It just feels like I'm being kicked when I'm down, you know?'

He frowned, sitting opposite me at the breakfast bar. 'You know I'm here for you, right?'

'I know. But what can you do? What can anyone do?'

*

Neither of us had answers, of course. Partially because I didn't really know what I wanted. Everything felt too raw. I'd had my post-college life planned out until a year ago: get good grades, go to uni, be with Josh. Dominic had ruined those plans and my powers had all but destroyed the rest. I'd never be able to have a normal life.

And apparently I couldn't even have decent grades.

I must've been fidgety in the night, as Tilly hopped off the bed after a couple of hours and lay on her bed under my desk. She always preferred mine or Mum's beds to her own, so her relocating to an actual dog bed spoke volumes.

Spectre floated above my wardrobe, as if on guard.

When I finally fell asleep, I dreamt Thomas was floating above me.

'Oh my god, Edie! I love it! I can't believe I waited so long to leave the graveyard! The outside world is amazing!' He floated in a circle above me. 'I went to this music concert, where they all had really brightly coloured hair, and wore a lot of black, and they seemed to scream more than shout, but it had such a fun atmosphere! There was a big group at the front, dancing. At least, I think that's what they were doing.'

Dream-me forced a smile.

'Why don't you go out? Do some more stuff?' he suggested, still circling above me as I lay in bed. It felt almost Peter Pan-like.

'I'm fine here,' I said, pulling the duvet higher up.

'You're missing out on so much!' said Thomas. 'So much!'

The Poltergeist's Ship

His voice trailed off as I woke up. Of course the dead Victorian child would enjoy modern life more than me. Sigh.

8
Niamh

We got access to our room about an hour after embarkation. Our suitcases were just inside the door, beside a small wardrobe. Opposite that was the entrance to the bathroom. It was tiny, just about big enough for one person to move around in, but it was clean and modern. And we *were* on a cruise ship. Some things were bound to be small.

At the far end of the cabin were the balcony doors. I hadn't been able to bring myself to book an interior cabin even though it was cheaper. My sleeping pattern was bad enough at times. I didn't want to make it worse for a week then have to spend a month fixing it. I'd never been one of those people who could magically change their sleeping patterns – it always took me at least a week to unlearn bad habits but one night to break them. It was much better for me if I could tell where the sun was.

A paper itinerary lay on the bed, towels shaped into swans beside it. I couldn't even fold paper neatly, so the towels were pretty impressive.

Ben picked up the itinerary, kicked off his trainers, and lay back on the bed. 'They have a cinema? *And* a theatre? There are towns with fewer facilities than this! *Our* town has fewer facilities than this!'

'Yeah, it's mad.' I stood by the window, looking out at the other ships at the port. We hadn't left yet as other people were still boarding, so I was enjoying the view of the Barcelona port instead. I was surprised by how many other ships there were. Everything was so much bigger when you left the Midlands.

Ben pushed his glasses up his nose. 'I swear the children's area takes up most of the ship.'

'Only on one floor,' I said sitting beside him, 'and they have their own section. You're missing this bit.' I pointed to an area of the map I remembered from looking online.

'Adults only,' he said.

I smiled. 'Which means quiet. There's also a library with daily puzzles to keep you occupied.'

Ben grinned. 'I do love crosswords.'

'I will stick with word searches.' I leaned back, resting my head against him.

It wasn't a huge room, but it was enough for both of us. The bed took up most of the space, with the rest of it taken up by a sofa that looked on to a wall-mounted TV. Underneath that was a small chest of drawers. A wardrobe sat opposite the bathroom.

'Thanks for inviting me. Not that you had anyone else who could come at such short notice, but still,' said Ben.

'I'm glad you're here,' I said. 'I wouldn't want to be here with anyone else. Well, except Edie. But this will be a different kind of cruise. More of a relaxing couple's cruise instead of mother/daughter bonding time. And at least it was easy enough to turn the two single beds into a double.'

Ben put the map on the floor beside him and climbed on top of me, a cheeky grin on his face. 'Yes, that does make life easier.' He leaned down and kissed me.

It wasn't long until we left the port and our cruise officially began, so we had quick showers to freshen up, then got changed and went to the adults-only area to watch the sail away.

Lying back in our loungers, drinks in hand, we looked up through the glass ceiling. The sun was still bright – Ben had his prescription sunglasses on – and it was around 25 degrees celsius outside. Just right. Even better because we had air conditioning nearby.

Some of the ghosts floated above the harbour, glowing against the azure-coloured water. I was more fascinated watching them than the disappearing Barcelona skyline.

The farther away from shore we got, the more ghosts that got pulled back to the people they haunted. One by one, until no one was left.

*

After the sail away, we had to do a safety drill so that we knew how to use our life jackets, where to convene if something happened, things like that. While there, we met our cabin steward, Niall. He was a blond, Irish guy, who had more energy than any puppy I'd ever met.

The Poltergeist's Ship

I'd thought being a cabin steward had meant that he just cleaned our rooms and made towel animals, but he explained it involved more than that, and that we should go to him directly or speak to Guest Services if we had any issues.

He also said to avoid Guest Services before or during meal times as that was when it was busiest, so we'd lose time on the ship. Since they were open all hours, we were better off going at other times if we could, like before bed or first thing in the morning.

We explored the ship, signed up for some excursions and speciality restaurants, then headed to the buffet for dinner.

'Do you think she's all right?' I asked, checking my phone again. Nothing from Edie. I hadn't heard from her all day. We'd paid for the WiFi package, but it was slow. Should I have tried her before we left port?

Ben reached across the table and put his hand on top of mine. 'She'll be fine.'

We were having a late dinner for Brits but an early one for Europeans, so there weren't that many people around. It gave us time to appreciate the balance between humans and ghosts. Most of the ghosts hadn't realised we could see them yet, but those who did waved at us then carried on their ways. Everyone – human and ghost – seemed more relaxed. I could get used to this.

The buffet was filling with people, creating a gentle hum around the room as everyone talked and laughed.

I shifted in my wooden seat. 'It's just, this is the first time she's been on her own overnight before. What if something happens to her?'

'She can look after herself, she's proven that.'

'It's not her I don't trust. It's everyone else.' I knew we'd had the same conversation in the car, but I couldn't shake the feeling something bad would happen without Ben or me there to protect her. Ben's forcefield had saved us more times than I could count.

'Given everything that's happened, some quiet time might help her process it all. It's good to slow down sometimes. And she's been pretty much non-stop for a year.' Ben was right, of course he was. He was Mr Logic. My brain was not. 'What did you do when you had to leave her alone while dating your ex-husband? You kept her away from him initially, right?'

I flinched at the mention of Dan. 'We met up when she was at school or at a friend's house and she never knew about him until things got serious.'

A smile flickered over Ben's face.

'What?'

'Does Edie knowing about me mean we're serious?'

I ran my finger over his hand. It was dry from all the DIY he'd been doing at the bookshop. 'Well, we're on a cruise together, you spend half your time at my place, and we fought a psychopathic necromancer *and* a murderous poltergeist together. I'd say that's pretty serious, wouldn't you?'

His smile grew. He leaned over the table, ruffling the white tablecloth as he did so, and kissed me. 'Yeah, you're right.'

'Did you know it's been almost a year since we met?' I said.

'Only a year? It feels like longer.'

'Should I be insulted?'

The Poltergeist's Ship

He backtracked: 'I mean it feels like we've known each other longer. In a good way. I couldn't imagine my life without you.'

Good save. I squeezed his hand. 'Me neither. It's nice to have another grown up with powers around again. And when you do that thing…'

He smirked, a flirtatious glint in his eye. 'I can do it later, if you ask nicely.'

I tilted towards him, smirking. 'Asking nicely.'

He leaned in to me, his lips caressing mine. 'I'll think about it.'

'Tease.' I shook my head, pulling away.

He grinned.

9
Edie

'Morning,' said Fadil, walking into the bookshop.

I suppressed a yawn, flicking on the coffee machine. 'Morning.'

The green paint had arrived yesterday afternoon, which meant it was officially painting day. We were going to cover the coffee machine in a sheet to protect it from the paint, but I was holding off on doing that until the last minute because life. We'd already covered the floor with some old duvet covers to keep the paint away.

Fadil was dressed in his overalls ready to go, and I had on a pair of scruffy jeans and an old top that was covered in cream paint from decorating Mrs Brightman's.

'How come you're so tired?' Fadil asked, perching on the stool. He stretched his arms above his head.

'I didn't get to sleep until about three.' It was just after eight, and I'd gotten up around five. 'It was weird, sleeping home alone.' Wait. Who was I talking to? 'Sorry, that was stupid of me to say.'

Fadil shrugged. 'It wasn't like I had a choice. If you're not used to being alone, it's scary. You notice every noise.'

The Poltergeist's Ship

I nodded, placing Fadil's mug under the machine. It had a cartoon mummy on it. Ben had found it at a car boot sale. We still found it funny. 'Yeah. It doesn't help that Tilly flinches at every noise, so if I react, she goes into guard dog mode.'

Fadil snorted. 'Yes I'm sure an intruder would be terrified of a ten kilo ball of white fluff.'

I rolled my eyes. 'She thinks they will be. And to be fair, her bark *does* scare some door-to-door salespeople. They're always surprised at how small she is.' I put the coffee in front of Fadil then reached for mine. I'd made it when I'd first walked in an hour ago. As soon as the first sip hit my mouth, I spat it out back into my westie mug. 'Gone cold.'

Fadil laughed. 'What time did you get in?'

'About six,' I said. 'I got bored of sitting around so I walked and fed Tilly then figured I might as well do something productive. I wasn't tired then, but now…'

Fadil nodded knowingly. 'Give yourself some time to adjust. Eventually you'll be so tired you'll just crash.'

Yawning again, I went into the small kitchen in the back to discard of my cold coffee and rinse my mug. Gwendoline, Shane, and a couple of other ghosts were in there talking. They greeted me then continued with their conversations.

It was weird how quickly we'd adapted to there being ghosts in the back room all the time. We barely even noticed them anymore. And they barely noticed us.

I returned to the shop front. 'I hope you're right. I don't think I've ever felt this tired before.'

'I can stay over if you want.'

I smiled. 'Thanks. I'd like to give it another night first to see how I get on. I've got to get used to it eventually, right?'

He nodded. 'But if you're not ready yet, there's no shame in that.'

'Isn't there?' I put my mug under the coffee machine and pressed the button to start it. Nothing happened. I pressed it again. Same result. 'Please don't tell me it's broken. *Please*.'

Fadil hopped off his stool, put his drink down, and came to stand beside me. 'If in doubt, turn it off and back on again.' He turned it off at the plug. 'And no, there's no shame in not being ready to sleep on your own overnight. Especially after everything you've been through. Go easy on yourself.'

I grunted. I was eighteen. I should've been able to do whatever I wanted on my own, no matter what I'd been through. How else could I prove to my parents that I was independent? Maybe a week alone was slightly too much for the first time.

Shifting from foot to foot, I glanced at the coffee machine, then at the plug. 'Can we turn it back on yet?'

'Give it a minute. I'm sure it'll be fine.'

I flapped my arms in the air. 'What if it's not? What if it's really broken? It's like a month old!' It was one of the first things Ben had bought and we'd used it almost every day since it'd been set up.

Fadil lowered my arms. 'Then it's still in warranty and we'll send it back or get someone out.'

The Poltergeist's Ship

He was right. There was a simple fix. Even if we couldn't fix it before Ben got home, he'd understand it wasn't our fault.

Fadil turned the plug on and we tried the machine again. Nothing.

'Well isn't that just great? Can we even do anything if Ben isn't here? Does he need to be the one to contact them?'

'I can do it,' said Fadil. 'I don't get to use the phone very often. I'll just pretend to be Ben, and hopefully they'll send a replacement or someone out to fix it.'

I shook my head. 'This is the worst timing.'

Fadil put his arm around me. 'Hey, don't worry about it. We can figure this out.'

'Do we have a choice?'

'Well, we could get upset about something out of our hands, or we could find a solution so that we're not wasting energy worrying about it.'

'You really need to stop reading psychology books.'

Fadil grinned at me. 'Or maybe I need to read more of them.'

'What would you do without access to books, podcasts, and videos?'

Fadil paused, pretending to be deep in thought. 'It would be worse than spending four thousand years trapped in a sarcophagus unable to move. At least then I didn't know what I was missing out on. Now, I'd know how much I'd lost.'

'Well there's a sad thought.'

He shrugged. 'Things were simpler then.'

'In a good way?'

He tilted his head from side to side, as if to say 'maybe' or 'sort of'. 'There are pros and cons to both. Neither is better. It's just different.'

'Yeah, you're definitely too wise for your own good.' I shook my head as I laughed at him.

'Don't worry. You'll catch up with me one day.'

'God, I hope not. I don't want to be as annoying as you.'

He stuck his tongue out at me. 'You'd be lost without me and you know it.'

'True. Very true.' I hugged him, resting my head on his shoulder.

10
Edie

Fadil went back to Ben's to find the contact details for the coffee machine company. I carried on with the painting, blasting loud rock music through some portable speakers. I was buzzing with nervous energy and redecorating to music felt like a good outlet. With the weather being unseasonably warm, I wanted to get a coat done before it got too hot and affected the paintwork.

And all right, I was dancing as I painted. Sue me. It made me feel better.

I'd locked the door after Fadil had left, that way nobody could come in without me noticing. He'd be back later after finding the paperwork and having a rest. To help his aching muscles, we'd agreed to make up our schedules as we went along. As long as we got everything done before Ben got back, that was all that mattered, right?

I continued dancing, banging my head to the music in between brush strokes. I was almost done with the first coat of green. Seeing it alongside a couple of bookcases Fadil had built yesterday, I got why Ben had chosen it now. The green complemented the walnut of the shelves, adding depth and making the space feel cosy.

The dancing improved my mood, giving me a physical outlet for all the self-hatred I'd been bottling up. I hadn't realised just how much I'd been carrying until I stopped dancing and started panting. Anyone walking past would've just been able to make out a blurry figure moshing to music. I hoped they enjoyed the entertainment if they did look in.

When my favourite song came on, I put the paint brush down and began leaping around the room like I was doing a bad job at ballet or something. There was a reason I hadn't stuck with it beyond aged six.

I was so into my dance routine that when Fadil opened the door, I jumped so far I smashed into the bookcase. It toppled, crashing through the window. A stream of books fell to the floor.

Frazzle.

*

'What am I supposed to do, Maggie?' I bawled. In a panic, I'd called her, not knowing who else was responsible and calm enough to help. She worked in a kitchen and had two children. This was nothing compared to the level of stress she was used to every day.

Fadil was as freaked out as I was and blaming himself for making me jump, building the shelves before we'd done all the painting, and wanting to put books on there. None of it was his fault, but for some reason he often felt guilty for things he hadn't done.

The Poltergeist's Ship

While we'd waited for Maggie to arrive, we'd picked up the bookcase and the books. The bookcase was in tatters and would need to be replaced. Some of the books had ripped or had their covers bent at weird angles.

'I can't let Ben come home to this!' I leaned against the doorframe, away from anything else I could damage, and blew my nose on a tissue. 'But I can't afford to replace it, either.'

Fadil stood beside me, flicking through the phone book that, up until that point, we'd been using as a step to get to the higher shelves.

Maggie inspected the damaged window. 'It could be worse.'

I flapped my arms by my sides, the snotty tissue still scrunched up in my hand. 'How? How could it be worse! There's no window left!'

'Sure there is,' said Fadil. 'A window doesn't have to have glass in it.'

I glared at him. 'That's not helpful.'

He shrugged, returning to the phone book. 'Got something. Day and Night Windows. No job too big or small. Based just around the corner. And they do commercial. Want me to ring them?'

'Yes. But how do we pay them? I can't expect Ben to pay for this! Or put it on his insurance! A claim like this when he's not even open? His price would go through the roof!'

'There's a joke in there somewhere about it going through the window instead…'

'Fadil,' said Maggie, scolding him. It wasn't quite her Harsh Mum voice, but it had a clear warning to it. Which he totally deserved.

He retreated slightly. 'You're right. Sorry. That was too soon.'

Maggie walked over and rubbed my arm. 'I'll pay for it.' She put her hand up as I went to say she couldn't. 'And you can pay me back when you have the money.'

I wrapped her in a hug so tight I was pretty sure she couldn't breathe, but I didn't care. 'Thank you thank you thank you. You're the best.'

She gave me a squeeze. 'I know.'

*

The window fitter showed up half an hour later. Was it weird they were that fast?

I didn't care. I was desperate. Their online reviews had been decent. Maybe they just had a big team and I'd sounded desperate enough on the phone that they'd taken pity on me.

She strutted down the pavement from the direction of the tram and train station. I knew it was her because she wore a black baseball cap with 'Day and Night Windows' written on it. Everything she wore was black, and she was covered from head to toe: a long-sleeved cotton *Supernatural* top, black jeans, black boots, even black gloves. Her eyes were covered with Jackie-O style sunglasses. Underneath her baseball cap poked out thick, coily ash blonde hair that was tied into a low ponytail. She had on a lot of layers for August, especially during a heatwave. Maybe it was job-related?

As she reached Maggie and me and studied the damage, she whistled, long and low. 'What happened here?'

'Bookcase fell into the window,' I grumbled.

She stepped closer, looking at the edges of the shattered window. Her sunglasses were so dark, and her baseball cap so low, I was surprised she could see anything.

That wasn't the only thing that was odd about her, though. Her life essence felt...different. Like it had been split in half or something. It had a low-frequency to it. And it was a lot quieter than what I was used to. Usually, I had to tune out people's life essences so that I could focus on what I was doing. This time, I had to focus so that I could feel hers at all. Was it because Fadil was using some of my powers? Or was her life essence really that...*odd*?

As long as she could help me, I didn't care what her life essence felt like. Or what it meant.

Because I'd been so afraid of my necromancy powers, I hadn't developed the full scope of what someone's life essence could tell me. I knew there was the potential to learn how to sense different things – the Book of the Dead had a guide on it – but I didn't want to follow that path. It made me too nervous.

'I see,' she said.

What did that mean? How bad was it? Could she fix it?

'I'm Maisie, by the way. I run Day and Night Windows with my Dad.'

A father/daughter business? Cute.

'Edie. And this is my aunt, Maggie.'

Fadil had been so upset about the window situation that Maggie had sent him to walk Tilly before Maisie had arrived.

Maisie shook our hands, her leather gloves warm to the touch. Was she really wearing gloves in August? When the temperature was in the mid-20s?

Maisie took her phone from her jeans pocket and typed away. 'What sort of replacement are you looking for?'

'As close to the original as possible, please,' I said. That way Ben would hopefully never notice what'd happened.

She raised her head, as if to study me. 'You don't want something better quality?'

'I don't want the shop owner to know what happened while he was away,' I mumbled.

'Gotcha.' More typing on her phone.

I glanced over at Maggie, who gave me a meek smile.

'When is the shop owner back?' asked Maisie.

'Six days,' I replied.

She pursed her lips, trying to hide a frown.

'What? Can you help? Is it doable?' I said, my tone frantic.

She drummed her fingers on the back of her phone. 'It should be. Give me a minute?' She raised her phone to her ear and walked out of earshot.

I turned to Maggie: 'What if she can't help? Then what do we do?'

The Poltergeist's Ship

'Then we'll speak to someone else,' Maggie replied, still the picture of calm. How did she *do* that? Could I bottle her calm and drink it with my morning coffee? Maggie would probably tell me my excessive coffee and sugar consumptions were part of the problem if I asked her that. But I was not letting them go.

Maisie returned a moment later. 'We can do it. It'll cost extra for a rush job, though.'

I glanced at Maggie.

'That's fine,' she said. 'The shop is due to open soon. We can't afford to wait.' Or let Ben down any more than I already had. I was so glad Maggie was there to help. I wasn't sure what I'd do without her.

'All right. I'll send you a deposit invoice through when I get back to the office, then come back with a couple of the gang later to board it up.'

'Thank you!' I was so excited I could've hugged her, but that felt weird when I barely knew her. Especially when she was so covered up, and her life essence was so unusual, that there was clearly something different about her. It had to be related to her (lack of a) life essence, didn't it? It felt like too much of a coincidence otherwise.

But all that mattered was getting the window fixed. She could be a demon for all I cared. If she could help me, I'd sell her my soul.

OK, maybe not quite. But I *was* desperate.

She took a card from the back of her phone case and passed it to me. 'If you have any questions, give me a ring. I'll be in touch later.' With that, Maisie headed back through town, towards the tram and train.

'There was something odd about her, but I liked her,' I told Maggie once she was out of earshot. I could've sworn I saw Maisie's shoulders move, as if she was laughing. Could she hear us?

Maggie tilted her head. 'Odd in what way?'

'I think she might be one of us.'

Maggie narrowed her eyes. 'A part of your world?'

I nodded. '*Our* world. Just because you don't have powers, doesn't mean you're not a part of it.'

'Do I...feel different to you? Since the coma?' Maggie asked as we climbed through the broken window and went back inside.

'Why do you ask?'

'Your mum, Alanis, Ben...they've all mentioned how dark the curse Dominic cast on Josh and me was. I wondered if that'd changed anything.'

I hadn't been hugely sensitive to life essences when it'd happened last year, but I could definitely feel an underlying darkness to Maggie and Josh that hadn't been there before. Some days were better than others, but I couldn't deny that it was there, no matter how much I tried to ignore it.

'It doesn't change how good of a person you are, or how strong your life essence is. I guess your average, non-magical person would call it your spirit. You've always had a strong one. I don't need powers to see that. But does something that traumatic leave a mark? Yes. It would on anyone.'

Maggie bent down to pick up a paperback that'd been left on the floor, her brown hair falling over her face and shielding her expression from me.

'It doesn't change who you are, Maggie. Not if you don't let it.'

She held the book to her chest and steeled herself. 'Don't worry, I won't let him win.'

11

Niamh

'So, how'd you sleep on your first night on a cruise ship?' Ben asked, rolling over and putting his arm across my stomach.

We were lying in our cabin, the only light coming from the sun on the other side of the thin curtains. We had blackout curtains, but we'd left those open to help us wake up and gradually adjust our sleeping patterns.

The ship rocked gently, footsteps from the people in the cabin above us echoing.

It was still strange, being there with Ben instead of Edie. How was she? What was she up to? Was she sleeping all right on her own? I'd given up trying to contact her via the useless WiFi.

I'd slept all right, but not amazingly. Every so often, people walking up and down the corridor had jolted me awake. I was pretty sure some ghosts popped in at one point, but I couldn't be sure I hadn't dreamt it. I had had some weird dreams lately. Usually after too much sugar before bed or when I was on my period.

The ship was going to arrive in Palma de Mallorca for its first stop at eight that morning, giving us time to shower and have breakfast.

The Poltergeist's Ship

I placed my hand on Ben's and sighed. 'Better than I thought I would. You?'

He yawned. 'Not great. Apparently I get seasick.'

I sat upright, frowning. 'You never mentioned that!'

He joined me, resting his head on my shoulders. 'I didn't know. I've never been on a boat before.' He yawned again. 'I'm going to go for a shower, try to wake up before breakfast.'

'You sure you don't want to just relax for a bit?'

He hopped out of bed like an excited child. 'Are you kidding? We're on a cruise ship! I want to explore!' He pursed his lips for a moment, looking slightly green. 'And I will *not* let seasickness stop me!'

I laughed at his enthusiasm. 'All right.' I kissed him, then pulled the duvet over myself as he collected his toiletries then went in the shower.

While I was waiting for Ben, I decided to catch up on my favourite podcast. I hadn't had time to listen to it while travelling because I'd been too busy talking to him. But since he wasn't there, I put my earphones in, found the latest episode, and hit play.

The intro music kicked in. But then it stopped. I checked my earphones' battery levels and my phone said they were fine. So I tried again. A few seconds played. Then white noise replaced the folk music of the theme tune.

I paused it, went back a few seconds, and hit play again.

This time, white noise – much louder than the volume I'd chosen – shot through my ears. I ripped my earphones from my ears and threw them on the bed. *Ow.*

'What's up?' Ben asked, emerging from the bathroom wrapped in a towel. He rubbed at his freshly washed hair with a smaller one.

'I was going to listen to a podcast but it's just playing static,' I said.

'Maybe the download's corrupted? Try redownloading it when we reach Mallorca. You can borrow my headphones and see if that makes a difference as well if you want.'

'Thanks,' I said. 'You sure you'll be all right?'

He grabbed some jeans and boxers from a drawer, then put them on. 'I'll be fine. I'll take a seasickness tablet before our next sail away.' He picked out a T-shirt from the wardrobe and pulled it over his head. 'I'm not letting it ruin our holiday. I'm excited to explore Mallorca.'

'For the history or the architecture?'

He grinned. 'Both, of course.'

*

People always assume historical places are the most haunted, but I've always found them to be the opposite. Once the people responsible for someone's unfinished business have crossed over – whether it was resolved or not – in most cases, that ghost crosses over, too. The only exception tends to be when they don't *want* to cross over, like with Gwendoline and her fellow miners, or when the unfinished business is with another ghost, like with Thomas.

That doesn't stop the rumours, of course. People seeing grey ladies or murder victims or executioners floating around near where they were killed or did their business.

Mallorca was no exception. With a beautiful, historic castle overlooking the sea, it was rife with ghost stories.

But I actually found it peaceful.

Not because it wasn't full of people, but because it was more devoid of ghosts than many places I'd been to. Ghosts haunted the living, but the more historic parts of town, where no one lived, were a lot quieter than busy city centres or cruise ships.

The cathedral combined Gothic and European influences, making it unique in its style. The light-coloured stone was balanced out by bright green palm trees and the bright blue of the water. We saw so few ghosts walking around it I wished we could've stayed.

We got back on to the ship that night, sore from walking too far but content from exploring. We were going to get changed for dinner, then go for burgers.

Once I'd called Edie while I had a signal. It was the longest I'd gone without speaking to her and I was worried, especially after how much she'd been beating herself up about her exam results when we'd left.

Although I couldn't imagine cruising with anyone other than Ben now that we were on the ship.

'How's the cruise?' Edie asked, her face alongside Tilly's on my phone screen. Tilly nudged it.

I smiled, showing her around the room from my spot on the sofa. 'Good. Relaxing. How are you?'

'How are things going at the bookshop?' asked Ben from beside me.

'Good,' said Fadil from off camera. Edie exchanged a look with him. What did *that* mean? I daren't ask. The less we knew, the better.

'Maggie came to check on us. And Tilly had a bath yesterday,' said Edie. The little dog jumped off the sofa and disappeared out of sight.

'Why?'

'She rolled in Eau de Fox.'

'Lovely.' Typical westie.

Edie glanced at something behind her phone. 'Tilly thinks you're trapped in my phone. She's circling the table and staring at it, as if she's trying to find a way to get to you.'

I smiled, missing how cute they both were. But Edie seemed much happier at home. Having Tilly, Fadil, and Spectre with her was no doubt helping. Bringing Ben and leaving her at home had been the right choice.

'What time do you leave the port?' asked Fadil.

Ben checked his watch. 'In the next half an hour, I think.'

'I wonder what happens to people who don't make it,' said Edie.

'They get left behind,' said Fadil.

Edie turned to look at our research-obsessed friend. 'How do you know that?'

Fadil smirked. 'Saw it online. But I figured neither of you would do that. Especially not Ben.'

Ben grinned. 'Of course not. You know me better than that.' He was Mr Reliable, and it was one of the many things I loved about him.

'Have you ever come across someone you think is one of us but you can't be sure before?' Edie asked, changing the subject.

'Probably, but I wouldn't have known since this is all new to me,' I said.

'All the time,' replied Ben.

'Really?' Edie and I chorused.

'I can't sense life essences, obviously, but after a while you start to notice behaviour patterns. But if you don't know what to look for, that person might just seem a bit quirky. Why do you ask?'

'I met someone who I think might be one of us, but she feels totally different to anything I've ever felt before. So I have no frame of reference for figuring out what she is,' Edie explained.

What had she been doing to meet someone so unusual? Were there really that many people with powers in our hometown? How had I grown up so oblivious?

My mother. That was how.

'Have you checked the Book of the Dead?' asked Ben.

Edie grunted. 'No, I was trying to avoid translating any more of it. It's not a big deal, anyway. She seems nice enough and is fine with the wards.'

'That's what counts, right?' said Ben.

The wards had never failed us before, so that was a promising sign.

'How did you meet her?' I asked.

Edie and Fadil exchanged weighted looks again. What did those silent conversations mean? I'd never know.

'She was interested in the bookshop and stopped to ask us about it,' said Edie. Why did I feel like there was more to it than that, based on the loaded looks between them? Not that it mattered when I was thousands of miles away.

'How nice,' said Ben. 'Hopefully she'll become a patron when it's open.'

'Something tells me she'll become a regular,' said Fadil.

12

Edie

'Can we go to the pub?' Fadil asked, no hint of sarcasm in his voice.

We were sitting on the floor, organising the pile of damaged books. It wasn't looking good. I stopped sorting the books into damaged and undamaged piles and stared at him, wondering if he'd drunk some of Ben's craft beer with his lunch. Or were the glue fumes from the boarded-up window going to his head?

'Why?' I stretched my legs, my feet having gone numb from me sitting on them.

Fadil continued sorting. He sat on his feet, turning a book over in his hands. 'I've never been to one before. I want to see what it's like.'

'It's the middle of the week. It'll be deserted.' I picked up a hardback and examined it, bringing it closer and smelling the vanilla-like pages and fresh hardback glue. The spine was ripped. Frazzle.

Maybe I could acquire the damaged ones for my collection?

I probably couldn't afford all of them.

'Exactly,' said Fadil. I supposed it being quiet meant it'd be better for both of us. 'Come on. Don't you think it'd be good to get a distraction after a rough day?'

I was still feeling sorry for myself after what'd happened. I'd just been starting to feel better for my stupid grades. Breaking Ben's shop window had made me start to spiral again.

At least Fadil had had some luck with the coffee maker. They were sending someone out look at – and hopefully fix – it later this week.

He crawled over to me and rested his head on my shoulder, looking up at me with puppy-dog eyes I'd thought only Tilly was capable of. '*Pleeeeeeeease.*'

It was hard to say no to that face. Even harder when I remembered how isolated he'd been for most of his life and how he was still trying to make sense of the modern world. Some things would probably never make sense to him. That was why he had us.

I really didn't want to go out after having slept so badly, and having had such a stressful day, but I knew it'd be good for Fadil. And maybe he was right that the distraction would help me, too.

'All right. Fine. But if it gets too much for either of us, we leave.'

Fadil held his hand out for me to shake. 'Deal.'

*

After locking up the bookshop and changing into something less dusty and paint-covered, we headed to the pub. It was about a fifteen-minute walk from mine. And dog-friendly, but we chose to leave Tilly behind so that Fadil could absorb the atmosphere without being distracted by her. She was happy enough watching TV with Spectre for a couple of hours anyway.

The Poltergeist's Ship

We walked into the Victorian-era pub, heading into the restaurant area at the back. It was separated by a circular bar in the middle, with half of it visible on this side and half on the other. When it was first built, the divider had been to prevent different classes from being able to see each other. Nowadays it separated the main bar and restaurant areas, like in a lot of other British pubs.

'What do you want to drink?' I asked Fadil as we stood at the bar.

The mahogany wood framed the dozens of drinks on the back bar. Glasses hung from the ceiling. A jar of dog treats sat beside the beer taps.

Fadil stared at the back bar, his mouth agape. 'There's so much choice. What should I have?'

'They might let you try some of the beers on tap if you wanted to give those a go,' I said.

Fadil shook his head. 'No, I can't do that.' He had his ID in his hand, but he was uncomfortable using it because it was technically Dominic's. 'I'll just have lemonade, please.'

'All right.' I went for a rum and coke, feeling smug when the bartender IDed me. It was the first time I'd been out since turning eighteen. I'd had no one to go with until now. I'd never thought of inviting Fadil before because he often seemed so reluctant to go out, and I wasn't going to tag along with Mum and Ben. Gross.

After getting our drinks, we found a table near the back, by some black and white photos of local, long-dead celebrities.

Fadil leaned back in his wooden chair, taking everything in. 'So this is a pub.'

'This is a pub. It's a fairly stereotypical one, but it's decent enough.'

'You've been before?'

'For Sunday dinner with Mum and Tilly, yeah.' Mum had tried to motivate me to revise for my exams with a Sunday carvery. Some difference that'd made.

The side door opened and three familiar figures walked in: Josh, Melanie, and Laura. Frazzle. Fadil and I were sitting at a fairly large table. We'd thought we could get away with it because it was quiet. But there was enough room for them to sit with us if they wanted to. Josh and I might've been civil, but that didn't mean I was comfortable hanging out with him. This was meant to be a relaxing night out. If they joined us, Fadil and I would have to be careful what we said and did.

Melanie spotted us first, walking over without saying anything to the others.

'Hey Edie!' she said, a huge grin on her face. She held her hand out for Fadil to shake. 'I'm Melanie.'

'Fadil,' he said, shaking her hand as the other two joined us.

'He's my mum's boyfriend's cousin,' I informed them.

Josh smiled at Fadil. They'd only met a couple of times, but they got along fine. Josh knew who Fadil really was, but he went along with our cover story.

I glanced up at him, wistfulness washing over me. We locked eyes for less than a second before he looked away. Way to make me feel even worse about things between us.

He looked smart in his navy shorts and light blue cotton shirt. It wasn't the kind of thing he normally wore, but in the unexpectedly hot and humid weather, most people were dressed differently so that they didn't melt. Desperate times and all that.

I suddenly regretted wearing a mini skirt. I felt self-conscious. Exposed. Twisting in my seat, I tried to hide my pale, freckled legs, but what difference would it make? I couldn't change into trousers.

'Mind if we join you?' Melanie asked, pulling out a chair to my left before Fadil or I had answered. Why'd we have to sit at a round table?

Josh and Laura exchanged awkward glances but didn't say anything.

I didn't know Laura that well, but since we'd exorcised Melanie last year, she and I spoke a couple of times a week. She knew about ghosts and that I could see them, but not the full extent of my powers. The less she knew, the safer she was. That didn't stop her from being curious, of course. But I tried to keep things on a need-to-know basis. Like she didn't know who Fadil really was.

I glanced at Fadil. He shrugged. It was hard to say no without seeming rude, I supposed. Especially as they could tell we'd barely touched our drinks.

Laura sat beside Fadil, then Josh sat beside her. He stared at the table, barely looking at anyone.

'How've you been since results day? You disappeared before we could talk,' said Melanie. If she sensed the awkwardness, she didn't say anything.

'You know,' I said. 'Helping finish Ben's bookshop before it opens next month.'

'Exciting!'

Melanie had really opened up since Tessa's death, as if Tessa had suppressed who she really was. I almost felt bad thinking that, but Tessa had been oppressive, like humidity on a hot day. She'd just had such a presence about her. Living and dead.

'So, Fadil, tell us more about you,' said Laura, leaning into him. Her honey blonde hair fell out of place and tickled his shoulder.

Fadil shifted in his seat, tugging at the neck of his brown T-shirt. 'What do you want to know?'

'Where are you from?'

He opened his mouth, no doubt to say Egypt, then abruptly closed it, looking to me for confirmation.

'He went to boarding school,' I answered for him. 'Very sheltered.'

Fadil turned to me, a look that was somewhere between grateful and scornful on his face. Where else would he have had a sheltered upbringing, though? It wasn't like he could really say Egypt – the place was a bit different to when he'd grown up there. He had no idea what it was like now. And I couldn't help him because I had no idea either.

Laura seemed intrigued. Frazzle. 'I'll bet your parents must be really well off, right?'

'We don't speak anymore,' said Fadil. Well, that was true.

'Oh. I'm so sorry. I shouldn't have brought it up.' Laura reached out and stroked his hand. 'You're skin is so soft. So many men don't understand the importance of good skincare.'

Fadil jerked his hand away, his eyes wide with horror. He shifted in his seat, his gaze darting around the pub like a frightened dog. He chugged his lemonade, almost choking on it. 'I'm going to get another drink. Edie, can you come help me decide what to get, please?'

'Um, sure.'

What was wrong?

I figured him wanting to get a drink was code for needing to talk, so we got up. I went to the bar, but Fadil went through the corridor, as if heading to the other side of the pub. The bar there had more drinks visible, so we could use that as an excuse if anyone asked about it.

Except he stopped in the empty corridor and leaned against a wall just to the side of the stairs. His breathing was rapid, as if he couldn't fill his lungs with air.

I put my hand on his shoulder. 'Are you all right?'

He shook his head. 'I can't...I need...'

'Come on.' I grabbed his hand and guided him outside into the fresh air. It was still a little stuffy out, but it was sunny and nowhere near as humid as it could've been.

The pub was unusual in that it sat just off a four-way junction. So there wasn't a lot of space for a seating area, and the outside was quite busy at times. There was a small row of fenced-off picnic benches to the side of the pub, so that's where we sat. It was the other side to where we'd left everyone, so they wouldn't see us through the window.

Fadil put his hands face-down on the table as if he was trying to steady himself. He shook his head. 'I can't do this.'

'What do you mean? This was your idea.'

He shook his head again. 'No. I mean. With Laura.'

'What about it? She likes you.'

He took a deep breath. 'Yes, I'm aware. I've watched enough romance films.'

'You're not interested in her?'

He half-laughed, raising his head. His expression was one of disgust. 'How can I be? I'm old enough to be her great-great-great-great a million times great grandfather! For all I know, we *are* related! There's no way to trace my family tree!' He stared at the table. 'She'll never get it. She'll never be a part of our world. Look at what's happened to everyone who is, or finds out about it. Maggie, Josh, Melanie. She's safer if she doesn't know.'

'Who says she has to know? You can pass for someone from the 21st century now.'

He sighed. 'That doesn't change who I am or where I come from. I'll never completely fit in here, no matter how much I try to assimilate. You get it. Your mum and Ben get it. Even Josh does to a degree. But most people never will. I have all the love I need from the people already in my life. I don't need a romantic relationship to feel fulfilled.'

'So don't make it about that,' I said, leaning back in my chair.

Fadil shook his head. 'You don't get it. I'm not interested in that, either.'

'No sex?'

The Poltergeist's Ship

'I went four thousand years without it.'

I pursed my lips. That was an awfully long time to be celibate.

'My point is, I don't miss it. And I don't want it again.'

I reached out and touched his hands. 'If that's what you want, then of course we'll support you. And we'll get Laura off your back.'

'How? You don't even know her that well.'

'Don't need to,' I said with a smirk. He had so much to learn.

13

Edie

We returned to the table with refreshed drinks. Laura's heavily mascaraed eyes looked up at Fadil.

I sat beside her while Fadil sat in my old seat, creating a barrier between them. She pouted. Pretending I hadn't seen it, I met Melanie's gaze and gave my head a small shake, then glanced at Laura. Was my message subtle enough that Laura wouldn't notice, but Melanie would understand?

She nodded, so I figured she had.

'Say, Law, did you see that cute bartender?' asked Melanie. Yep, she'd got it. Phew.

Laura took her eyes from Fadil and focused on her friend. 'No. Tell me more.'

I nudged Fadil under the table. He didn't respond. Josh sipped his drink, oblivious to what was going on. There was a time when he would've been the person I'd asked for help, but that time had long passed.

Plus, Melanie was Laura's best friend. She was the best person to deflect her friend's attention.

'Come on, let's go get a drink and see if we can get him to serve us,' said Melanie with a mischievous smirk. The two of them left, leaving a bemused Josh behind with Fadil and me.

The Poltergeist's Ship

'Why do I feel like I'm missing something?' Josh asked. He quickly looked at me, then looked away. I wasn't sure if his habit of barely making eye contact with me would ever fully go away.

Fadil's shoulders lowered. 'Am I a bad person?'

'No! Never!' I said.

Josh glanced at the door Melanie and Laura had just walked through. 'Because you're not interested in Laura?'

Fadil nodded.

'She moves on pretty quickly. She'll be fine,' he said.

That seemed to perk Fadil up. 'She does?'

'Yeah,' said Josh. He ran his finger around the rim of his cider glass. 'She has a tendency to lay it on a bit thick.'

'You don't say,' said Fadil.

Josh gave him a downturned smile. 'It must be hard, being in a situation like yours with everything.' More people had entered the pub since we'd got there, so I appreciated Josh being vague and I knew Fadil would, too.

'You have no idea,' said Fadil. 'Why do I have to want romance to feel whole?'

'You don't,' said Josh. 'If that's not for you, there's nothing wrong with that.'

I smiled at him, pleased that Josh accepted what Fadil was saying.

'Thanks,' said Fadil. He nudged me. 'And thanks for understanding, too.'

'Of course. I want you to live whatever type of life makes you happy.'

'I don't know what that is yet, but I do know it'll include you.'

I smiled. 'Fine by me. You're going to find it pretty hard to get rid of me.'

*

Melanie came back a few minutes later, sans Laura. 'She stayed to flirt with the bartender. You're safe.'

Fadil rested his head on the old wooden table, clearly relieved. 'Thank you,' he said to the table.

Melanie smiled as she sat down. 'She's like a small child, easily distracted from things that she needs to stay away from. No damage done, don't worry.'

Knowing he hadn't hurt her definitely made him feel better. But it had tainted our night out. It was pretty obvious Fadil didn't want to stick around, so we left soon after.

On the walk home, a familiar face rounded the corner on to the bypass. Maisie. She was striding down the opposite side of the road, wearing grey jeans and an *Ash vs The Evil Dead* T-shirt. No gloves, hat, or sunglasses this time. Strange.

I could finally make out her features properly. Her thick hair came to her shoulders. She was taller than average and had a muscular frame and looked a couple of years older than me.

Noticing us, she raised her head in greeting. I smiled back, crossing over so that we could talk to her.

'Nice top,' I said.

'Thanks. It's one of my favourite shows. And films. I do love anything where evil gets fucked up. It's a reassuring message in modern times.'

'Tell me about it,' I said.

Fadil stood beside me, his hands stuffed into the pockets of his straight-leg jeans. He looked around, as if he were trying to stay out of the conversation or didn't know what to say.

'How come you're out so late?' she asked.

'What, should I have a curfew?'

She smirked. 'Well, I figured bookish types like you two…'

'You're not wrong,' Fadil mumbled.

She smiled again. It was a smile that seemed to light up her whole face, returning personality and temporarily distracting from the greyish hue of her brown skin.

'We went to the pub,' I said.

Maisie checked her watch. 'In that case, you're out early. Leaving at ten?' She tutted. 'You've got another hour and a half! And you're not nearly drunk enough.'

'Excuse me,' said Fadil. He walked away, as if he wanted to be alone.

Maisie watched him round the corner. 'He OK?'

'Rough night.'

'Oh. Sorry. Did I just make things worse?'

'He'll be all right,' I said. 'He just needs a comfort film and a hot chocolate.'

'If you say so.' She glanced around, as if looking for something but not finding it. 'I'd better get going. Look after yourself, yeah?'

'You too.'

I turned back as I walked off. She was watching me. She gave me one last wave, then continued in the opposite direction.

Fadil was just round the corner, leaning against a wall. 'Sorry. I didn't mean to bolt like that. You could've talked to her a bit longer.'

'It's fine. I was worried about you,' I said.

'I guess Laura just made me realise some stuff about myself that…I guess I'm OK with, but saying it aloud made it more real, if you get me? It's something I've wondered for a while, but now I have confirmation.'

'It's OK. You're allowed all the processing time you need.'

'Am I? It doesn't feel like it.'

'Why?'

He twisted his foot against the pavement as we stood in the pedestrianised street. 'Everything moves so fast in this time. Is there ever time to really sit on decisions or process them?' He clasped his hands together, then began to massage one of his palms.

'There is if you need it,' I said. 'I'm sure Ben would understand if you needed to take a step back from the shop.'

'No! I need that!' He switched to massaging the other hand. 'It's just other stuff, I guess. I don't know. Maybe I'm overthinking things.' He seemed to be putting a lot of pressure on that hand.

'Are you all right?'

'My hands are just really sore, that's all. They feel… tight and tingly and they're pulsing.'

'Maybe we should get Doc to check you out.'

He stopped massaging his hands and tightened his jaw. 'No. Definitely not.'

14

Niamh

'What the—' Ben jumped out of the bathroom, cringing. His hands were turning an angry red.

I peered into the bathroom. The room was filling with steam as boiling water gushed from the tap. He turned it off. Had something happened to the hot water since we'd had our morning showers?

'You all right?' I asked.

'Yeah, fine,' he said, rubbing his hands. He turned the tap back on to see if cold came out the second time, but almost immediately, boiling water came out again. 'That's so weird.'

'Maybe it's just having a moment,' I said. I got some calendula cream from my first aid kit and handed it to him.

'Thanks. I'm sure they'll get it sorted. With so many things to manage on this ship, little things like that are bound to go wrong.'

'Yeah.'

'I was going to fill my water bottle from the bathroom, but I think I'll pick up a drink on the way instead,' he said.

I tried to convince myself that he was right, that things broke all the time. It was how I paid my bills. I should know. But I couldn't shake the feeling that it wasn't a fault on the ship.

*

'Hello hello hello,' said the steward who was taking us on a behind-the-scenes tour of the ship. She was a twenty-something blonde with a spring in her step. 'My name's Aly. I'm so happy you could join us! We're going to check out some staff-only areas, where the crew sleep, and go say hi to the captain on the bridge. So let's get this started!'

There were only a handful of people on the tour, but they ran them throughout the cruise and in different languages, so I supposed with it being our first sea day it wasn't at the top of most people's list of priorities. Ben and I were interested in how the ship was run so we'd decided to check it out.

We followed Aly through the ship while she talked about the history of cruising. Apparently when flying was invented, ocean liners were repurposed into cruise ships, turning the former mode of transport into a destination instead.

Our first stop was the staff cafeteria, where they had their main meals. There were no windows on this floor, but there were screens around the room that emulated the weather outside. Currently, it was bright sunshine with a handful of clouds.

The room itself was orange and blue, with tiled flooring. Several different buffet areas were laid out around the huge space, allowing staff to help themselves to food. Aly explained that on some days, they had themed meals or party nights to celebrate staff, since they technically didn't have a day off the whole time they worked on the cruise.

This far down the ship, the bobbing in the waves was considerably more noticeable. Ben looked a little green, so I figured the seasickness tablet he'd bought hadn't fully kicked in yet. Based on the set of his jaw, the nausea wasn't going to stop him.

Off to the sides of the huge cafeteria was a shop where the crew could get snacks and toiletries, and through another door was a nightclub. Since it was the middle of the day it was empty, but they were clearly going for the vibe of an upmarket club with its sleek dark wood furniture and black walls.

After showing us the gym, we went up a floor to the staff bunks. I shivered.

'You all right?' asked Ben.

'Yeah, just a chill.' Except it didn't feel like that. It felt more unnerving than that. More tainted than that. It had to just be a coincidence, though. It couldn't be a poltergeist or a demon.

Could it?

I couldn't see any ghosts. Although that didn't mean they weren't nearby. I shivered again. There had to be another explanation. There couldn't be a poltergeist on holiday. We deserved a break, dammit.

'This is one of the vacant bunks,' said Aly. It had a TV and a few other amenities, but I was surprised at how small the staff bedrooms were. I supposed the cruise company wanted the crew to only have the basics and therefore feel compelled to work as much as possible.

The Poltergeist's Ship

'If you'll follow me up these stairs, we'll head to the captain's quarters next.' It wasn't just up some stairs. It was through a labyrinth to get there. But the view from higher up on the ship, of the bright blue sea and skies, was worth it. 'We can't go into the captain's quarters, but we can go see her on the bridge.' Aly opened a door and we stepped on to a glass-fronted area that looked out to sea. It hung slightly over the edge of the ship to give the staff on the bridge a better view. They all looked up and waved, then turned back to what they were doing.

'This is the centre of operations,' Aly explained. 'As you can see, we've got an amazing view out here. And, if you come a bit farther...' We followed her deeper onto the bridge. Some of it had a glass floor so that we could see below into the ocean. I stepped back, feeling a bit woozy.

'This helps when we're pulling into port. Some people don't like standing on it, but the glass is over an inch thick. It's completely safe.' She jumped. Several of us, myself included, gasped. But of course, nothing happened.

The captain came over, today wearing a white shirt and navy trousers. 'Hello everyone, I'm Captain Sofia Ricci. How's the cruise? Is Aly taking good care of you?'

No one answered.

'She is,' said Ben, avoiding leaving the captain hanging any longer.

The captain smiled. 'Well, I'll leave you to it. Have a lovely cruise. And don't forget to try the tiramisu in the main restaurant. It's my favourite!'

Everyone mumbled that they would, then the captain returned to talking to one of the other crew members on the bridge.

Aly beckoned us closer conspiratorially. 'If you come here and peak through this door, you can see into the captain's office. Just through the door on the other side are her quarters. She stays close because, while she's here, she's always on call, even during her downtime. So the closer she is to the bridge, the better.' Given how far we'd walked to get to the bridge, I wasn't surprised the ship was designed to keep the captain right next to it. We must've spent half the tour walking from one part of the ship to the next.

I shivered again. Were we following the path of a poltergeist?

A figure moved in my peripheral vision. I turned, but it was gone before I could register anything other than that it'd definitely been a ghost. Fingers crossed it was a nice one.

Although judging from what I could sense, I didn't think it was.

The door that led to the captain's quarters was closed, but we could see into the office. It was full of tech and paperwork. Like any other office, but more high-tech. I could see Ben peering through the window, trying to work out what each piece of equipment did. It all went over my head, but he seemed fascinated.

I stepped closer to try to work out what was so interesting. And if I could see the ghost again. Another wave of evil hit me, stronger than the last. I gasped, stepping into another passenger behind me.

'Sorry,' I said.

The Poltergeist's Ship

He put his hand on my arms to steady me. 'It's all right. Just need to find your sea legs.'

Oh how I wished that was my problem.

15
Edie

I opened Ben's front door, breakfast hooked over one arm and Tilly's lead on the other. Before I could call out to let Fadil know it was me, Tilly was yanking on the lead to get to him and barking excitedly, so I figured he'd know.

Stumbling through the door, I let her off. She catapulted herself up the stairs to Fadil. I heard him yelp in surprise, then start making baby noises at her. Smiling, I put her lead on the coat rack then followed her upstairs.

Fadil lay in bed, huge bags under his reddened eyes. 'I feel terrible, before you ask.'

'Will breakfast help?' I asked, holding up the bag. 'I bought cherry Bakewell waffles or blueberry pancakes.'

He sat up in bed, the prospect of food seeming to have perked him up. 'Pancakes please.'

'Do you want to eat in here, or?'

'No, I'll come downstairs. I don't like eating in bed. But give me a minute? I might need a crane.'

'Do you want some help?'

He shook his head then seemed to regret it, clutching the bed to steady his spinning head. 'I'll meet you downstairs.'

The Poltergeist's Ship

'All right. Give me a shout if you need me.'

'Will do.'

I left him to his search for a crane, then laid our breakfasts out on the table. I didn't bother dishing them up on to plates in case we lost some of the maple syrup or almond butter on the breakfasts, so instead I just put some cutlery out and made us each a cup of tea.

Tilly barked. It was her excited bark, so I figured it meant Fadil was out of bed. A moment later, he plodded down the stairs, then hobbled into the kitchen, hunched over and clutching his back. Tilly was close behind, never letting him out of her sight.

'My back has seized up.' He sat down. 'Why do I feel so sore? And so ancient?'

I bit my lip.

Realising what he'd said, he laughed. 'You're right. I *am*. I just don't normally feel it this much.'

'Do you think your past is catching up with you?'

He shrugged, choosing to start eating and avoid my question.

Halfway through his pancakes, he said: 'thanks for yesterday.'

'You don't have to thank me for anything.'

'I do, though. Not everyone would understand.'

I rested my cutlery on my takeaway box. 'Not everyone is me.'

He smiled. 'No that's very true.'

'I'll take that as a compliment.'

'It was meant as one.'

We finished our food in comfortable silence, then I left him and Tilly to rest while I headed to the bookshop.

*

'Come *on*!' I banged my head against the bookshop door. The boards that Maisie and her colleagues had put up the day before were covered in graffiti. It wasn't particularly pretty or any form of art: it was some black scribbles on the plywood. That was it. I wouldn't have minded so much if it'd looked good.

Could things get any worse? It was one thing after another. I was exhausted.

I sank on to the ground, resting my head against the ugly wooden board. Why was I even bothering? It felt like one step forwards, twelve steps back. I'd never get anywhere at this pace.

With Fadil resting, I didn't even have anyone to help me clean up the ugly scribbles. And I really didn't have the energy to do it. I'd hoped to finish painting today.

Stupidly frustrated, I cried. It was a drizzly day so there thankfully weren't many people around to see me bawling. I didn't even care that I was getting wet. What difference did it make? That was the least of my problems.

'You OK?' asked a familiar voice.

I looked up to see Maisie. Great timing. As if she didn't already think I was a failure for breaking Ben's window. Too drained to speak, I just shook my head.

She was covered from head-to-toe again, wearing the same branded baseball cap as yesterday, and huge sunglasses despite the cloudy day. Her coat made her look like she belonged in *The Matrix*.

She sat beside me, mimicking my knees-to-chest pose. Tapping the board with the back of her head, she said: 'This is only temporary. Don't let it get you down.'

'How can I not? It's one thing after another after another. I'm not sure how much more I can take.'

Maisie stood up and held out a gloved hand. 'Come on. Let's go talk somewhere dry.'

'I don't want to disrupt your day.'

'Are you kidding? I was going to the bank.' She faked a yawn. 'You're doing me a favour.' She smiled. It was a genuine smile, too. At least, as far as I could tell. My judgement wasn't exactly reliable.

I took her hand and she helped me up. Her strength startled me. It was like I weighed nothing to her. I mean, I wasn't heavy, but I wasn't light by any means either. Curiouser and curiouser.

We walked a couple of doors down to the nearest coffee shop. Stepping inside, we shook the rain from ourselves then joined the queue.

'I'll get the drinks, you go sit down. You look like you need it,' said Maisie.

'Do I look that rough? I mean, I only woke up two hours ago. If I look that bad already…'

She gave me a sympathetic smile. 'I wouldn't say you look rough. I'd say you look fed up.'

I clicked my tongue, pointing at her. 'Got it in one.'

She frowned. 'What do you want to drink?'

'Coffee. Black. Strong.' I needed something strong to wake me up and make me feel less crappy.

'Coming right up. Gimme a minute and I'll come join you.'

I grabbed a table near the back of the long space, sitting facing the huge window at the front of the shop. Normally, I found coffee shops comforting. I was pretty sure I was beyond that.

Self-hatred and pity plagued my thoughts as I rested my head in my hands. The same worries danced around and around in my head, like I was trapped on the world's worst merry-go-round. What was wrong with Fadil? Would we get the bookshop window fixed in time? Would we finish redecorating? Building furniture? Finishing the website? Should I resit my exams? How was Mum? Was she enjoying her cruise?

'So,' said Maisie, putting our drinks on the table and pulling me off the merry-go-round of nightmares. 'What's wrong?'

I looked up at her, pulling my massive filter coffee to me. 'I don't want to burden you.'

She sat opposite me, removing her baseball cap and placing it on the table beside her espresso. 'A problem shared is a problem halved.'

'Is that really true?'

She tilted her head. 'One way to find out.'

There was something about Maisie that made her easy to talk to. I'd felt like that about Dominic, too, but she felt different, somehow. Like she just actually wanted to listen. No pretence. No judgement. Just a friendly ear.

But could I really trust my instincts? They hadn't exactly served me well…ever.

Could I trust the wards more? They hadn't steered me wrong yet…

'I've just had so many things go wrong lately, this feels like the icing on the cake.'

Maisie suppressed a chuckle. 'I mean, it *is* kind of like icing. Since it's on top of the boards…'

I shook my head, trying not to laugh. 'That was bad.'

Her grin widened. 'Made you smile.'

'You're terrible,' I said, still trying not to laugh.

'You know, the boards are only temporary. They'll be gone in no time. And so will that bad graffiti. The artist could've tried a bit harder to make it look good.'

'Probably didn't feel it was worth it since they're only temporary,' I said. 'Used them as a canvas to practise their skills instead.'

Maisie smirked. 'See? I knew you had some humour in you somewhere!'

I tapped my giant mug of black coffee. I wasn't so sure that *was* funny, but talking to her was making me feel a bit better. 'Will it really be done before Mum and Ben get home? I can't have them find out. They already think I'm a failure.' I chugged some coffee, hoping it'd help. Instead it almost burned my mouth as it was still too hot to drink.

'Firstly, I'm pretty sure no good parent would ever think that about their child. Secondly, yes, it will be. They'll never find out.' She smirked. 'We all have our secrets, right?'

Was she alluding to her own?

Her hand went to her face. She scratched, then jerked her hand away as if she shouldn't be doing it.

''Scuse me.' She grabbed her bag and hat and went into the toilets.

I sipped my coffee, leaning back in the seat and watching the rain tap against the window. A thunderstorm had been forecast but hadn't manifested. I was disappointed. There was something soothing about them, especially the way it smelled after.

Maisie emerged a moment later, rubbing something into her hands.

'Hand cream?' I asked.

'Sunscreen. I'm really sensitive to UVA rays, so I have to reapply it all the time.'

'Even in winter?' I asked.

'Yeah. Unlike UVB rays, UVA rays don't change based on what time of year it is. They can do a whole lot of damage all year round if you're sensitive enough. Even in cloudy, English weather.'

'That must suck.'

She nodded, sighing as she sat down. 'It does, but it also means I've got killer skin.'

'Is that why you cover up so much?'

She held her baseball cap by the brim and shook it about. 'Yeah. It's really annoying and gets me some weird looks, but what can you do? At least in the UK the UVA levels never really get that high compared to some countries.'

'It still sounds like a lot to manage.'

She shrugged. 'I'm used to it. Now: back to you. What else has been on your mind?'

'I failed my exams.' How had I confessed that so easily to her, but I'd struggled to talk to anyone else about it?

'Did you fail, or were your expectations too high?'

That was a question I hadn't considered. But everyone wanted good grades, didn't they?

'I didn't get high enough grades to go to uni,' I said.

'Do you want to go to uni?'

'No, but that's not the point. I was classed as one of those "gifted" students, you know? And I feel like the last year, I lost it.'

'Ah, the curse of the gifted student. I know it well.'

'You have my condolences.' I finished my coffee. 'I'm sorry, I'm just offloading on you and that's not fair.'

'Didn't I invite you for a coffee so that you could offload?' She twisted her espresso cup around. She still hadn't drank any of it. 'Can you resit?'

'Maybe. But what's the point? How do I know I'll do any better?'

'I can help you study, if you want? As long as it's not, like, music or something. I have no musical talents.'

I laughed. 'No. Not music. I also have zero musical talents.'

'In that case, I can probably help. And listen, don't be so hard on yourself. Exams are stressful. And something tells me you've been through a lot lately. Not everyone understands that, but what happens outside of academia or work has a huge impact on our ability to recall information. And exams are basically one big recall exercise. It's exclusionist, if you ask me.'

Had she been talking to Ben and Fadil? Because what she was saying reminded me a lot of what they'd said a few days ago. Had it really only been a few days?

'It is. But if I ever change my mind about working for Mum, I need a back-up plan. And that starts with improving my grades.'

Maisie tapped the edge of her untouched espresso. 'Well then. When do you want to start studying?'

16

Niamh

Because Ben was a huge nerd and loved showing off his knowledge – and I loved seeing him show off his knowledge – we went to trivia night in one of the ship's pubs that evening. The theme was the 90s, which, in theory, we'd both be good at. In practice…there were a lot of people on the ship.

We got one of the last tables, not having realised it would fill up quite as quickly as it did when there was still half an hour to go until it started.

But they'd already set everything up, with the screen at the front announcing that the next activity was the trivia.

When it got nearer the time, someone handed out the sheets of paper for us to fill in.

'What shall we call our team?' Ben asked, holding the pen above the paper, ready to write our team name down.

'Ben and Niamh?' I suggested.

Ben rolled his eyes. 'So unoriginal.'

'I hate naming things,' I said. 'What about Nen? Or Biamh?'

'They're terrible 'ship names,' said Ben.

'I agree. So I'll leave the name to you.'

Ben hid the paper from me then scribbled something. He removed his hand, then leaned back and grinned. *The Ghost Hunters*.

I stared at him. 'Could you be more obvious?'

'No one is going to believe that's what we actually are. Especially not when the autumn and Halloween decorations are practically everywhere by the end of July, and it's already the end of August.'

He was right. It was like autumn got earlier and longer every year, and the minute Halloween was over, the Christmas decorations came out.

Right now, the bar didn't have any decorations up. It was designed to look like an English pub with mahogany wood, green leather, and real ale on the bar. The biggest difference to an English pub was the air conditioning unit above us, which provided us with a refreshing breeze. No English pub would fork out for an air con unit. They were too expensive and we only needed them about two days a year.

Although looking at the weather forecast for Hucknall, it looked like they were having a heatwave and we were missing the one week of good weather England had every year. I hoped Edie and Tilly were OK, and Edie was wearing her sunscreen.

Our quiz host, who also happened to be Aly from earlier, hopped on to the stage. Was she even old enough to remember the 90s? And was everyone who worked on the cruise filled with so much energy? Or just the crew members we seemed to keep running into? 'All right everyone, we've got our teams ready. Are you excited for our 90s-themed quiz?'

The crowd cheered.

The Poltergeist's Ship

'Awesome. Our first lot of questions are music related. Question one: what was Geri Halliwell's – aka Ginger Spice's – famous Union Jack dress made out of?' asked Aly. The question appeared on the screen behind her in several different languages.

'A tea towel and a black Gucci dress,' I mumbled to Ben, to make sure no one sitting nearby could hear me.

'Really?' said Ben.

I nodded.

'How do you know that?'

'Do you really want to know?'

'Yes. I never painted you as a Spice Girls fan or a fashion fan. So now I have to know,' he said, scribbling down my answer.

'It was the former. Geri was my favourite. She made red hair cool.'

'Red hair's always been cool.' He kissed my cheek. 'Anyone who doesn't think so needs to borrow my glasses.'

I squeezed his shoulder. He always knew what to say.

'Our next question is a clip from a song. One point for the artist, one for the song title.' Aly hit play on the remote in her hand. A music video started to play on the screen, but it was broken by static. The audio was distorted and fragmented, making it impossible to tell what it was. The clip stopped.

Was the static part of the quiz? It'd been so brief I couldn't tell.

Ben wrote down the answer, clearly knowing what it was from the five seconds Aly had played.

'You could tell what that was?' I said incredulously.

'Yeah. Everyone knows that song.'

I glanced at what he'd written down. There was no way I would've gotten The Verve's *Bittersweet Symphony* from that.

She did three more music questions — none of which I could figure out, but Ben got all three — then changed categories.

'Now we're on to movies! For each question, you'll get one point for the movie title and another for the actor's name. And that's the actor, *not* the character they play.'

She hit play on the remote in her hand. The image and the sound were distorted again. It was louder this time. Wasn't it bothering anyone else? I cringed, looking away and covering my eyes. Surely this wasn't part of the quiz? Nobody else seemed to react to it. But it couldn't just be me, could it?

'Are you all right?' Ben whispered into my ear.

The clip, thankfully, finished. I removed my hands and relaxed.

Until a face appeared on the screen. It took up the whole thing, its jaw tight and its nostrils flaring. Their eyes darted around the room, as if searching for someone. I turned away, trying to look like I couldn't see them while keeping the screen in the corner of my vision.

'Do you see him? On the screen?'

'I see a clip from *Pulp Fiction*.'

Great.

I looked at the screen again. The face was gone. So was the static.

'Did you not hear the static?' I continued, really hoping it wasn't just me seeing and hearing things again.

'What static?'

'Was the clip distorted for you at all? Were any of them?'

'No. What did you see and hear?'

'All the clips were just static. The noise was so loud I could barely hear them. I couldn't tell what they were meant to be.'

Ben frowned. 'There was nothing there. It was just a clip from a…well-known nineties horror movie involving a witch in the woods that we never see,' he said, clearly referencing *The Blair Witch Project*.

'I didn't see or hear that. At all.'

'Do you want to go?' asked Ben.

I really didn't want to, but I couldn't put up with the noise. It was painful. And loud.

But that wasn't what was really bugging me.

Who was the face on the screen? And why was I the only person who could see them and the static?

17
Edie

Tilly barked. I jumped awake. Gwendoline was hovering at the foot of my bed. 'Sorry to wake you,' she said, looking genuinely guilty. 'I didn't know who else to tell.'

'What is it?' I said, sitting up, immediately alert. It was two in the morning. She only would've woken me in an emergency.

'Shane was out and noticed your friend Maggie's husband behaving erratically.'

'Erratically how?' I asked as I reached for my phone, ready to call Maggie so that she could pick him up.

'Like he was drunk or something.'

Harry didn't get drunk. Or at least, I'd never seen him drunk. The most I'd ever seen him drink was a fancy glass of wine or one of those real ales with a meal.

Maggie answered after the second ring. She sounded groggy. 'Edie? Whaswron?'

'Sorry to wake you. A ghost saw Harry in town and thinks he's drunk.'

'My husband? *Drunk*?' I could hear the sounds of her moving around and getting dressed, ready to pick him up. And the incredulity in her voice. 'Do you know where he is?'

'Gwendoline does.'

Maggie had never spoken to Gwendoline before, since she couldn't see ghosts, but she knew of her existence because she'd helped us more times than we could count. And this was probably going to be another one of those occasions. It was a shame they couldn't speak as I thought they'd get along.

'Do you want me to meet you there?' I offered.

'No! I'll come get you. I don't want you wandering the streets this late on your own. Your mother would murder me.'

'No she wouldn't. She loves you too much.'

Maggie scoffed. 'She loves you more.'

*

I left Tilly to nap and climbed into Maggie's car. She seemed more awake now. Before I'd even fastened my seatbelt, she was pulling away, having not turned the engine off to wait for me.

'Gwendoline has just gone to check he's still there,' I said. 'But if you head in the direction of town, that should give us a good start.'

'He's still in town,' said Gwendoline, appearing behind us in the backseat. 'By the Lord Byron statue.'

'Great. Thanks,' I said to her. 'He's by the Lord Byron statue.'

'What statue?' said Maggie.

I snorted. 'Really? You've lived here forever and never noticed it?'

'It's two in the morning,' she reminded me. 'I just about remember my own name.'

'Right. The one on the building opposite the church where Lord Byron is buried.' It was a pretty big statue built into the side of a building. It looked over to the church where he was buried, and the graveyard behind it that Thomas had once haunted.

'Oh. *Oh!* That statue. I know the one you mean now. Opposite the car park. Perfect. Easier to get him into the car. In theory.' We drove in silence for a minute. 'Hm. I didn't think about what we'd do if he didn't want to get into the car.'

I cleared my throat, shifting awkwardly in my seat.

Maggie chanced a look at me as she turned into town. 'No. *No.* That's another thing she'd murder me for.'

'I'd only do it a little bit so that he was more cooperative.'

Maggie inhaled through her teeth, her grip tightening on the steering wheel. 'Let's see what happens first.' She pulled into the car park. There was no one else there, since it was so early. Or late. Whatever you classed two in the morning as.

The gates to Thomas's old graveyard were closed; the library lights switched off. The only lights were the security lights of the shops in town and the orange hue of the street lamps.

Maggie turned off the engine. We sat for a moment, listening.

There was an eerie silence, broken only by the wind rustling the leaves on the poplar trees in the graveyard and in front of the library. I suppressed a shudder.

Even though I could see ghosts, that didn't make the atmosphere any less eerie.

'There!' pointed Gwendoline.

I looked over, tapping Maggie on the shoulder and pointing in the same direction. A figure that looked remarkably like Harry was now stumbling down the pedestrianised high street. He was stumbling so much I was surprised he was even still upright. *Was* he drunk?

'Is that really my Harry?' said Maggie.

'You've never seen him that drunk before?' I figured it'd happened, just not in my lifetime. Or not around me, at least.

'No, never. He told me once that he got so drunk at his first Freshers' Week he spent all night vomiting into a toilet and it put him off. So now he only has the odd one or two.' She got out and headed towards him. I exchanged worried looks with Gwendoline, but we followed. What else could we do?

Shane and another ghost that haunted the bookshop watched on helplessly, walking alongside drunken Harry. They weren't powerful enough to materialise and do anything. But at least they could talk to me so we knew what was going on.

'Do either of you know what happened?' I asked them.

'No,' said Shane. 'This is how we found him. Gwendoline recognised him so went to find you.'

'Thanks,' I said, then relayed what they'd told me to Maggie.

Maggie approached her husband, her hands hovering above him. 'Harry? Let's get you home, shall we?'

'Huh? Mags? Is that you?'

'It's me,' she said, her voice soothing.

He staggered towards her open arms, but before he could reach them, he tripped and fell to the floor.

Maggie reached down to help him up, but when he stood, he was like a different person. 'I'm fine. I'm fine,' he snapped. But he wasn't fine. He still seemed disorientated. 'How did I get here? What's going on?'

'We're taking you home so you can sleep whatever this is off,' said Maggie, her hand hovering behind his back as we returned to the car.

'What *is* this? Why do I feel so strange?'

'How do you feel?' I asked.

He looked me up and down with disdain. Always good to know when someone appreciated your help. 'Peculiar.'

I suppressed a laugh. Of course he'd say that. Both not helpful and indicative of Harry being Harry.

Harry refused our help to get into the car, swotting our hands away whenever we reached out to him. And, of course, he insisted on sitting in the passenger seat so I went behind Maggie. I couldn't sense anything off about him. Maybe he was just drunk to cope with work stress? He reeked of alcohol, so it wasn't a huge stretch.

But there was something about his erratic behaviour that didn't feel like it was just alcohol. It didn't feel like drugs either, but maybe it was. I didn't have much experience with that sort of thing, so it wasn't like I had anything to compare his behaviour to.

Maggie turned on the engine and we drove away from town in silence. I assumed she'd go back to hers, but she dropped me off at mine first. 'Are you sure you don't want my help?' I offered.

She glanced over at Harry, who was asleep beside her. 'There's nothing you can do. He just needs to sleep it off. Josh can help me get him out of the car.'

'All right. You know where I am if you need anything else.'

She gave me a meek smile. 'Thanks.'

Once I was inside, she drove off. The house felt empty without Mum there, but Tilly greeted me with a sleepy version of her excited hello.

Spectre watched from the top of the stairs, a curious expression on his feline face. The three of us fell asleep, curled up on the sofa.

18

Niamh

I didn't sleep well that night. How could I, knowing I was hearing things again? Worse, I was *seeing* things this time too.

The last time I'd heard things no one else could had been during Goodfellow's killing spree. I'd known when he was about to murder someone because he'd whistled to torment them first. I couldn't go through that again. I was still recovering from the last time.

But what else could the static be a sign of, if not a ghost trying to cause trouble?

I was up and showered early, so I left a note for Ben, then went in search of caffeine. There was no point spending all night tossing and turning when there was always something to do on a cruise ship. I might as well make use of where I was.

I found one of the coffee shops on the boulevard open, so went in and ordered a drink. I wasn't hungry, just bored and restless.

There was something soothing about being on a ship with thousands of people but nobody being around. The huge boulevard was eerily quiet, just broken up by the sounds of the coffee shop and cleaners. Above me, the stars twinkled down on us, reminding me of just how small we really were.

Even though we were at sea, I couldn't feel the ship moving. It almost felt like I was on land. The ship was so huge, and we were so high up, right in the middle, it was less noticeable.

Ben seemed to be adapting too, although he had a stash of seasickness pills from Guest Services that I carried in my handbag just in case.

I leaned back in my chair, waiting for my coffee and watching the trees swaying. Who'd have thought you could basically grow a park on a cruise ship? It made me realise how much I appreciated dog walks with Tilly. How was she? How was Edie?

I checked my phone. She'd last messaged me yesterday morning, to tell me how their pub trip had been. It didn't seem like either of them had enjoyed it as much as Fadil had thought. I hoped it didn't put them off going out more. It was good for them.

My phone screen flickered. Dammit, not that again. I turned the screen off and back on, but it continued to flicker. Could I not get five minutes with technology behaving anymore?

Annoyed, I pocketed my phone and returned to watching the trees.

A couple of women walked past, laughing. They both looked pretty drunk, but not totally off their faces.

Mid-laugh, one of them slipped and fell, hitting the ground at a weird angle. If I hadn't known better, I would've said that she'd been tripped. But there was no one else around, and her friend was about a foot away from her.

Or was there someone else around? Someone even I couldn't see?

Something did feel off. There was a ghost nearby. But it wasn't just that. It felt dark. Wrong.

Fiddlesticks. It was similar to what I'd felt on the tour, but stronger this time.

I shuddered.

No ghosts were visible nearby, but it seemed like there definitely was an invisible one causing mischief. Where was Tilly when I needed her?

The coffee shop server ran to the woman and tried to help her up, but she shoved him off. He stumbled backwards.

'This ship is unsafe!' she insisted. 'The floor must've been wet or something. How else could I have slipped?'

It definitely wasn't wet. I'd walked on that same patch a minute ago.

'I'm sorry, madam. Would you like me to get someone to help you to the medical centre?' he offered.

'No! I want an apology!'

Ah, she wanted money. Freebies. Discounts. To cause a scene and be *seen*.

'I'm very sorry. Let me get you a drink.' He turned to go back to the safety of the coffee machine.

'No! I want to speak to the captain, tell him how unsafe his ship is!'

Sigh.

'She's very busy and doesn't generally deal with customer service queries, but I'm sure I can get the—'

'No. I want to speak to the captain. I deserve to speak to him.'

'Her,' he corrected again.

'Pardon?'

'The captain is a woman,' said the barista.

'Well. That explains it, doesn't it?'

'Explains what?' asked the barista. This was getting juicy. But also painful.

'The standards. Women just aren't cut out to be leaders.'

For the love of cruise ships.

'What does that have to do with you slipping on the floor?' asked the confused barista. Frankly, I was confused, too. Was this woman drunker than she looked? Or just deluded?

'The standards are lacking because she's just not suited to being in charge,' said the drama queen.

All through this exchange, her friend had watched on, taking neither side and maintaining a poker face. I wanted to shake some sense into her; get her to drag her friend away.

Why was it that sometimes women's biggest enemies were other women?

I couldn't sit there any longer. I was nervous, tired, and grumpy. But what really annoyed me was seeing her back that poor barista into a corner with her blatant sexism. 'Why does a woman in charge mean standards are lacking, exactly?' I asked from my chair, my voice as calm and level as I could make it.

'Who are you?' she asked.

'An observer,' I replied omnisciently.

'Well. How else could this have happened?'

'You tell me. How *could* you have slipped? Could it be that we're on a cruise ship, which isn't exactly steady ground? Could it be that you've had one too many and weren't walking in a straight line as you walked over here? Could it be that you tripped? Heck, we've all stumbled after one too many.'

She stared at me, blankly. 'I...'

The barista looked to me, trying to hide his smile. He simply mouthed *thank you*. I nodded in response. Didn't want the woman knowing I felt smug.

'Women just can't lead things this big,' she said, digging herself in further. I wasn't sure whether to give her a shovel or a bulldozer.

'What evidence do you have for that, exactly? Other than that you slipped with no other female around except for your friend, who was right beside you, and me, who's sitting in this chair?' And a ghost whose gender I didn't know. 'And since the captain is likely asleep right now, and the cleaning crew haven't come through here yet – which is evident by the fact that the bins haven't been emptied – what does you losing your footing have to do with standards?'

'Um...'

The friend, finally realising her protesting companion wasn't getting anywhere, grabbed her by the arms and shot us an apologetic look as she dragged the drama queen away.

'Thank you,' said the barista. 'You saved my ass and schooled her.'

'When you've worked on as many building sites as I have, you get used to BS like that. Doesn't make it any less annoying, but it does teach you how to handle it.'

'Oh my god, I totally forgot your coffee! Can I get you some biscuits or something as well?'

'I mean, I'd never say no to one of those chocolate chip cookies…'

'Coming right up.' He made my drink, then returned with it, two cookies, and a small card. 'Drinks card. One free drink per stamp. It's the least I can do.'

'You don't have to thank me like that. I would've done it just to see the look on her face.'

He grinned. 'And that's why we need more people like you in this world.'

*

After enjoying a relaxing and event-free coffee, I returned to our room feeling smug. I'd made a new friend and got fifteen free coffees. Considering only the filter coffee was included and that wasn't what either of us drank, I was extra pleased I'd schooled the casual misogynist.

Ben was awake and reading on his phone in bed when I walked in.

'Cookie?' I offered, holding the second out to him. I'd eaten the first with my coffee.

'For breakfast? Don't mind if I do.' He took it from me and bit into it, making satisfying noises as the chocolate and dough melted in his mouth.

'I went for a coffee and had a fun conversation,' I said, relaying to him what'd happened while he drank his free coffee.

'And to think. I dreamt I was swimming alongside the cruise ship. Your morning sounds much more eventful.'

'I'd say so. We should be coming in to port soon. Do you want to go grab actual breakfast before we leave?'

'Yeah.' He threw the empty paper bag towards the bin, just missing it. He kissed my cheek, put it in the bin, then went for a shower.

While I waited, I turned the TV on and started channel hopping. The signal was better than I'd expected, although half the channels were in languages I didn't speak so my options were limited.

Admitting defeat, I settled on BBC News. While I liked being away with Ben, I still felt a little homesick. BBC News was my way of feeling close to the UK again.

My eyes flitted shut as I listened to the presenter talk about the latest political drama. Mid-sentence, his voice was replaced by white noise.

I jumped up, opening my eyes and reaching for the remote. His face had been replaced by static. The white noise shrieked. Trying to turn it down seemed to make it more aggressive and my headache worse.

A face appeared on the screen. The same one from trivia night. I pushed myself back against the headboard, which wasn't far, but it gave me some distance. I couldn't make out the ghost's features. 'Stay away,' the voice said, over and over. It was a deep, gravelly voice. One that was designed to intimidate. And it worked.

My hands shaking, I turned off the TV. What the hell had just happened?

Should I tell Ben?

No, it was a holiday. At least one of us should be able to enjoy it without worrying. We could ignore the ghosts. He said that. It was safer if he didn't know. I didn't want him to get involved if the ghost was only trying to contact me.

I didn't want to get involved. I was doing exactly what the ghost had asked me to do.

I told Ben I was going for a walk, then darted out of the door before he could reply.

Pacing the corridors calmed my brain a little, but not much. That wasn't a poltergeist. Was it? No. It couldn't be a poltergeist. It wasn't allowed to be. Hadn't we taken down enough of them?

But the repeated static, and the woman slipping over, and the darkness on the ship, made it look more and more like one of the ghosts on our quiet cruise ship had an agenda.

The ship felt claustrophobic, like the corridor was closing in on me. It didn't help that I had a terrible sense of direction, so instead of being able to look out to sea, I kept ending up in another internal corridor.

Even if I'd wanted to go back to our room, I wasn't sure I could find it. I was officially lost. And since I'd been so worked up about the spectral message, I hadn't picked up the stupid map to help me navigate the gigantic ship. Big mistake.

Leaning against a wall, I tried to remember what direction I'd turned in when I'd left the room. Had I gone left or right? Had I come across anything I could use as a landmark? Was there a map nearby I could use?

I closed my eyes, trying to picture something.

When I opened them, a ghost was walking down the corridor, away from me. Where'd he come from? Maybe he knew something.

'Hey!' I called out.

He didn't turn around. Instead, he rounded the corner.

I jogged to keep up with him, but when I got there, he was gone.

Well that wasn't helpful.

I'd lost the ghost and *I* was still lost. There was a lift in the middle of the corridor, so I got in it and headed for the floor I hoped breakfast was on. With my phone still in the room, I was totally helpless.

There was a map inside the lift door, so I studied that as I tried to work out where I was. I couldn't have been the first person to get lost on a cruise ship, surely?

The door opened on to the floor I'd selected. It didn't open out on to where I'd thought, though.

Ben was on the other side, looking confused. 'Where did you go?'

'Funny story…'

Ben stared at me, waiting for me to explain my 'funny story.' Fiddlesticks. What was I supposed to say?

'I couldn't find something so I went to try to find it.' Yeah, great answer Niamh. Well done. Round of applause. Standing ovation.

Ben lowered an eyebrow. Yeah, I didn't believe myself either. 'Why didn't you ask if I'd seen it?'

I stared at my green Converse, barely able to look at the man I was on holiday with. That I was in a relationship with. Why was I lying to him? 'You were in the shower. I didn't want to bother you.'

'I wouldn't have minded,' he said, making me feel worse. There was an opportunity to flirt in there, but he hadn't used it, which meant that he definitely didn't believe me and was definitely annoyed with me. Great. 'You could've texted me to meet you after.'

The lift doors started to close. I stepped into the corridor. They closed behind me. 'I was in such a panic when I realised I didn't have it that I left without grabbing my phone.'

'And what *is* "it"?'

Right. I hadn't actually explained what I'd lost yet. This was getting worse by the second.

'I, uh, realised I was out of shampoo so I went looking for some.' Possibly the worst lie ever, and I hated myself for lying, but I wasn't ready to tell him what had really happened.

Ben frowned. 'That's the worst lie I've ever heard.'

He was right. I could've borrowed his shampoo. And I'd already showered that morning so didn't even need it.

I ran my hand over my frizzy hair, not sure what to say. I'd dug myself into a hole and I wasn't sure how to get out of it.

'What actually happened?' He looked hurt that I'd lied to him. Something twisted inside of me. What was I *doing*? Ben deserved better than this.

'Can we not do this here?' I looked around. The corridor was quiet. Almost *too* quiet. Which meant that if there were any cameras nearby, they'd pick up on what we were talking about.

'Let's go for breakfast and I'll explain later,' I said.

Ben pursed his lips, looking down at my outfit. 'Might want to change first.'

'What?' I followed his vision. Oh. I'd been so tired when I'd left, I'd put my green top on inside out. Good look. Not. At least I'd been sitting down while in the coffee shop and hardly anyone had been around to notice.

We rounded the corner and headed towards our room. It seemed Ben already had a pretty good idea of how to navigate the ship while I was still clueless, so I let him guide me. I hadn't fully shaken the claustrophobia that'd come with being unable to get back to our room or find fresh air.

I pressed the button for another lift, checking my reflection in the mirror beside it. How had I not noticed my top was inside out? Muppet.

A huge face appeared in the mirror. It stared at me with piercing eyes. It was so huge it took up all of the floor-length mirror. It watched me. Waiting. Laughing.

Before I could react, it flew at me. I stumbled into the wall behind.

The mirror shattered.

19
Edie

I'd always planned to have breakfast at Maggie's that morning, so it was only about six hours later when I turned up at her front door. She insisted on looking after me while Mum was away, so had invited me over for breakfast to make sure I was eating properly.

While I had the urge to point out that I could look after myself, I wasn't stupid enough to turn down free food, especially not food cooked by a professional chef. So I turned up at eight before heading to the bookshop.

Abigail opened the front door, greeting me with squeals and a bear hug. I hugged her back, pleased to be able to spend time with her again.

'Abi, she needs to breathe,' said Josh, rolling his eyes. There was a jokey tone in his voice that reminded me a little of how things used to be. It filled me with warmth and hope. Could things go back to the way they were? Or was everything too far gone and too complicated for that?

I smiled at him as I closed the door, an excited six-year-old still clinging to me. 'I don't mind.'

'*See?*' said Abigail. She squeezed me tighter, sticking her tongue out at her older brother. 'I just don't want you to go again.'

I ruffled Abigail's curly hair. 'I'm not going anywhere.' Realising what I'd said, I glanced up at Josh. He gave me a nostalgic smile, then walked off. What did that mean? Had he come to accept that I wasn't going anywhere? Was he OK with me again? I could dream.

Abigail was so excited by my presence I hadn't had the chance to ask what'd happened with Harry. But his car was gone, and he usually left for work around seven, so I figured that was where he was. Surprising, given how drunk he'd been, but then Harry *was* a workaholic.

Abigail guided me into the kitchen, where a cup of tea was waiting on the side for me. 'I made it!' she beamed.

Maggie looked up from the stove and smiled, jerking her head at the new one-cup hot water dispenser behind her. 'She did. You're getting good at making tea now, aren't you?'

Abigail nodded. Then faked gagging. 'Still don't want to drink it, though. Tea's nasty.'

'You know,' I said, crouching down to her height. 'I used to think that when I was your age, too.'

She widened her eyes. 'You did?'

'I did.'

'What changed?'

I killed off a bunch of tastebuds eating food that was too hot and drinking too much coffee, probably. I wasn't going to say that. Instead, I stood up and sipped my tea. 'My tastes changed. They do as you get older.'

'Does that mean I'll like broccoli one day?'

'You'll *love* broccoli. And not just because it tastes great, but because it's super healthy,' I said. Weirdly, it'd always been one of my favourite foods, even when I was Abigail's age.

Abigail gasped in horror. She turned to her mum: 'Is broccoli really that good for you?'

'Yep,' said Maggie, taking some broccoli out of the air fryer. 'It's one of the best sources of vegetable protein, which helps your body repair itself. And it could even help you heal quicker from a cold because of the vitamins in it.'

Abigail sighed. 'Maybe I'll give it another chance, then.'

Maggie winked at me. 'That's my girl.'

Josh appeared in the doorway, a PlayStation controller in his hand. 'How long until food, Mum?'

'You've got time for one race but not a whole day on one of those simulation thingies,' she replied without even looking up. I loved that she sort of knew what games he played and how long different ones took. Josh had always been a big gamer, and I supposed he'd done it a lot over the summer while things were quiet. Why not? He still had his job at the coffee shop and he always helped with babysitting. He needed down time too and Maggie respected that.

'Thanks.' Josh disappeared again.

Maggie shook her head and shrugged. 'I'll never get the fascination with gaming, but if it makes him happy.'

Abigail tugged at my T-shirt. 'Can we play dolls?'

'We're about to eat, Abigail,' Maggie reminded her.

Abigail pouted, flapping her arms. 'But you said Josh had time for a game!'

'Josh's games are quicker than yours,' she replied, her tone even.

Abigail's pout deepened.

'Why don't we change their outfits before breakfast, then we can play after?' I suggested, trying to find a way to avoid an upset six-year-old.

Maggie nodded her approval at my suggestion, then returned to cooking breakfast. I didn't know what it was, but it smelled amazing. There were onions, eggs, broccoli, and peppers involved. That was all I could tell.

As we went into the living room, Abigail grabbed my mug of tea. 'Don't forget your tea!'

Smiling, I took it from her and drank some. It was pretty good for an early attempt.

Her dolls were stored in a yellow box that lived in the corner of the lounge. She took a couple of dolls from it and passed one with long hair and a fringe to me, then took a pink wardrobe out from the box and opened it. It was full of clothes.

The sounds of Josh's racing game echoed downstairs, as did his minced oaths as he started to lose. I missed playing those games with him.

'Why do you look sad?' Abigail asked.

I shook my head, trying to snap out of it. The last thing I needed was for her to think I was sad, even if I was. 'Just thinking, that's all.'

'About what?'

Bloody children and their questions.

'What outfit would look best with her hair,' I lied.

'I think blue,' said Abigail. It was her favourite colour, so most of the outfits were various shades of blue. 'Dad likes blue.'

'Where is he?' I asked.

'At work.' Already, like I'd thought. A sad look passed over her cute face. 'He works a lot lately.'

Harry had always worked a lot, so if Abigail had noticed he was working a lot by *his* standards, that had to be a bad sign. Even though he was a workaholic, he'd always doted on his kids.

'Do you miss him?'

She pursed her lips, as if in thought. 'Sometimes. But he's been different lately. I miss old Dad.'

The hairs on the back of my neck pricked up. She'd noticed his behaviour was weird lately, *and* he'd been drunk last night? Alarm bells started ringing in my mind. 'Different how?'

Maggie poked her head through the door. 'Breakfast is ready. Can you tell Josh, please?'

Forgetting our conversation and the dolls, Abigail ran out of the room to fetch her brother.

Talk about timing.

I went into the kitchen, where Maggie had laid the table and was dishing up.

'Stuffed peppers with onions, tomatoes, mushrooms, eggs, and a side of broccoli,' said Maggie.

'Sounds amazing. And smells amazing,' I said. It really did. My stomach let out a growl of longing.

'Of course it does. I made it.'

'Of course,' I said, hugging her and not caring if it made it harder for her to plate up.

She put her spare arm around me. 'I'm glad you're here.'

'Me too.'

*

'How are things going at the bookshop?' Maggie asked as the four of us finished eating breakfast. I was biding my time before bringing up Harry's change in behaviour, but I knew I had to talk about it soon. It was too suspicious not to.

'All right,' I replied, slicing into some broccoli. 'The paint is almost done and so is the website. The replacement bookcase arrives later in the week and we have a few more pieces of furniture to build. It's more work than I thought it'd be, but I'm enjoying it. I just want to do Mum and Ben proud, you know?'

She nodded. 'You will.'

I looked away, feeling my cheeks flush. I really hoped she was right.

'I'm sure it'll go well,' said Josh. 'Sorry I can't be there for the opening.'

I hadn't expected him to say that, that was for sure. I'd assumed he wouldn't care that he'd be at uni by the time we opened. But that comment made it seem like he was genuinely disappointed he couldn't show his moral support.

'That's OK. Uni is more important.'

What else could I say? It would've been nice to have him there, but I still didn't know where we stood. Maybe some time apart would be good for us.

'When do you leave?' I asked, changing the subject before my head exploded any more.

'I think it's the third weekend of September.'

The bookshop opening was the weekend after. A year after Josh and I had become a couple. Then had everything ripped away from us a month later.

Even though we hadn't always lived near each other, him moving out and going to uni felt different, somehow. I had no doubt that it would change him. I'd seen people from the years above us leave for uni then come back a semester later dressing – and even speaking – differently. They seemed more confident in who they were. It almost made me wish I was going, too. Even if I wanted to I couldn't, though. Not anymore.

'Can you excuse me for a minute, please?' I pushed my chair away from the table. Asking for permission to pee in a house where I'd spent so much of my childhood felt weird, so I didn't wait for a response, I just went upstairs.

As I reached the landing, a wave of something just… *wrong* hit me. I hadn't noticed it downstairs, but I couldn't ignore it upstairs. It filled the air like a fog. My chest was tight. Based on what Abigail had said about Harry, and how he'd acted last night, was something more sinister wrong?

Could I hold going for a pee until I got to the bookshop? The suppressive atmosphere was almost suffocating.

But I managed, because I was desperate.

After peeing, I scurried downstairs, trying not to gasp for breath and give away how awful upstairs had felt.

How could I warn Maggie without worrying Abigail? Could Josh help, somehow? I didn't have a different option this time.

Everyone's cutlery was together and they were leaning away from their plates. Giving me the perfect opportunity to get Abigail away so that I could talk to Maggie in private.

I met Josh's eye and jerked my head at Abigail, silently hoping he'd take the hint. Abigail was doing a monologue about what'd happened on her favourite TV show so wasn't paying attention to us. Maggie looked like she was listening, but I wasn't sure if she actually was.

Josh narrowed his eyes in confusion. So my hint wasn't working.

Distract her. Please? I mouthed.

He nodded. 'Hey Abigail. Do you want to do that tea party now?'

Abigail leapt out of her seat. 'Yes! Although I told you. It's a *coffee* party, not a tea party. I hate tea.'

Josh smirked. 'All right. Sorry. Let's go set up your coffee party.'

'Will you join us, Edie?' Abigail asked me.

'In a minute. I'll just help your mum clean up first.'

Abigail shrugged, walking off without me. I figured she wouldn't want to help clean up if she could get out of it.

Thanks I mimed to Josh. He nodded, then left.

The Poltergeist's Ship

'Why do I feel like I'm missing something?' Maggie eyed me sceptically. 'Josh doesn't do Abigail's coffee parties. She's been trying to get him to for months.'

I started piling the empty plates on top of each other. The crisp white crockery clattered. 'How'd things go with Harry last night?'

Maggie sighed. 'He crashed in bed as soon as we got home. When we woke up he was gone.'

'I know he's a morning person but don't you normally get up at like, half six?'

She tapped the side of her empty orange juice glass. 'Yeah. It's strange.'

'Abigail mentioned Harry has been working a lot lately,' I said, trying to sound calm and not reflect the internal panic that was building within me. 'And I remember how he spoke to Josh after Goodfellow's attack.' And he got drunk last night, and the upstairs of your house feels really weird.

Maggie stood up and also began clearing the breakfast table, scraping leftovers on to one plate. 'He's had a much shorter temper than usual recently. He blames work.'

I'll bet he did.

'He's been working much longer hours, too. I feel like I haven't seen him a lot lately.'

Sirens screamed in my head. Please, *please* don't let the Morgans be victims of something else supernatural. For the love of everything supernatural. *Please*.

'How would you feel about having some sort of protection again?' I asked. After the threat from Goodfellow had gone, Maggie had returned Mum's amber amulet, insisting we needed it more. Now I wasn't so sure.

Despite Mum's protests, and the fact that Maggie and Josh had been tortured by demons, she *still* hadn't let any of us ward their house again because she was more concerned about upsetting Harry. It looked like that had backfired. Again. Would she ever learn?

Maggie froze, clutching an empty bowl. 'You think something else is going on?'

Yes.

'I think it's better to be safe than sorry.'

And we really should've warded her place again after they'd redecorated last year. So much of the past twelve months could've been avoided with that one simple step.

She lowered her shoulders. 'I just don't want to upset Harry. You know how he feels about this stuff.'

I reached out and touched her hand. 'Yeah. But what's more important? Your safety, when you know this stuff is real, or his scepticism?'

If my suspicions were right, upsetting him was the least of our problems. But I couldn't tell her something was wrong with him until I had proof.

With their house not being warded, and me not sensing anything from Harry directly, I had circumstantial evidence at best. There was every chance a poltergeist could've visited their house, had a look around, then left without any of us knowing. How long the suffocating atmosphere lasted varied from ghost to ghost.

Not to mention there were too many questions I didn't have answers to, so I wasn't going to worry Maggie unnecessarily until I had evidence.

But that didn't mean I wanted her to be unprotected.

She put the bowl into the sink. 'Do you really think we're in danger?'

'I just think it's worth having some sort of protection. Mum would say the same and you know it. Dad would too.' I didn't like bringing them into the conversation to convince her, but I knew I was right. They always erred on the side of caution when it came to protecting the people they cared about. Less so when it came to themselves.

Maggie nodded slowly. 'Yes, I suppose you're right.'

20

Niamh

'Are you all right?' Ben asked, helping me stand.

'Are you?' I asked, brushing shards of glass from the back of his hoody.

Glass crunched under our feet as we walked tentatively to the mirror to examine it.

'Was that the same ghost from trivia night?' asked Ben.

'You saw them that time?'

'Yeah. I've read about them changing shape and size before, but never seen it in real life.'

'Have you ever seen them shatter a mirror into a gazillion pieces before?' I asked.

'Never to this extent.'

I rubbed my forehead. There was a sharp pain between my eyes, as if pressure was building there. I took a few deep breaths.

The mirror, which had been taller and wider than me moments before, now consisted of an empty red frame. The shards of glass were all over the red carpet, grinding underneath our feet as we looked around. It hadn't broken into just a few pieces. It was in smithereens.

The Poltergeist's Ship

'Oh my god!' Of course our cabin steward rounded the corner right then. Niall ran over. 'Are you all right? What happened? I heard a noise and came to investigate but I didn't expect *this*. Did you fall into it?'

'No, we were coming from the other direction and heard it so came to investigate, too,' I lied. Even if I'd gone along with his story, there was no chance I could've done that much damage. I was less than half the mirror's size!

Niall narrowed his eyes. I wasn't sure he believed us. But what evidence did he have? Even if there were cameras around that showed the corridor, it wouldn't pick anything up. They'd be the wrong kind to pick up on any ghosts.

He gestured to a piece of glass on Ben's shoulder. 'May I?' Ben nodded. Niall picked up the glass and studied it, as if it held all the answers. 'How odd. Anyway, don't worry about this, we'll get it all cleaned up. You go enjoy some breakfast!'

*

Before breakfast, I went back to get changed so that I wasn't walking around with the seams of my clothes exposed.

But that wasn't the only reason Ben wanted to go back to our room.

'So, are you actually going to tell me what happened?' he asked as I picked some clothes from my suitcase. He reached into my shower bag and threw my bottle of John Frieda shampoo at me.

Javi's mum had gotten me into their stuff in the nineties and I still used it. It was cheap, cheerful, and effective. Everything I needed to tame my wiry ginger curls. At least when it wasn't super humid because I was in the middle of the ocean.

Javi. Javi was the reason I hadn't wanted to involve Ben in what was going on. He'd been killed by a poltergeist, taken away from Edie and me far too young. Ben wasn't much older than Javi had been, but he was definitely wiser.

After Dominic had used my lies against Edie and me, I'd promised her I'd be honest with her, no matter what. Javi and I had always had the same policy in our relationship. I'd lost that when I'd married Dan, and it'd backfired in so many ways I'd lost count.

I sighed, sinking on to the bed I shared with Ben. Sometimes, I couldn't let go of the fact I wouldn't be with him if it wasn't for Javi's death. It made me question who I loved more. It was hard to remind myself that I could still love Javi and move on with my life, especially now that Javi was such a big part of it again.

And, as he liked to regularly remind me, he was Team Ben. He *wanted* me to move on because even though he could come and go as he pleased, he'd long crossed over and wasn't meant to get involved in anything – or with any*one* – in the real world. My world. Whatever it was called.

Ben sat beside me, waiting.

Voices of a couple arguing echoed through the thin metal wall. That had been Dan and me. We'd never been able to fully enjoy ourselves anywhere because our ideas of fun had been so different.

We'd been so different, and not in a yin and yang kind of way. More like a scream and shout kind of way. That kind of drama was exhausting. It wasn't the type of relationship I wanted. I was too old for that.

Ben deserved better.

So did I.

The last time I'd faced a poltergeist, he'd almost killed Edie, Ben, Josh, and me in the local graveyard. He *had* killed Tessa and Thomas. Along with several others.

The time before that, a poltergeist had bruised – maybe broken – my ribs. I'd been too stubborn to get X-Rayed and get the damage confirmed. My ribs had only fully healed because Edie resurrecting me had healed all my past injuries and ailments.

And the time before that, a poltergeist had killed Javi, depriving me of my first love and Edie of her father. In living form, anyway.

Wherever poltergeists went, trouble and pain and suffering followed.

Some relaxing holiday this was turning out to be.

I put my hand on Ben's lap. 'I'm sorry I lied. And it was such a bad lie. I should've just told you the truth. I just…panicked.'

He frowned. 'Why?'

'You know the ghost we just saw?'

'Yeah…'

'I saw them on the TV while you were in the shower.'

Ben took the light blue shampoo bottle from my hand, which I hadn't realised I was practically hugging, and put it on the side. He held my hands in his. 'Why didn't you tell me? We're a team, right?'

I wiped at my eyes with the back of my fist as they threatened to fill with even more tears. 'Yes,' I whispered. 'But…' I snivelled. 'Did you see the black eye a poltergeist gave me? Or the bruised ribs?'

'Is that what this is about?'

'How Goodfellow nearly killed us? And it took five of us to stop him?' I twisted the edge of my T-shirt between my fingers. 'They just love causing trouble, taking things away from you. Everything went wrong because of a stupid poltergeist. Dominic never would've been able to brainwash Edie if it hadn't been for a poltergeist.'

Ben didn't say anything. He watched me, waiting for me to continue.

'Javi and I were so cocky. We thought it'd be just like any other haunting. But he was smarter than us. Faster than us. More powerful than us. And I lost my husband because of it.'

Ben put his arm around my shoulder. I leaned into him, still curled up, but wanting the comfort of his touch.

'I can't lose you, too.'

Ben stroked my hair. 'You won't.'

'But you don't know that.'

'You should know better than anyone that we can't control death. Or life.'

Well, technically Edie could, but this felt like the wrong time to be a smart arse.

The Poltergeist's Ship

'No, but that doesn't mean I don't want to try to avoid something else going wrong,' I said.

Still stroking my hair, he kissed my temple. 'You know, Javi's a great guy. I'd never want to compete with him. But I'm also *not* him. I don't have the same powers, I don't think in the same way, and I don't do things in the same way.'

'And you have a forcefield,' I mumbled.

'Exactly. It's done a pretty good job of keeping us safe so far, hasn't it?'

I nodded, clutching his hoody. His forcefield had been crucial to us defeating Goodfellow. We couldn't have taken him down without it. 'But it only takes one ghost to get through it.'

'It doesn't work like that.'

'But you don't know that. Javi and I messed up because we were young and thought we were invincible.'

'You were a lot younger then. Things were different.'

I sighed, knowing he was right but still not being able to shut my brain up. 'Growing up, my family was Javi, and Maggie, and Manju. Their parents raised me better than my own. I always felt like Mum thought I was a failure because I wasn't as powerful as she was. I wasted too many years seeking her approval.' Curling into Ben further, I rested my head on his broad chest.

'I get it,' he said. 'Coming from a witch family, I was always looked down on.'

I lifted my head to face him. 'What? Why?'

'Well, you know how witch families are matriarchal? Well, turns out they saw my defensive power as useless and the fact I was male as equally pointless.' He sighed, pausing for a moment and pulling me closer. I hadn't known any of this about his upbringing. I'd always assumed he'd had a happy childhood, with his stereotypical two point four family. 'I tried really hard to prove I was a good little witch, but it didn't matter what I did, my sister was always the favourite. When I told them I wanted to study Parapsychology at uni, well, I might as well have told them I was emigrating to Australia. They didn't get why I'd do something so far removed from how I'd been raised. For me, it felt like a natural progression. But they'd always lived in their fairly insular world of witchcraft and didn't see the need to change it. I wanted to get out and explore, show people that those of us who believed weren't mad after all.'

'Did they come around to the idea?'

Ben scoffed. 'No. We've barely spoken since. There's a reason my brother-in-law doesn't ask them to babysit the twins. He has no powers, and he's a single dad to twin witches, so it's hard, but he'd rather keep them away from the toxicity that's masqueraded as love and protection.' He stood up, pacing to the door and back to the bed. I almost reached out to him, missing his touch, but I stopped myself because he was clearly restless. 'Not all witch families are like mine, but I come from two very long lines of witches. That's a lot of responsibility to carry.'

I nodded, remembering what it was like growing up as part of my mother's necromancy lineage. I hadn't even known I was a part of it at the time, but she'd sure made me feel like a failure for not being as powerful as her anyway. 'It's not your fault, you know. None of it is.'

'No,' he agreed, 'but that doesn't mean I don't feel guilty. Or responsible. Or…' He stopped pacing, shaking his head as if he was trying to get rid of a thought going around it. 'When Lindsay died, you know who they blamed? Me. I wasn't even there, didn't know what she was doing, but they blamed me for not protecting her. I was the big brother. I had the forcefield. It was my *job*. And I couldn't do that one thing.'

My heart broke as I stood up and hugged him. 'Lindsay doesn't blame you, you know that, right?'

He nodded, then sniffled. A tear trickled down his cheek, landing on my neck and tickling it. I wiped it away, guiding him back to the bed where the two of us curled up together, both fighting off tears.

Ben hardly ever spoke about his parents. Now I understood why. I'd had no idea they'd treated him so badly, or how similar our upbringings were. Just because his parents were both still alive and together, that didn't make his childhood any healthier than mine. Having powers didn't excuse parents from toxic attitudes.

Ben snivelled, wiping a tear from his cheek. 'I get it, Niamh. I may not have lost the love of my life, but I lost my best friend. Half the reason I lost her was my fault, too.' I tried to interrupt him to tell him otherwise, but he cut me off. 'It was, though. If I hadn't stopped speaking to her, I might've noticed more and been able to stop her from ending up sacrificing herself to save us all from Dominic.'

I rested my head against his, my legs tucked behind me. 'I know it doesn't seem like it, but she did save us. Not from his manipulation, but can you imagine what he could've done if he'd still had his active necromancy powers? As well as spell casting and his manipulation skills? We struggled to take him down as it was. Lindsay saved us.'

Ben cried harder, not even trying to hide it anymore. His body shook as the tears ran down his reddened cheeks. I wiped them away. This was the most open we'd ever been with each other. It was a fragile but special moment.

'You're right,' he said through sobs. He leaned his forehead against mine. 'When I walked into the apartment and saw you lying there…' He shook his head. 'I thought I'd lost you, too. I know Edie saved you for herself, but, selfishly, I wanted her to as well.'

I swallowed down the lump that was forming in my throat. 'Oh, Ben.'

He tucked my hair behind my ear, kissing me lightly, tenderly. 'I'm scared of losing you, too, Niamh. I can't let that stop me from helping people, though. That's all I've ever wanted to do, whether that's helping them find a book to escape reality with a few hours, or saving them from a haunting. It's who I am.'

I took a deep breath. 'For a long time, I tried to convince myself it wasn't me. That I could live a perfectly normal life away from ghosts and everything else paranormal.' Although at that time I'd really only known about ghosts. And wished I still did. 'I really, really tried. It didn't kill me physically, but mentally and emotionally, it almost destroyed me. And Edie.' I rubbed my face with my hand. 'When I met you, and found out you didn't just understand our world, but you were a part of it, too, it felt too good to be true. Could I really get lucky twice, finding two people to love who'd help me make sense of my life? To spend my life with?'

Ben tilted his head to the side, a smile creeping across his face. 'You love me?'

I stroked his cheek. 'More than I ever thought I could. You saved me from myself. You still do. Every day.'

Ben pulled me closer, kissing me again. 'I love you, too.' He tucked my hair behind my ear. 'Even people who don't have gifts like ours take risks every day. We can't predict what's around the corner, powers or not. We just have to make sure we have the right people around us and do the best we can.'

'How do you always know what to say?'

He chuckled, pecking my lips. 'Family trait. Sometimes more useful than a forcefield.'

As his lips touched mine again, my anxieties melted away. It filled my body with a fire only he could. We missed breakfast.

21
Edie

'We have to find out what's going on with Harry,' I said as Fadil and I painted the skirting boards. All the furniture we'd built was far, far away from the window this time. Not that it mattered as much when it was already boarded up.

Before heading to the bookshop, I'd gone home, found the amber amulet, and given it to Maggie. Knowing she had some form of protection gave me one less thing to worry about. I wished I had something for Josh and Abigail, too, but we'd agreed Maggie spent the most time around Harry, so if something was wrong, she was the most at risk.

Fadil shook his head. 'No. Noooo we don't.' He crossed his arms, paintbrush pointing at his face. Centimetres from painting his tanned complexion...

'If we don't, who will?'

He slammed his paintbrush into the tray. White paint spewed onto the beige cloth it was resting on. A little went on the cuff of his jeans, too. He didn't seem to care. 'Anyone but us. Absolutely anyone.'

'There *is* no one else,' I reminded him. 'Josh, Maggie, and Abigail need us!'

'Or do they need us to back off? You said it yourself: he has a stressful job. Works a lot of hours. That eats away at a person.'

I wrinkled my nose as I put some more paint on to my brush.

'If he's stressed or anxious or depressed or burned out or all of the above, he'd pull away from his family either out of embarrassment, shame, or a desire to protect them.' Of course he knew that.

'You have got to stop watching psychology videos on YouTube.'

'Never.' It was like watching them brought him comfort or something. 'All I'm saying is that not everyone acting weird is possessed.'

'But,' I continued, to Fadil's dismay, 'in my experience, it is more often than not. The difference is, most people can't see it. We can.'

'You're aware we're not in my generation and not everything is the result of a demon or a curse, yes?'

I'd never heard him use 'my generation' like that before. I supposed it was the only way he could talk about when he was previously alive and avoid saying 'Ancient Egypt,' which annoyed him.

I returned my brush to the tray and crossed my arms. 'You're aware what world we're in and everything that's happened so far, yes?'

Fadil tensed his jaw, oozing disapproval.

'He *never* gets drunk but was stumbling through town in the middle of the night. And I felt something weird upstairs in their house this morning. That has to warrant investigating before it spirals into something else, doesn't it?'

'But—'

The bell above the door jingled, cutting off Fadil's response. Maisie walked in, a spring in her step. She froze when she saw us. 'Did I just walk into something?'

'No,' I said at the same time Fadil said, 'Yes.'

'Oooook then,' she said, stuffing her hands into her pockets and rocking on her heels.

Fadil stormed off into the back room.

'He all right?' asked Maisie, walking over to me.

'Just scared, I think. And maybe protective.'

'Interesting combo,' she said. 'Anything I can help with?'

Could she? Would she? No. I couldn't ask her that. She didn't even know the Morgans. And I had no idea if she actually was a part of our world or not. I had suspicions, but if I was wrong…

'Don't worry about it,' I said. 'What brought you here?'

'Just checking a couple of measurements for the window. Don't worry, it'll still be here in plenty of time.'

'Good. I can't handle any more stress right now.'

She patted me on the back. 'I got ya.'

*

'This is such a bad idea,' said Fadil as we sat on the tram on our way into Nottingham city centre.

'He'll never know we were there,' I said. The plan was to visit Harry at work – without him seeing us – and monitor how he behaved. If he was off or acted unusually, or I could sense anything from him, we knew something was going on.

Ideally I would've taken Tilly, since she barked at demons or people who were possessed – pretty much the only thing that made her bark other than dogs and posties – but she wasn't allowed in the bank. So my powers would have to do.

I was kicking myself for not taking her with us last night, but when I'd left the house I'd just thought Harry was drunk.

'But if he *is* possessed, wouldn't *he* sense *us*?'

I hadn't thought of that. We had no idea who – or what – was possessing Harry, if anything. I probably should've done more research before executing the plan. Fadil was going to kill me.

'You don't know, do you?' he said, shaking his head in disbelief. Fadil hadn't actually met Harry yet. On the rare occasion he went to Maggie's place, it was long after Harry had left for work. And since Mum and I had repeatedly told Fadil he wasn't missing out on anything, he was in no rush to meet Maggie's husband.

The tram jolted as it pulled up at the next stop. The doors opened, letting a brief but refreshing breeze into the stuffy carriage.

I was convinced Fadil was going to get off. But he didn't. He stayed sitting in the seat opposite me. And glared at me instead.

Since it was a quiet weekday lunchtime, we had a set of four seats to ourselves and there was still plenty of room for people around us.

Nobody got on or off, so the doors closed again and continued along the tracks.

Fadil shook his head, staring out of the window and not speaking. The judgment radiated off him and was getting on my last nerve.

'What do you want us to do? Just sit around and hope for the best?' I snapped.

He grumbled.

'I'm serious. After everything we've witnessed, you want us to be passive bystanders? Like everyone else who walked past you for two hundred years was?'

'That's a low blow.'

'Imagine how Harry feels if he is trapped in there. How scared he must be.' Even people who didn't like Harry couldn't say that was a pleasant or fair fate. Incorrigible and sceptical he might've been, but he wasn't evil. He didn't deserve to lose control of his body like that.

Fadil crossed his arms. 'I thought you said he didn't believe in any of it?'

'It's kind of hard not to by now, isn't it?' Then again, with Harry's level of denial, who could be sure?

Fadil shifted uncomfortably in his seat. 'I still don't like this.'

'Neither do I. I just don't feel like we have a choice.'

*

Harry worked for a large, international bank in the city centre. It was in a busy part of Nottingham, near clothing shops, other banks, and cafes. The ground underneath us was cobbled, which seemed to make Fadil more shaky on his legs, so he leaned on me for balance.

Reaching the bank, we tried to peer in through the glass windows. Nothing. There were too many people inside, and too many ATMs in front of the windows, for us to see him. Stupid old-style building with massive windows but not a lot of space to build hefty ATM machines into walls.

'We'll have to go in,' I said, heading towards the door.

Fadil grabbed my hood and pulled me back. 'Do you even use this bank?'

'Er…'

Fadil shook his head. I was tired of him judging all my plans without having an alternative. 'You know he could look that up and find out that you're not a customer in seconds, right? Don't you think he'd get the tiniest bit suspicious, especially since it's mostly older people who go into banks these days?'

'I don't like doing things online, though,' I said. It was why I'd never bothered with group chats at school or college and avoided social media unless doing research.

That reminded me: I needed to check Harry's social media accounts. If he had any. I didn't actually know. He seemed like the type to avoid social media.

I had something in common with Harry? Frazzle.

'So what's your cover story?' Fadil asked me.

I stared across the road at Pret, where busy office workers were rushing in and out with their coffees and croissants. A few people sat outside, hunched over their phones as they munched on wraps, sandwiches, or soups. Must get food after investigating Harry.

'Hello?' said Fadil, pulling me away from a cyclist who was about to crash into me. The delivery person stuck their finger up at me as they cycled away towards one of the many food outlets in the city centre. Rude. But then I had been in the way because I'd been thinking about food.

'I want to open a new account. And since I was walking past I thought I'd go in and see what they can do for me.'

'Why were you walking past?'

'Shopping. And Pret.'

He rolled his eyes. 'What kind of account?'

'Oh my god why are you asking so many questions!'

Fadil looked like he was about to give up, but pressed on anyway. 'Why are you so unprepared? Haven't you learnt *anything*? We need to prepare before diving into things like this!'

I huffed. No I did not want to prepare. I wanted to march in there and see—

'Edie. Hello.'

Fadil and I turned to the sound of the voice. Harry. Standing in the door of the bank behind us. Frazzle.

If we hadn't been so busy arguing, we might've noticed his approach and been able to hide.

Harry mostly looked the same as usual, but there was a curious glint in his eye that I wasn't used to. His posture was more upright than normal, like someone had attached a broom to his back and a coat hanger to his shoulders and he was going to start ballroom dancing. He'd never had bad posture, but never posture good enough for dancers or military personnel, either.

'Harry. Good to see you. This is my friend, Fadil.'

Harry nodded in greeting. His suit looked more polished. It was like there was a sheen to him or something. He reminded me of a door-to-door salesman. Which is not how I normally would've described him. Normally I would've described him as a stereotypical, boring accountant. Which was exactly what he was. But something about him just felt off. I couldn't put my finger on it.

'Pleasure.' His tone didn't match his word choice.

'How are you feeling?' I asked.

'Fine. Why wouldn't I be?'

Because he'd been stumbling through town less than twelve hours ago?

It was like he had no recollection of what'd happened the night before. It was so odd. Before I could elaborate, he continued: 'What are you doing here?' Harry had never been particularly talkative around Mum and me, but the conversation had never been *this* stilted. It was like he barely knew how to conduct small talk.

'Just doing a bit of shopping,' I lied.

'Why stand so close to the bank, then?' he lowered his eyebrows in confusion.

'Just talking out of the way,' said Fadil. Considering he hadn't needed to lie to a stranger and think on his feet much, he was surprisingly good at it. What had he done in his previous life? Maybe one day he'd tell me.

'I see,' said Harry. 'Well, I'm *just* going to get some lunch. Enjoy your shopping.' He didn't wait for us to respond. He walked off down the hill, towards the bustling Old Market Square.

'That was so weird,' I said.

'But was it out of character?' asked Fadil. 'How was his life essence?'

'He spoke differently. Stilted. Formally. It was like having a conversation with AI. And that crack he made, about how we overused "just" when talking to him? He wouldn't normally make a joke like that.'

'What joke?' said Fadil.

'You know, where he emphasised *just* because we said it one too many times. It's not his usual sense of humour.'

Fadil pursed his lips. 'And his life essence?'

'Seemed normal.' To my dismay.

'So he's totally fine.'

I still wasn't convinced. Thomas had hidden his powers, his life essence, for over a century. So we knew it was possible. What if whatever was inside of Harry could do that, too? But it couldn't hide the traces of power it left behind, like at the Morgans' house? The situation had just reached a whole new level of complicated.

22

Niamh

After an eventful morning, I was glad to be off the ship. Although given how tired I was, I wasn't sure how much of Pisa I was going to remember.

We sat on the bus on the way to the Leaning Tower of Pisa, and even though I hadn't stood that much the last few hours, I was grateful for the seat. I rested my head against the window, barely registering anything as we drove past the cream-coloured buildings.

All I could think about were poltergeists. Were we about to face another one? What would they want this time? *Who* would they want? And could we really take them on, just the two of us?

I'd assumed the panic had been why I'd had an increasingly nasty headache on the ship and why my chest had felt tight. But the farther away from the ship we got, the more my headache seemed to calm down. I was still tired, but I hadn't realised how much the energy on the ship had exhausted me.

'Does the air feel different to you?' I asked Ben, trying to be subtle as the bus was full.

'Different how?'

'*Different* different,' I said, hoping he'd understand my emphasis. It felt like a weight had been lifted from my chest.

He paused, closing his eyes and taking a few deep breaths. When he reopened them, he said: 'now that you mention it, it does.'

Fiddlesticks.

'Do you think it's a staff member?' asked Ben.

'Or someone who didn't get off at the port. Not everyone does.'

'We should get some stuff, just in case,' he said.

'You didn't bring anything with you?' The last thing I wanted to do was spend my ghost-free excursion searching for ghost-hunting equipment.

'No. Hard to explain at customs,' said Ben. Ugh. So it looked like that was how we were going to spend it.

'Do you think it's the same as with Goodfellow? I can hear him because Edie resurrected me?'

Ben frowned. 'Could you hear stuff like this before? Or did Tilly ever react to things you couldn't see or hear?'

'She barked at thin air a couple of times. We always assumed it was an invisible ghost.' It was common among dogs, especially more reactive breeds like westies. 'Or another dog walking past.' I ground my teeth together. Why did ghosts have to ruin *everything*? Every time?

He squeezed my hand. 'There won't be another Dominic or Goodfellow.'

'Won't there? We both know we're targets. I'm not as much as of one as you or Edie, and I'm not as smart as you are, but—'

The Poltergeist's Ship

'Niamh—'

'It's OK, I know I'm not. But that doesn't mean I can't be fast or strong.'

The Leaning Tower of Pisa came into view. Its four-degree lean looked more significant than it sounded. It was weird, seeing a piece of history that had been built so many centuries ago and still stood tall. It came from a time when people had still believed in ghosts and witches and magic. When there was no technology for ghosts to interfere with.

'Maybe you should take some self-defence classes,' he suggested.

I was the most physically fit because of the manual nature of my job. Why hadn't I ever learned to protect myself or those around me using my muscles, not my magic? 'Now there's an interesting idea.'

*

To not completely waste our holiday, we did a very short tour of the Tower and one of the nearby museums, then decided to scope out what we needed.

Ben seemed to be almost excited at the prospect of spending our second stop shopping for ghost-hunting equipment instead of sightseeing like normal people. What were the odds of Pisa having a ghost hunting shop, though?

'New gadgets? Of course I'm excited!' said Ben as we stood to the side of the Tower. He slipped his hand into mine.

As much as I wanted to pretend ghosts didn't exist while we were away, it was too late for that. Doing some good old-fashioned ghost hunting was the only thing that would make me feel like I had some semblance of control over the situation. At least then we'd know what we were up against.

'Yeah but how do we find all that?'

'That's part of the adventure!'

'I appreciate your optimism.' I did not share it. We were in Italy. Neither of us spoke Italian, and the odds of a tourist town having anything even close to what we needed were slim.

Although, to be fair, I'd been buying supplies online for years. It was easier and quicker than having drawn-out conversations with shopkeepers.

'We may not find an EMF metre, but we'll find something useful,' he insisted.

Someone walking past shot us a sceptical look. Of course they spoke English and knew what an EMF metre was. Oh well. At least we'd never see them again.

'So what do you expect to find?'

Ben stopped walking and studied our surroundings. Lots of people. Gothic-style architecture. Grassy areas sectioned off so that people didn't walk on them. Pristinely trimmed hedges. A few food and souvenir stalls. Nothing helpful.

'And how can we track activity on a ship with literally thousands of people on it?'

Ben put his arm around my shoulders. 'What you're missing is that you're already helping with that.'

'What do you mean?' I said, enjoying his touch but hating his vagueness.

'Well, for whatever reason, you have a connection with our spectral friend. Which means we can narrow down our search area by using you.'

'How? I can barely use my phone. I can't use headphones or watch TV. Surely that'd be all over the ship.' I'd even tried Ben's headphones at one point and it hadn't made a difference. 'Hang on a minute.'

I took my phone from my bag and unlocked it. The screen was fine. I took a photo of Pisa. Still fine. I sent it to Edie. *Still* fine.

'Try your earpods again,' suggested Ben.

I did as he suggested, cringing in anticipation of the static I'd been unable to avoid. But it never came. The folk music theme tune of my favourite podcast played as it normally would. No white noise disrupting it, and no issues with my phone screen, either.

'So it's definitely something on the ship,' said Ben.

'But how can a ghost interfere with every electronic device on such a big ship?'

'Maybe they're not.'

'What are you saying?' I asked.

'Maybe they're just interfering with the ones near you.'

*

'I can't get a signal,' said Ben, shaking his phone as if that would make a difference. He put it into aeroplane mode for the fifth time, despite it having not made a difference the last four times he'd done it. But he had to try.

'Why don't you try?' he said, finally remembering I had a working phone.

'Why don't we just ask someone?' I suggested instead.

'Who? We don't speak Italian,' said Ben.

I walked a bit closer to a group of teenagers around Edie's age, who were talking nearby. They were flitting between English and Italian. Perfect.

Before Ben could talk me out of it, I marched over to them. '*Buongiorno*,' I said. 'Oh my god, your necklace is *bellissima*,' I said to the teenager directly in front of me. She was wearing a pentagram. They were all dressed in black with various supernatural symbols on their clothes or jewellery. They reminded me of Edie. Which was why I suspected they'd know if there was a shop that could help nearby.

The girl touched her necklace, smiling but looking confused. I didn't blame her. My approach was pretty random. '*Grazie.*'

'Where'd you get it from?'

Her friends watched our exchange, bemused. I was pretty sure Ben's expression behind me was as equally confused, but my plan was so far working. They hadn't stabbed us or turned out to be psychopaths yet, anyway.

'Just online,' she said.

Fiddlesticks.

'Ah, that's a shame. Is there anywhere around here that sells something similar?'

'Or something more…technical?' Ben said from behind me.

I looked at him over my shoulder and rolled my eyes.

'What do you mean by "technical"?' asked one of her friends, a guy with long, straight, black hair.

'Sound recorders, infrared cameras, that sort of thing,' said Ben. He was derailing my conversation here.

'You ghost hunting?' said a third friend, this one with crimson hair and a nose piercing.

'Yeah, but we left our equipment behind. Turns out, cruise ships are gold mines for ghosts,' said Ben.

The five of them nodded. 'There's a place around the corner. Should have something you can use.'

Bingo.

*

Our new friends guided us to a shop tucked away from the main tourist area, but not so far away that we wouldn't be able to get back to the bus, and therefore cruise, in time. They had a quick look around themselves, greeted the owner, then left us to get our supplies.

'So what do you want to get?' I asked.

Ben being Ben, he gravitated over to the shiniest tech. He studied a particularly expensive-looking recording device. 'Hmm. I suppose we can't go too mad.' Checking the price tag, he flinched. Must've been a step too far. He moved on to the item beside the expensive recording device. 'What about this? A spirit box?'

I glared at him.

'What? They pick up—'

'I know they pick up frequencies that spirits sometimes communicate on. You know what else is good at communicating with spirits? Our powers. And they don't make awful, grating noises that give me a headache.'

'It might help the passengers and crew communicate with the ghosts.'

I continued to glare at him. 'Isn't that our job?'

'So…no spirit box?'

'Sure. If we're on different cruises.'

Ben rolled his eyes. 'Fine.'

'What about these?' I said, gravitating to the other side of the shop where there were a bunch of dowsing rods. I knew what he was going to say, but it was too good of an opportunity to miss. Especially after he'd suggested using a spirit box despite knowing how much I hated them.

Ben shook his head. 'Are you kidding me? Do you know how useless those things are? They were debunked years ago. I don't get why people still bother with them. It's like spirit boards. Our muscles involuntarily twitch sometimes, which is what causes both of them to move. It's why most of us can't use those stupid steady hand games at the funfair.'

I patted his shoulder, laughing.

'Moving on.' He returned to the tech section.

The shopkeeper watched us with narrowed eyes, his shiny head reflecting the harsh LED lights. I couldn't work out if he was listening to our conversation or not. I hoped he found it amusing. Even if I had goaded Ben into insulting some of his stock. He had a bunch of spirit boards on the back wall.

'Does Edie still use that infrared app?' said Ben.

'Yeah. I think it's only as good as the camera on your phone, though.'

'How old is your phone?'

I took it from my pocket. It was a smartphone, but definitely not as recent as Edie's or Ben's. 'Um…a grandparent smartphone, maybe?'

Ben took it and studied it for a moment. 'More like the Fadil version of smartphones.'

'That's insensitive to Fadil.'

'He'd make the same joke. He has a more recent phone than you and only about four contacts in it.' Of course he did.

'It functions better than yours right now,' I said, sticking my tongue out at him. 'And I only need to ring people on it!' What was the point in buying a new phone every year if my old one still worked? I just needed something that functioned and took cute dog photos.

'Don't you email clients?'

'Not if I can help it. I usually text or call them. It's quicker. Most of my clients are Mrs Brightman's age, so they only really speak on the phone or in person.'

'So we'll keep that as an option to try on my phone, at least. I still have the app from when Edie was experimenting with it last year.' Without my permission, but I supposed her intentions had been good.

'My phone isn't *that* bad,' I said, feeling the need to defend it.

He lowered an eyebrow.

'It *isn't*.'

'If you insist,' he said.

I smiled and gave him a playful nudge. 'OK, being serious. What might actually help us communicate with, and stop, this ghost?'

23
Edie

Back at the bookshop that afternoon, I couldn't shake the feeling that something was wrong with Harry even though his life essence had felt normal. Whatever it was I couldn't put my finger on, we needed to be prepared for it.

If something happened while Mum and Ben were away, we were vulnerable. I was the only one with useful powers that could protect us. While Fadil could see ghosts, his spells so far hadn't worked. Ben had suggested it might be because of his lack of confidence in the same way mine hadn't worked well against Goodfellow. Hmph.

Fadil and I had tried to do some online snooping about Harry when we got back, but all we found was an out-of-date headshot on the bank's website and a couple of family photos on Maggie's profiles. It was unusual to look someone up and find hardly any online presence, but he'd always been a private person, so I figured he just didn't want to share his personal life with the internet.

Giving up on our research, and satisfied that the paint was dry, Fadil and I started tidying up. As we pulled masking tape from the walls, I used the opportunity to tell Fadil an idea that was starting to feel less like an idea and more like a necessity. 'I want to practise using my powers. Make sure I can get the most out of them.'

Fadil pulled off a strip of masking tape from by the front door. It made a satisfying noise. 'What do you mean?'

'I need to be able to protect us if something happens.' I pulled another strip off a few feet away, by the back door.

His disapproval and disdain were palpable even though I couldn't see his face. 'We don't know that there's anything wrong with Harry. You said his life essence was fine.'

We didn't not know, either. 'Even so, it won't be long until the next threat. Gran all but said I'm a walking target.'

'So you want to write some more spells?'

'No,' I explained. 'I want to learn how to use my necromancy.'

Fadil inhaled sharply. 'Is that…a good idea?'

'I don't think I have a choice. If we're caught unaware again and I don't know how to use my powers, there's no guarantee things will go as well as they did against Dominic or Goodfellow. We had more backup then.'

Fadil sighed, sitting cross-legged by the window and resting his chin in his hands as he watched me.

'Are you all right?'

'Just sore. And the paint fumes are giving me a headache.' He squeezed his eyes shut and reopened them. 'I'll be fine. You were saying?'

'I need to learn how to use my powers.'

He leaned against the boarded-up window. 'So you need a guinea pig?'

'Maybe.'

'Use me, then.' There was no hesitation in his voice.

'No. Absolutely not.'

'Why not?'

'I don't want to hurt you.' Any more than he was already hurting. Which, judging from his posture and strained expression, was a lot.

The bell above the door jingled. Fadil flinched. Josh entered, looking concerned.

'Hey,' I said.

'Sorry to interrupt. Can you talk?'

'What's up?' I said.

Fadil pushed himself up. It looked like even that took a gargantuan effort. 'I'm going for lunch.' He walked past Josh and left us to it.

'He OK?' Josh asked, pointing to Fadil through the glass door. People seemed to be asking that about him a lot lately.

'He's in a lot of pain.' I gestured to a clear spot on the floor, since we'd put the stool in the back out of the way of the paint. We both sat down. It gave me flashbacks to when we were younger and used to sit in our living rooms playing dolls or Lego. If only life were still that simple.

'I hope he feels better soon,' said Josh.

'Thanks. Me too. So…'

Josh frowned, running his fingers over a knot on the wooden flooring. 'I'm worried about Dad. Something about him seems off.'

I tried to fake calmness, but alarms started ringing in my head. 'Off in what way?'

'On the rare occasion we do see him, it's like his personality has totally changed. I remembered how Abigail changed when she was possessed, and I wondered...'

Josh wondering the same thing as me, when he knew his dad so much better, made me nervous. If his change in personality wasn't a sign of possession, I didn't know what was.

But why couldn't I sense anything unusual with his life essence? Was the ghost possessing him another necromancer? Thomas was the only ghost I'd ever met who could hide who he was, and that had been because of his powers.

'I've been wondering that too,' I said. Might as well be honest with him. I owed him that much. 'But when I saw him earlier, his life essence felt fine. His personality on the other hand...'

'You *saw* him?' said Josh.

'Fadil and I went to do some investigating. But we didn't really get anywhere.'

Josh's shoulders dropped. He stared at the floor. 'So you don't think anything is wrong with him?'

'I didn't say that. His behaviour was definitely weird. But I haven't worked out how else we can investigate yet.'

Maggie had the amulet but we only had the one, meaning Josh and Abigail were still unprotected. The best option seemed to be to ward their house. But I wasn't sure we had the ingredients to do it.

Josh fidgeted. 'Is there anything you can do?'

The Poltergeist's Ship

There was definitely something we could do. But Fadil was going to hate me for it.

*

'You hate me,' said Fadil as we trudged through the woods. 'That's the only reason you'd make me come out here.' He shuddered, wrapping his arms around himself. I couldn't tell if he was doing it because he was in pain, he was cold, or was uncomfortable with where we were going. Probably all of the above.

'He's an alchemist. We know he's about two hundred years old. That makes him the best person to advise us right now.'

'Ben has a library full of books! He has a *bookshop* full of books now! There's a library down the road! You have a Book of Shadows *and* a Book of the Dead. And they're both a gazillion years old. And you're telling me you can't get what you need from any of those things?'

'Not unless a book can magically make a warding potion, no.'

Fadil grunted. 'He killed Thomas! How is it a good idea to ask a *murderer* for help?'

'He didn't kill Thomas. He just didn't stop Goodfellow from killing him.'

Fadil rolled his eyes. 'Semantics, Edie! The guy is a *psychopath*.'

'If you have another suggestion for someone who can help us, by all means, let me know.' I sure didn't, and I wasn't going to waste my time trying to find a better source when one was just down the road. We didn't have time to waste.

'The internet! What's the point in the 21st century if you can't use the internet!' He huffed as he stamped through the freshly fallen leaves, his arms crossed over his massive coat. Even though it was hot and humid, he seemed to be unable to feel it. If he didn't speak to Doc soon, I was going to reach out to him on Fadil's behalf. It was definitely not massive-coat-wearing weather. I was sweating in jeans and a loose-fitting top.

'How do we know anything we read on the internet is true? So much of it is made up. And if we order something, we have no idea how long it'll take to show up or even if it's legit.'

Fadil waved his arms in the air. 'How do we know anything the alchemist says is true?'

'Simple: he wants repeat business. If he lies to us he doesn't get that. Also, he's never technically lied. Just avoided the truth.'

Fadil still wasn't impressed. 'That does not make him a good person! Or someone we want to work with! *Ever*!'

Why was he making this harder than it needed to be? Tobias was a morally grey person, sure, but so far, when we'd needed him, he'd come through. What more did Fadil want?

'We're not in league with him. We're going to see if he can help and then maybe pay him for his services. You're really overthinking this.'

Fadil marched ahead, which seemed contradictory when he didn't actually want to see Tobias. But, judging from his reaction, I was pretty sure he knew we didn't have a choice but he was going to protest until we reached the front door anyway. He'd done the same thing last time.

I mean, Tobias had peeled Fadil's skin off and replaced it with Dominic's. So I supposed he had more of a reason than anyone to hate Tobias.

I ran ahead to catch up with him. 'How do you walk so fast when you're in pain?'

'Momentum!' he snapped. 'If I don't keep the momentum going my legs will give way and I'll fall over.'

'Oh. I never thought of that. I'm sorry.'

My apology seemed to diffuse some of the tension that'd been building between us. Fadil took a deep breath. 'Apology accepted.'

'You'll get to see Dave again,' I reminded him.

He smiled at the mention of Dave, Dominic's dog. Fadil had fostered Dave until he'd moved into his permanent home with Tobias. They'd gotten along well, although it'd been months since they'd seen each other. Would Dave remember either of us?

We had no idea if Tobias would even be home when we got to his cabin. It wasn't like he had a phone we could ring. But he also rarely went out, so it was pretty likely he'd be in.

A twig snapped under my feet as the cabin came into view. A moment later, Dave barked.

'Here's hoping that's an excited bark and he hasn't since been trained to maul anyone who walks through the front door,' mumbled Fadil.

I rolled my eyes, not justifying his cynicism with a response.

The cottage door opened. Tobias stood inside, looking as grey as ever: grey hair, grey suit, grey skin. But he did seem more jovial than usual. The dog effect.

'Edie! Fadil! What pleasant surprises.' He held his arms out in greeting, as if he were welcoming us to a circus big top. He was normally more subdued than that. I was definitely blaming Dave. The border terrier emerged from behind his owner's legs and ran at us. I'd never seen him so excited to see anyone before.

We bent down to fuss him, forgetting why we were actually there for a moment.

'It's been a while,' said Tobias. 'I assume you need my help again.' He didn't sound mad about it. More intrigued.

My cheeks burned. Stupid natural ginger hair. 'We have some questions about warding, actually.'

He grinned. It didn't reach his eyes. 'That I can help with. Why don't you come in?'

24

Edie

'So, what do you need to know?' asked Tobias as we settled into his cottage. It hadn't changed much since I was last there in December, except for the copious amounts of dog toys. The cushion Tobias had made for Dave using leftover fabric was in the corner, next to Tobias's armchair.

Fadil and I settled on the faded sofa, as we always did. It had a yellow throw over the top that looked new. I'd never seen anything new in Tobias's cabin before. Definitely the dog effect.

'We ran out of warding paint and I don't have all the ingredients. I was also wondering if you knew of any ways we could enhance it,' I said.

'Why didn't you ask Ben?'

'He's on holiday and I didn't want to bother him,' I said.

Fadil shifted, gently nudging me and widening his eyes. Clearly he didn't like Tobias knowing Mum and Ben weren't around, but I didn't see a reason to lie.

'I see. What are you looking to protect yourself against?'

Wasn't that the question?

'Um...bad stuff?' I said.

Tobias sighed. 'So you don't know.'

'Not exactly.'

Tobias crossed his legs, clasping his hands in his lap. 'What signs have you observed so far?'

'The atmosphere in the house feels off, and so does the person in question, but his life essence seems normal. Do you have any idea what that could mean?'

'It could be a number of things,' he responded. 'Has anything else happened?'

'The person I'm suspicious of was stumbling around drunk in the middle of the night. But he barely drinks. I'm conscious that our friends could be in danger and feel like the longer we leave it, the more danger they're in.'

Fadil shifted uncomfortably again. I understood his concerns, but Tobias couldn't help us if he didn't know what was going on.

Tobias got up from his chair and walked over to a bookcase on his left. His eyes scanned the shelves. The whole wall was covered in books. Some looked even older than ones in Ben's library. I wanted to go study them, but something kept me on the sofa. And no, it wasn't Dave. He was nudging Fadil's hand every time he stopped fussing him.

'What do you normally use?' asked Tobias.

I handed him a scrap of paper I'd written our usual recipe on to. 'Mum's finding some of the ingredients increasingly hard to get hold of. And we can't wait to have them imported from Australia.' Or afford the cost of importing them.

He nodded, stopping at a book with a faded golden spine.

'If we made it, could we water the paint down? Make it go further?' I asked.

Tobias pursed his lips, then pulled the book from the shelf and blew the dust from it. 'Do you know what happens when you drink too much water?'

Was that a trick question? What was he getting at?

'It dilutes the salt and electrolytes in your body,' said Fadil. 'So then you get water toxicity and it can kill you.'

Tobias nodded. 'And when you don't have enough?'

'The body needs water to function otherwise toxins build up. And it can kill you.'

'Exactly.'

How did Fadil know that? And what did it have to do with warding paint?

Walking over to a table by the window, Tobias gestured for us to join him. We did, but we also gave him a wider berth than we would've most people.

'So you're saying if we water it down, it's less likely to work? And if it's too concentrated, it's also less likely to work?' I said.

'Yes. You're better off finding substitutes or additional ingredients. There are many similar ways to do things that come with different properties, like using mustard instead of pepper when cooking. They're not identical switches, but each brings different properties to a dish and sometimes those substitutes end up working better than you'd anticipated.'

'So we can change the recipe?' I said, feeling hopeful.

'Of course. It would help if we knew what you wanted protection from, of course. There are specific ingredients that tailor a potion to different beings.'

'I think a ghost. Possibly a necromancer one, if that matters.'

'A necromancer ghost,' he repeated. Tobias flicked through the book and pointed to a page. I didn't recognise some of the ingredients. 'What about this?'

'I don't think Mum has these ingredients at home.' I wasn't sure Maggie did, either. Some of the names looked like they were in Latin, so I couldn't even understand them.

'Probably not. There are one or two unusual ingredients here, but they'll make this potion stronger than the one your mum has been using. And they happen to be ingredients I like to keep in stock. I could make it for you,' offered Tobias.

Of course he had the ingredients we needed in stock. I could sense Fadil rolling his eyes beside me.

I didn't like the idea of relying on him any more than we already had, but I didn't need to remind Fadil how desperate we were to protect the Morgans. In for a penny…

'When could you make it for?' I asked.

'How much do you need?'

'At least enough to do a four-bedroom detached house,' I replied.

Fadil coughed. He clearly didn't like how specific that was to the Morgans actual house. But it wasn't like I'd given Tobias their address.

'Let me see what I have out the back.' He disappeared into the back room, the one where he'd traded Fadil's mummified skin for Dominic's fresh skin.

Fadil shuddered. 'I thought we were just coming here for advice!'

'If he can't make it fast enough we'll go somewhere else,' I said. Although I didn't know where that 'somewhere else' would be. Our only other option was Alanis the healer, but I doubted she'd have anything for warding a house. 'What are the odds of him having enough of everything?'

Fadil grunted.

'Good news!' Tobias said, emerging from the back. 'I can make warding paint for you. It'll take a couple of days. We just need to discuss the matter of payment.'

Fadil turned his back to Tobias, pursing his lips and glaring at me. I'd never seen him so annoyed at me. It hurt, but I had to focus. The Morgans needed our help.

But how could we pay Tobias? I hadn't even considered payment. Last time, he'd taken Dave in exchange for helping Fadil. There was no way I was giving up Tilly or Spectre, if that was what he was considering.

'Cash or card?' asked Tobias.

Of course he took money. Why hadn't I considered that? Idiot.

25

Niamh

When we got back to the ship, we placed a camera discreetly inside the door to our room and another by the balcony. They were small, so we hoped nobody would notice them.

While we'd been in Piza, Ben had also talked me into getting the spirit box. He thought it might help us communicate more clearly with said ghost, since they clearly had a fondness for technology. Time would tell if it'd be worth it. Most tech sounded like a spirit box to me lately anyway.

Since the cruise was filled with people, it was harder to conduct an investigation than usual. We couldn't put cameras up just anywhere; there was a high chance an attentive staff member would find it and we'd get kicked off, maybe even banned for life. It wasn't like most people would accept ghost hunting as an excuse for putting cameras up in public without permission. I was paranoid enough leaving them in our room, but at least we could pretend that was for content creation or something.

Edie called as Ben fitted a camera on top of the TV. I didn't want to answer, but I'd promised to be honest with her, for better or worse. So, cringing and ready to hand the phone to Ben, I answered. 'How's things?' I asked. Crackle. Fizz. Static. Fiddlesticks.

'Why did you just inhale really funny?' asked Edie.

I sighed. 'There's a ghost interfering with electricity on the ship.'

'Seriously? Can't you get a break?'

'No, apparently not.' I rolled my eyes.

'Do you know who? Or why?'

'I wish. We've just put some cameras up to see if they pick up on anything. And Ben's going to try that infrared app you showed him.'

'Will that even work on your phone?' she asked.

'Yes, it works fine thanks,' I said. My phone really wasn't *that* bad. 'Sorry, what did you say? The static is really bad.'

'I asked if it's every time you use your phone.'

'It's every time I go near any sort of tech while on the ship,' I explained, holding my phone at arm's length for a minute because the white noise was getting so bad.

'Maybe the ghost has a message,' she suggested.

'I really, really hope so,' I said. 'I have to go, the noise is killing me. We're in Rome tomorrow so I'll be able to talk better then. Look after everyone, yeah?'

'Will do. You too.'

*

Once we were happy with the camera setup, we decided to try the infrared app in the casino. It buzzed with energy from humans and ghosts. Some people cheered, others cried. Chips clattered on tables and music blasted from speakers. The bright lights, patterned carpets, and loud music turned it into sensory overload.

But there seemed to be an abundance of ghosts there, as if they were watching people gamble out of schadenfreude or living vicariously through them, so it felt like the perfect trial location. We probably weren't going to find a bigger concentration of ghosts in such a small space.

They hovered over people, shouting at them for picking the wrong card, or gambling too much, or not gambling enough.

After checking out the casino, we went for a walk down the boulevard. It was filled with shops and cafes and where I'd earned my free coffee the other day. Made to look like a park, the plants and trees looked even more spectacular in the sparkling sunset as the smell of pollen tickled my nostrils.

Ben's phone poked out from his shirt pocket, the back camera facing outwards and the infrared app open on the screen.

'The zip liner fascinates me,' he said, pointing up. It covered the length of the ship, probably offering some of the best views for anyone who could keep their eyes open for long enough.

'Nope. Hard no from me,' I said, focusing on the shops at eye level instead.

'You don't like heights?'

'No.'

'But you were fine on the plane,' he pointed out.

'That was a means to an end. And has some serious engineering behind it. But a zip liner? That does not have the same engineering as an aeroplane so I shall be keeping my feet firmly on the ground. Er, ship. That feels a lot like the ground because it's so huge.'

Ben put his arm around my shoulders and looked up. 'I'm not saying I'd go on it, but I think it's a cool concept. Makes things more interesting, you know?'

I shrugged his arm off my shoulders. 'For people who like thrills, yes. I don't know about you, but I get enough of those from things that go bump in the night.'

'Hey look, someone's going on it.' Ben guided me to a nearby bench. We sat down, Ben looking up at the zip liner and me staring straight ahead because just looking at the thing made me feel dizzy. I focused on a giant plant pot just in front of me. Something unmoving seemed safest.

'She's being strapped in. Looks pretty secure,' said Ben. 'Oh no.'

'What? What does "oh no" mean?' I chanced a look but didn't process any of what I saw.

'I think I see someone else up there.'

Ben pointed his phone at her. I leaned over his shoulder so that I could see the screen. He zoomed in. And sure enough, the cold figure of a ghost hovered beside her. Fiddlesticks.

Reluctantly, I tilted my head and looked up, clutching to the edge of the bench with one hand and Ben's thigh with the other to ground myself.

A spectral form floated just beside the woman being strapped on to the zipline. It was hard to work out who it belonged to from so far away. The camera app could only make out a blurry outline. They were a good ten or more storeys above us, but the glowing, floating figure was impossible to miss. To people who could see ghosts, anyway.

It flickered in and out of view. I couldn't work out if the ghost was intentionally trying to make themselves invisible or there was something wrong with them.

The woman stepped off the edge of the platform and zoomed down the zipline. Halfway, right above the boulevard, she stopped. Like she'd hit a wall.

'That's not meant to happen, right?' I said, my grip still tight on Ben's thigh.

'No,' said Ben. He pointed his phone at her again. The ghost was there, invisible, but very real.

A few of the people eating and drinking and walking around us noticed what was happening. They looked up, gasping and shouting as the woman kicked and screamed. It didn't help. It was like an invisible force held her back.

Except said force wasn't invisible to Ben and me. There was a ghost right behind her. And said ghost looked a lot like they were holding her back.

'We have to do something,' I mumbled to Ben.

'I don't know if I can reach her from here,' he said. He'd used his forcefield to move objects before, but they'd been much closer.

'Try,' I mumbled as I stood up and walked to where a couple of ghosts were talking. I had to be discreet. But thankfully, most of the humans nearby were too busy looking up or minding their own business to notice what I was doing. I took my phone from my pocket and pretended to be on it. 'Hey.'

The Poltergeist's Ship

The ghosts ignored me, not realising I could see them.

The woman's screams echoed through the cruise ship. The talking around us was being replaced by gasps of horror. I didn't need to look up to know that whatever was happening to her was so much worse than I could envision. I really hoped the ropes held.

The ghost wouldn't be able to get hold of any tools to cut the ropes, right?

Right?

'*Hey*,' I repeated to the ghosts through gritted teeth. 'Yes, I see you. And please can you go help that poor woman. You're the only ones who can.'

The ghosts hadn't even noticed her. Now, they looked up. Their expressions of shock reflected those of the living passengers.

They rounded up a couple more ghosts from the busy boulevard then floated over to where the woman was still stuck. Phew.

When the ghost holding her back noticed they had opponents, they vanished, leaving the other ghosts to push her to the end. Everyone onboard seemed to let out a collective sigh of relief.

'Thank god that worked because I was useless,' said Ben as I sat down.

'No you weren't.'

'What I tried didn't work. That's the definition of useless.'

I rubbed his shoulder. 'You were too far away on a moving ship. She was several storeys up. It was always going to be a stretch.'

'I suppose,' said Ben. 'At least now we know for sure there's a ghost wanting to cause trouble. And we have no idea who or why.'

'My two least favourite mysteries.'

Ben patted my leg and stood up. 'We'd better go find some answers then, hadn't we?'

As much as I wanted to reply with something sarcastic, I knew he was right. We *did* have to find some answers. Because if we didn't – and soon – someone was going to get into far more serious trouble than being stuck on a zip liner.

26
Edie

Surprisingly, Tobias took card payments. So I paid him then tried to work out how to come up with a way to disguise the wards in the Morgans's house to appease Maggie – and by association, Harry.

Of course, if there was something inside of Harry and the wards repelled him, we had bigger problems than if he saw them in the corner of a room and got annoyed.

When we got back to the bookshop, I felt a little more optimistic.

Gwendoline was floating around, examining what we'd done so far. 'It looks lovely.'

'Thanks,' I said, feeling proud of our work. It definitely had the cosy vibes Ben wanted.

'I hope you don't mind me looking around while you were out.'

'Not at all. It's your home, too,' I said. Just because the back room was the designated ghost area, didn't mean they couldn't leave. Especially not when customers couldn't see them anyway. And we were closed.

She hovered closer. 'I couldn't help but overhear you talking about practising your powers earlier, and I think you're right. I'd like to volunteer myself.'

I didn't know what to say. I was making everything up as I went along. Practising on a ghost hadn't even occurred to me.

But could I?

'Think about it: you can't hurt me. I can't feel pain, I can't die. There's no downside.'

'It makes a lot of sense. Removes a lot of the risk,' agreed Fadil.

'But what if I can't stop myself?' I said, remembering how addictive that power was and how much it'd messed with me. I knew I needed to practise, but I was still afraid of what I might do.

Gwendoline put her hand on my shoulder. 'You will. But the consequences are low. I'll recharge.'

What she meant was that if I couldn't stop myself I'd turn her into a glowing orb for who even knew how long. She wouldn't stay that way forever, but the guilt would never leave me if our experiment went wrong.

Shane floated in, oblivious to the weight of the conversation. 'Yo, what's up? What we all gathered in here for?'

Gwendoline narrowed her eyes at him.

'What'd I do?'

'Nothing,' said Gwendoline. 'Do you think you could watch the door for us, please? Make sure no one else comes in?'

'Sure. Why?'

We briefly explained the plan. He didn't know a huge amount about what I could do or what was going on, but he'd seen the state of Harry and understood the need for protection.

'Got your back.' He gave us the thumbs up.

The shop door locked, and Shane keeping an eye out, we relocated to the back room where there was no risk of anyone seeing us. I sat at the table, knowing I needed to learn more about my necromancy powers but terrified of them all the same. I wasn't sure I'd ever like that part of myself.

But I was painfully aware that one day, it could be the part that saved not just me, but the people I loved.

'Do you want my part back?' offered Fadil from his seat beside me.

'No!' I snapped. 'I mean, no. Sorry. I think it's better I learn to use it like this. Then we still have you around as backup.'

'OK.'

If he still had some of my powers I couldn't be consumed by them. In theory.

'Whenever you're ready,' said Gwendoline. She hovered in front of us, looking all calm and serene and trusting. The opposite of what I felt.

I closed my eyes, sensing the life essences in the room. There was Fadil's, fragile and brown, taking some of my own. A thin sliver of smoke tied us together.

Gwendoline's life essence was a light blue, as calm and serene as she was. I lured it towards me, feeling soothed by its embrace. It followed my guidance, recharging my own batteries and making me feel powerful. In control.

I opened my eyes. Gwendoline was faint. Fainter than I'd ever seen her. Fainter than many ghosts I saw. But I could keep going. If I just kept going a little longer—

No! I had to stop.

Stop.

Stop!

My body jolted as her life essence stopped flowing into me. 'Are you all right?'

'I feel a little light headed, but otherwise fine,' said Gwendoline. Who even knew ghosts could feel light headed?

'Right. Now time to reverse it.' I closed my eyes again and focused on how Gwendoline felt. She was so much weaker. My body didn't want to give up what I'd taken from her. It felt too good. But I had to. I pushed it from me, back in the direction of her body. It pulled at me, almost physically moving me across the room.

When I opened my eyes again, she was back to her usual self.

'Well. That was an experience,' she said, straightening her top.

'How do you feel?' asked Fadil.

'Wonderful, actually. Lighter than I have in a long time. It's almost like Edie cleansed my life essence before giving it back.'

Ironic, considering I felt like Gwendoline's life essence had cleansed me.

'How do *you* feel?' Gwendoline asked me.

'A little tired,' I said, yawning. 'Like I need a really good nap.'

The Poltergeist's Ship

'Maybe we should get you home,' suggested Fadil. 'I can walk Tilly while you rest.'

'Yes, rest. That sounds like a good idea.' I yawned again.

*

I got home after our experiment and crashed, not even noticing when Fadil got back from walking Tilly. She settled on the bed beside me and we fell asleep.

She woke me up a few hours later by jumping off the bed. And pawing at my bedroom door. It was three in the morning. Did she need to go out? Ugh. My head throbbed and I could hardly keep my eyes open; I really just wanted more sleep.

Tilly opened the door with her paws. And bolted down the stairs.

Then barked.

Who was she barking at?

In the middle of the night?

Spectre stared down at me from the wardrobe, unmoving.

I followed Tilly downstairs. She was barking at something on the other side of the front door. Was someone there?

My whole body shaking, I peered through the peephole. Or tried to. A figure blocked my view.

I jumped back.

There was someone there.

Someone was trying to break in!

I grabbed Tilly and held her to me.

I was home alone and *someone was trying to break in*. What was I supposed to do? What could I do? Would the wards protect us? Did I have enough energy left to use my powers if they didn't?

The person on the other side grunted. They'd been in shadow, so I hadn't been able to see who it was.

Curiosity getting the better of me, I looked through the peephole again. The figure was sitting with their legs out, rubbing their back, as if something had thrown them backwards.

Their hood created a shadow from the street lamps and obscured their face. But the figure looked male. The grunt I'd heard had been male, too.

Unable to look away, I watched as the figure stood up, groaned, and hobbled away.

*

I didn't get back to sleep. I was pretty sure Tilly didn't, either. What had the figure wanted? Were they human? I'd been too scared, too distracted, too drained, to use my powers to find out. Was it a coincidence someone had tried to break in while Mum was away? It felt like too much of one after everything that'd happened in the last few days.

Had Fadil been right, and we shouldn't have trusted Tobias or told him I was alone? Was I right about Harry? Or was it something else?

A key fumbled in the front door. Was the person trying to break in again? They wouldn't have a key though, surely? I'd used my powers to unlock doors before, but that place hadn't been warded. It had to be someone I knew. Mum wasn't home early, was she?

Someone closed the door behind them then crept up the stairs. I knew those footsteps.

Tilly jumped off the bed and pawed my door. This time, she seemed excited, not afraid.

Fadil opened the door, two takeaway coffees in hand. 'Good morning.'

Relief washed over me at his friendly face. I hadn't realised until then how much I'd needed someone else there with me.

I yawned. 'Does it have to be morning already?'

'How did you sleep?'

'Horrifically,' I replied.

He handed me one of the coffees then bent down to fuss Tilly. She was excited to see one of her favourite people so early in the day.

'Someone tried to break in.'

'*What?*'

I hugged my coffee. 'I didn't see who it was, but I think Moony or the wards hurt him. One minute he was right at the front door, the next he was a few feet away on the floor. Then he walked off hobbling.'

Last year, Ben had made gargoyles out of novelty gnomes. Ours was a mooning one I'd affectionately named Moony, to Mum's dismay.

Maggie had had one too, but she'd returned it after falling out with Mum and refused to take it back because it was impossible to hide from Harry. But how had Harry even known it was a gargoyle? Either she'd told him or she was paranoid he'd get even a whiff of the paranormal and it'd result in an argument. I loved

Maggie, but her conflict avoidance was infuriating sometimes.

What if it was Harry who'd tried to break in?

It *had* been a male figure.

He was the most likely suspect, even if Fadil would've preferred to be right about Tobias.

'Oh my god Edie. Are you all right?' Fadil sat on the bed with me. 'You should've rang me!'

I held my hand out to show him how much I was shaking. He put his hand on top of mine. 'I'm so sorry. But I'm really glad the wards held up. That explains why the gargoyle was lying down this morning, too.'

My back stiffened. 'Moony was what?'

'I put it back by the front door,' said Fadil. 'Aside from the broken foot it already had, it looked fine.'

The gnome might've been, but I sure wasn't.

'Did you see who it was?' he asked.

'No, but they were definitely male. And potentially older based on the sound they made when they fell back. It was deeper, if you get me?'

Fadil nodded. He hadn't touched his coffee since sitting down. Tilly must've sensed the tension as she lay in her bed under my desk, watching us. 'It seems a weird coincidence that'd happen now.'

'Exactly.' It was too much of a coincidence. But who was it? And would they try again? I yawned. 'What time is it?'

'Just past seven,' he said.

'You're up unusually early,' I said.

He shrugged. 'Couldn't sleep. Wanted to see how you were feeling.' The way he said it suggested there

The Poltergeist's Ship

was more on his mind than just that, but he didn't want to bring it up given what'd happened overnight.

I sipped my coffee while he played with Tilly, waiting for him to explain the real reason behind his early morning visit. The fact he wanted to talk about something was so palpable that I knew he wouldn't last long before he brought it up.

'I was wondering.' There we go. 'The thing you did with Gwendoline. Could you try it on me, next?'

'I'm not sure that's a good idea.' I really didn't want to hurt him. Or make his pain worse.

'Gwendoline, who's a perfectly healthy ghost, said she felt better after you gave her back her life essence. Your mum's injuries were healed. I was hoping…'

Oh. He thought I might be able to fix his chronic pain. How could I say no to that?

'I'm not asking you to do it all the time. Just once to see if it helps. The practise would be good for you, right?'

He was right, the practise would be good. But was it too soon after practising with Gwendoline?

'I'm not saying no, but I could really use more time to rest first. Especially after last night.'

'Of course! Whenever you're ready!'

I'd assumed he'd be deflated because I hadn't said I'd do it right away, but he seemed elated I'd agreed to it at all. But could it really help?

27

Niamh

'Is there anything in particular you want to do in Rome?' I asked Ben, flicking through the paper list of things to do. After the zip liner incident, I was desperate to get off the ship. The crew had closed it to investigate what'd happened but they'd obviously never find anything.

To help with the inescapable static, Ben and I had unplugged as much of the tech in the room as we could, but Niall seemed to plug it back in every time he cleaned. I'd have been more annoyed at him if it likely hadn't been part of his job. And if he hadn't left us with a different towel animal every day. The latest was a lion.

'Does it say how long each attraction takes?'

I scanned the paper. 'No.'

'I'll look on my phone, then. I think if we do more of the smaller things, we can cram more in. We can always come back another time to do Rome properly. I'm sure Edie and Fadil would love it.'

'Yeah, I think they would.'

How were they getting on? They'd seemed weird, distracted, the last couple of times I'd spoken to them. Maybe I was paranoid because I was worried. Ben and

The Poltergeist's Ship

Maggie would definitely say I was paranoid. And, given the way things had gone last autumn, I had every reason to be.

Ben kissed the top of my head. 'I'm going in the shower.'

'All right.' I stretched my legs across the sofa and opened the paperback I'd found in the ship's library. At least a ghost couldn't interrupt my ability to read a paperback.

I immersed myself in the magical world of fairies, forgetting about our real-world problems for a little while.

'Gah!' Ben ran out of the shower, stark naked. His arms and torso were crimson.

I ran over to him. 'What happened?'

He gestured to the shower, which was still running. The water was so hot the small room was clouded by steam. It was almost impossible to see the shower's switch.

I reached through to turn it off, barely avoiding getting burned myself. 'We'll have to talk to Niall. That can't be normal. Are you all right?'

'Bit sore.'

I dug into my first aid kit and handed him the calendula cream again. If this kept up, I wasn't going to have enough to last the cruise.

'Thanks.' He massaged the floral cream into his arms and torso. 'It stings, but it could've been worse.'

Always the optimist.

'It's got to just be a fault, right?' I said. 'You don't think…?'

'A ghost could do that? Yeah, I do. Especially after what we've seen so far. But first, we need to rule out a more innocent cause.'

*

Ben looked up at the screen on the stairs. 'Looks like we've got a couple of hours before the bus leaves for Rome.'

'Great,' I said through gritted teeth.

'What's wrong?'

'Screens.'

Ben frowned, putting his hand on me and guiding me away. The more time we spent on the ship, the noisier it got for me. The static meant it was hard for me to look at anything and was making me want to jump overboard to make it stop.

With so much tech on the ship designed to make our lives easier, it didn't matter where we went or what we did. Even in quieter areas, I could still hear static buzzing through inactive – but switched on – speakers.

The downsides of the modern world.

'You still can't hear it?' I asked.

'No,' said Ben.

'I'm grateful you don't have to put up with it and simultaneously annoyed you can't hear it.'

We reached the bottom of the giant staircase and moved off to the side so that we could talk. 'Do you think it's the ghost's way of communicating?'

'Communicating what, though? Last time it was a consequence of what Goodfellow was doing. It wasn't intentional. But for it to happen this often on a less aggressive scale doesn't fit that. It couldn't be from *all* the ghosts, could it?'

'I doubt it, but it's not impossible. It's usually a sign one or more of them is trying to communicate.'

I was about to ask what Ben thought the message could be when Niall walked over.

'Hey you two!' he said, bouncy as ever.

'Morning,' I said, not feeling remotely chirpy.

'Did you get any update on the hot water?' asked Ben. 'The shower's doing it now, too.' He pulled up his T-shirt sleeve to reveal the red mark that'd been left by the hot water. The calendula had calmed it, but it was still red.

Niall sucked air in through his teeth. 'Oh my. They said everything was fine, but I'll get them to take another look. Do you need any first aid?'

'No, it's fine, honestly. Just a bit annoying when you want a shower.'

'Definitely,' agreed Niall. 'Does it happen every time you put the hot water on?'

'No, I was fine to shower this morning, about half an hour before Ben. But it seems to be happening more frequently.'

Niall pursed his lips, then typed something on his phone. 'There are showers by the pool if you need to use them. I'll look into it and if we can't fix it we'll get you moved to a different room.'

'Thanks,' said Ben.

*

Moving to a different room seemed like a viable option. Until we were on the bus to Rome, where a couple nearby mentioned similar things happening to them. Then, a family also on the bus, joined in and agreed. Their rooms weren't anywhere near ours.

'So it's not just us,' said Ben. 'Meaning it has to be coming from somewhere else on the ship.'

Fiddlesticks.

'Like the pipework or something?'

'Yeah. But then that means we have bigger problems,' said Ben.

'Bigger problems than not being welcome in our own cabin?' I said.

Having been on the bus for about ten minutes, away from the relentless electronic buzzing, my headache was abating slightly. It was magical. It made me sad to think it was only temporary and whatever the cause was, it was ruining our holiday.

'It means anyone could be a target. If there even is one,' he replied.

'Well isn't that just great?'

28

Edie

While drinking our morning coffees, Fadil and I made a plan for how to explain to Maggie and Josh what was going on. It started with bribery. Between the two of us, Fadil and I were keeping the numerous local coffee shops in business.

Fadil still hoped that Harry was just stressed, not possessed, but he was starting to believe my suspicions. He at least believed that *someone* was after us.

I left him at the bookshop – where someone was hopefully going to repair the coffee machine – then headed with my bribery to see Maggie.

She opened the front door and smiled. 'Much appreciated.' She took one of the coffees from the cardboard holder, then stepped aside to let me into the hallway. She yawned, clearly not having slept well judging from the purple bags under her eyes.

'Is Josh here? I want to talk to both of you if I can.'

'He's just getting ready for work.' She jerked her head in the direction of the kitchen. I followed. 'What's this about?'

'I'd rather tell you together.'

She didn't seem to like it, but she accepted it. 'All right.' She shouted him from the bottom of the stairs.

As he walked into the kitchen, I held out the coffee to him.

'Um, thanks,' he said, clearly confused. He worked in a coffee shop. The bribery didn't make as much sense for someone who could get free coffee whenever he wanted it. But I wasn't going to leave him out either. That felt meaner.

'Edie wanted to talk to us,' Maggie informed him.

He pulled out a dining chair and sat down, waiting for me to explain. Somehow, I had to tell them they might be in danger without worrying them. And there was the fact that I couldn't prove anything. All I had were instincts and suspicions. But I couldn't not tell them. It was too dangerous.

When I'd finished my overcomplicated explanation, there was silence. I really hoped it was just because they were processing what I'd told them. I hadn't exactly explained myself well.

'So you want to ward the house again?' said Josh.

'I just think caution is better, especially with what's happened before. Wouldn't you prefer to be protected from a non-existent threat than unprotected from an actual threat?' I hoped I sounded logical.

Josh glanced at me. There was clearly an internal argument going on inside his head. He was worried too, especially since he was going to uni soon. But he was also fiercely protective of his family. There was no way he'd leave them unprotected even if he didn't like it.

'What would the wards do, exactly?' he ended up asking.

'Basically, they're designed to stop anything that wants to hurt someone inside of the house from getting inside.'

'So it's the quickest way to find out if something is wrong,' said Maggie.

I nodded. I really hoped, for their sakes, something *wasn't* wrong.

'How long until the paint is ready?' she continued.

'Tomorrow,' I said.

They both tensed.

'I know. It's not ideal. We all just need to play along and pretend everything is fine until then.'

Maggie shifted in her seat. 'I hate lying.'

'Well…'

'Well what?'

'Well if we're right—' and even though I didn't want to be, and we had no empirical evidence, I was convinced that we were '—we don't know how long he's been lying to us for.'

'This is horrible,' said Maggie. She rested her face in her hands.

Josh rubbed his mum's back. 'We'll get through this. We'll figure something out. Right?' He looked to me for reassurance. *Me?* After everything?

I supposed there wasn't anyone else this time.

'Right,' I agreed. 'We have before, we will again.'

'I hate this,' said Maggie, shaking her head. She pulled Mum's amber amulet from where it'd been tucked under her top. 'I think Abigail should have this. She's more important.'

'I agree,' said Josh.

'Where is she?'

'She stayed at a friend's last night,' said Maggie. Lucky.

'Could she stay there again tonight?' I suggested. That would mean one less person to worry about. And less to explain to a six-year-old.

'I'll check but I don't think they'll mind,' said Maggie.

'Awesome. So at least you have the amulet in the meantime,' I said.

'Do you not have anything Josh can wear?' she asked, silently pleading with me.

'Not that I know of,' I said, frowning. 'Sorry.'

'It's OK. I'll be fine,' insisted Josh.

Maggie pursed her lips. 'I don't like this. I don't like you not being protected.'

'Neither do I,' said Josh, 'but I'm more worried about you and Abigail. We only have to last a little while longer. We just have to keep acting like everything is fine until we can put everything into place. This is nothing in comparison, right?'

An unspoken conversation passed between them; shared trauma I'd never understand. But they both nodded in agreement. They'd survived worse. They could survive this.

*

When I arrived at the bookshop after breakfast, Maisie and a couple of others were fitting the new window. She was dressed in her usual all-black outfit, but her colleagues were wearing more weather-appropriate shorts and T-shirts. From what I could tell from their

The Poltergeist's Ship

life essences, they were human. Hers was a stark contrast and definitely *not* human.

'How's it going?' I asked as I reached them.

'It looks good,' said Shane, who'd floated over from the other end of the high street. I could've sworn Maisie looked right at him, but that could've been a coincidence given that people looked at ghosts without realising they were there all the time.

'Almost done,' said Maisie. 'Then I can start helping you with revision,' she added with a wink.

I shook my head, unable to hide my smirk. In a weird way, I was looking forwards to hanging out with her more. Even if that meant revision. 'Thanks so much for turning this around so fast.'

'Happy to help,' she said with a broad grin. 'And don't change the subject. I was serious about the revision. Quicker you start, the less painful it'll be.'

'Can't I enjoy my summer first?'

She glanced up at the cloudy sky, then back down at my pale skin. 'Something tells me your version of enjoyment involves reading a book indoors.'

'You got me.'

'She's right,' said Shane with a laugh.

I shot him a look. He floated off again in the direction of the tram.

Maisie smirked. 'I'll try to make it less painful, I promise.'

'How?'

'Haven't got that far yet. But I'll think of something.'

Fadil was inside, sitting in front of a half-built bookcase, when I walked in. His head was resting on one of the shelves.

'What's wrong?' I asked.

'Just taking a break,' he said.

'With your head in your hands?'

He shrugged. 'The light was annoying me.'

It was overcast outside and the ceiling light wasn't even on. What was *wrong* with him?

'Are you sure you don't want me to—'

'Say call Doc and you can build the rest of the flatpack yourself,' he said through gritted teeth.

'Make you a cup of tea?' I finished. Even though what I'd been going to say was exactly what he'd predicted.

'That would be nice, actually. Thank you,' he said. 'The coffee machine is fixed, by the way. One of the parts was faulty but the repairwoman just swapped it out and it's as good as new.'

Two things fixed in one day? Maybe things were looking up. Or maybe I was being unnaturally optimistic. But I needed to cling on to my last shreds of hope. I'd had enough of this week.

29

Edie

It was really hard to focus on anything while worrying Harry. But until the paint was ready, there wasn't anything else we could do. There was nowhere nearby I could get supplies other than Tobias.

So I spent the day sitting at the newly built counter, inhaling the smell of fresh paint, watching people walk past through the new window, and updating the website. I'd spent the afternoon working on the bookshop website, and it was finally almost done. Josh had designed the logo, and it now took centre stage on the site which allowed people to buy books and take a virtual look around.

I'd barely moved all day, incapacitated by my fear of what could happen next. If I stayed still, nothing could change, right?

If only.

'Um, Edie?' said Shane, hovering over to me.

I yawned, looking up from my laptop and at the nervous ghost before me. It'd been a long day, but Shane had always been nice and helpful, so I didn't want to be rude. 'What's up?'

'I know you've got a lot going on, so it doesn't have to be now, but I think I'm ready to talk to my girlfriend.

She needs to know some things so that she can move on. So that *I* can move on.'

If I asked why now he might second guess his decision. So I stayed quiet.

'If you need me to, like, guard the door again I can stick around a bit longer. It doesn't have to be straight away. Just don't ask me to watch that creepy guy.' He shuddered.

'What creepy guy?'

'Your friend's husband. No offence. Something about him was so weird. It was seeing him like that that got me thinking about crossing over.'

All right, this time I had to ask. 'Why?'

'What if he's possessed by a bad ghost? Was that bad ghost a nice person when they were alive, but the frustrations of being a ghost turned them into a poltergeist? I don't want that to be me.'

A perfectly good reason to confront his metaphorical demons.

'All right,' I said, closing my laptop and standing up. Helping Shane was the nudge I needed to leave the desk. 'Let's go talk to her.'

Shane's eyes went wide. '*Now?*'

'Yep. Get it over with before you can talk yourself out of it. Let's go.'

*

Shane obviously hadn't expected me to suggest we go *now*, but from the little I knew about him, if we didn't talk to his girlfriend right away, he'd procrastinate by

The Poltergeist's Ship

trying to find ways to be useful around the bookshop and talk himself out of seeing her.

Following his instructions, I walked to her house to meet her. She was on the outskirts of Hucknall, on one of the new builds. Not the one Mum had worked on where Dominic had disrupted the old mine, but one near the train station and tram stop.

It was hilly and green, juxtaposed by the humming of car engines on the train bridge.

'She has a spirit board,' Shane explained. 'She's used it to talk to me a couple of times but I haven't been able to move the pointer.'

This would've been so much easier if I'd been psychokinetic. Then I could've just moved the pointer and not had to have this conversation. Oh well. Couldn't have every power. Guess I had to settle for bringing people back from the dead instead.

'They're just a board game. Don't beat yourself up about it,' I said.

'Pot, kettle,' he said with a glint in his eye. Yes, he knew about my exam results. Every ghost in the bookshop did. There were no secrets around there, especially when over half its inhabitants could turn invisible.

'Failing exams is very different to moving a pointer,' I said as we rounded the final corner to her house. Cars were pulling into their drives as everyone got back from work for the day. Dogs barked in the background and children squealed as they welcomed their parents home.

'Is it, though?' he said, refusing to let it go. 'They both require conscious effort. Some people are naturally good at it, while others can study all they want. Doesn't mean we'll get any better.'

'So you're saying I shouldn't resit my exams?' If it wouldn't have looked weird for me to stop and glare at him, I would've.

'No, I didn't mean that. You should definitely resit.'

'Then what's your argument? Because I'm not getting it?'

He was a terrible counsellor.

'I meant that you did your best. You shouldn't beat yourself up.'

And with that I was done. With the conversation. Not beating myself up. That would probably go on a while longer.

'All right that's enough counselling for me today. Tonight it's all about you.'

Without asking if he was ready, I knocked on the door. There was barking and shuffling inside, then a petite blonde, around Shane's age, opened the door.

'Hi, Hilary. My name is Edie.' I glanced down at the dog behind her. It was a Yorkshire terrier. 'Cute dog. I have a westie.'

'Thanks. What do you want?' She looked tired and like she didn't really want to talk. I knew that feeling well.

'Tell her about the mole on her—'

'No,' I said to Shane over my shoulder.

Hilary looked around. 'Who are you talking to?'

Well this was going well already.

'Shane. I'm talking to Shane.'

She went to close the door on me. Her dog started barking, looking right at where Shane was standing.

'He asked if you're still wearing the necklace he gave you.'

He hadn't, but I remembered him mention it in one of our conversations at the bookshop.

'It was an aquamarine one, right? That he bought you on holiday?'

She followed her dog's gaze. The dog continued to stare at where Shane was floating behind me.

Without speaking, Hilary opened the door fully so that I could go inside. Inside, it was very monochrome. A lot of white, with spots of black and grey to break things up. It was a little sad to look at, actually. It was like all the colour had been sucked out of the house. The decor matched her fashion sense, which, at least for this outfit, involved a lot of high-quality tailoring and monochrome colours.

'How did you know that?' she asked.

'He's here,' I said. 'Behind me.'

She scoffed. 'Yeah. Sure he is.'

'He's been haunting the bookshop in town.'

'There is no bookshop in town.'

'It's a bookshop-in-progress,' I corrected. 'It opens next month.'

She didn't seem to care. 'Why is he here? Why are you here? How can you see him?'

So many questions.

'Shall we sit down?'

She gestured to the room on our right. The living room. I sat on the black leather sofa while Hilary sat on the reclining armchair opposite the TV. Her dog settled in her lap. Shane hovered from one end of the room to the other. The dog watched him, fascinated.

'I can talk to ghosts. Shane is here because he wanted to talk to you before he crosses over. To apologise.'

She wrinkled her nose. 'Is this some sort of sick joke?'

Always nice when people thought I was cruel enough to pull a prank like that.

'He said you've been trying to communicate with him using a spirit board, but he's not strong enough to move the pointer. He felt bad and wanted me to pass the message on for him.'

She gasped. 'How could you—I haven't told anyone that. Not even the dog has seen me do that.'

I pursed my lips, waiting for the information to sink in that her partner was really there in ghost form.

'Shane? Is it really you?' Her voice quivered.

He walked over to her and ran his hand over her face. She inhaled. 'I...what was that?'

'Ghosts can sometimes move the air around them. It's why some spaces feel cold or you might feel a breeze when one is around.'

She closed her eyes and inhaled. 'I miss you.'

'Tell her I'm sorry.'

'He says he's sorry for working so much. That he didn't value you enough.'

Her breath quivered as she tried not to cry. 'I know his work was important to him.'

'Not as important as you.' He hadn't moved from in front of her, and while she couldn't see him, she was looking right at where he was.

'He says you were more important.'

'The ring.'

'And he'd bought a ring for you. He stored it in an old shoe box, with his grandfather's things.'

'Wait here.' She went upstairs. Shane and I waited in silence while she rummaged upstairs. A few minutes later, she came downstairs with a decorated shoebox and a jewellery box. 'Is this it?'

Shane nodded.

'Yes.'

Opening it, she gasped. It was an aquamarine and white gold ring that complemented the necklace she'd put on while upstairs.

'I'm so sorry I never got to give it to you,' he said.

'He's sorry he never got to give it to you,' I repeated.

Hilary snivelled, putting the ring on her ring finger. 'It's beautiful.'

Shane watched, a look of sorrow on his face. 'I wasted so much of my life on work. And what for? They never cared about me. Not like she does.'

Starting to feel the weight of the situation, I wiped a tear from my eye. I had to remain emotionless and in control. I paraphrased what he'd said to her.

'Yeah, you did work a lot. And I'll always be annoyed at you for that because we could've done so much more together.' She snivelled again. The dog jumped up and licked a tear from her cheek. She gave a small laugh. 'But I love you too much to be mad at you. I always will.'

He stroked her cheek again. 'Take care of yourself. And don't be afraid to move on.'

The bright white light appeared behind him. The one that symbolised it was time for him to cross over.

'Look after each other,' he said to Hilary and her dog.

Then, he was gone.

30

Niamh

It was hard to enjoy Rome with Ben's revelation that the ghost may not be targeting anyone at all, but instead taking a sporadic approach to hurt anyone they could. Without a pattern to their behaviour, it made it a lot harder to stop them.

Bad news aside, Rome offered a screen break that lessened my headache for a few hours. And Ben's arm hadn't turned into a full-on burn. So at least a couple of things were working in our favour.

When we got back, we called Edie.

'Any update on the poltergeist?' she asked, never one to beat around the bush even though she likely knew I was ringing to check up on her.

'No,' I said with a sigh, barely able to see her face on the video screen because of the static. 'It's interfering with the water temperature, but it's intermittent.'

'How is it now?' Edie asked.

'Right now? It's fine. It doesn't make sense,' I said. 'There's no pattern to it.'

'It has to be to do with the ghost's location, right?' she said. 'Like it's interfering with your phone, so maybe it has a way to tap into technology, but it can't interfere with the water at the same time? Or it's in a different part of the ship?'

Ben, who was checking through the camera footage, nodded in agreement.

'Did you find anything?' I asked him.

'Doesn't look like it,' he said. 'Most ghosts just follow the people they're haunting, like we thought. A child ghost came in and seemed to be looking for something or someone, didn't find it, then left. That's it.'

While we didn't know much about the poltergeist on the ship, we did know they weren't a child. The figure we'd seen was too tall.

'Ugh.' I lay back on the bed, tired and frustrated.

'Mum? Where'd you go? The ceiling really isn't that interesting to look at.'

I picked my phone up and held it parallel to the ceiling. 'Sorry. Just fed up.'

'Did Rome help at least?'

'Thankfully. I've got some earplugs I can wear to get some sleep, too, but it feels like a catch-22 because with that and an eye mask on, I feel more vulnerable.'

'Could Dad watch over you?' she suggested.

'No! Absolutely not. He puts himself in harm's way too often for us. If he were a normal ghost, he wouldn't even be able to come and go as he wanted to.' I ground my teeth in frustration. The white noise was pissing me off. It was a constant hum. When I wasn't near it, like in Rome, I could *still* hear it. It was literally haunting me. Like tinnitus. 'How are you, anyway? How's the bookshop going?'

'It's looking really good,' she said. 'Did you see the photos I sent?'

The Poltergeist's Ship

I turned my phone around so that she could see Ben. 'The colour looks great,' he said. 'The furniture goes really well.'

'Yeah, it's super cosy. Just a few more pieces to do now. The website is practically done, too.'

'Amazing, thanks. I knew you two could do it.'

Edie smiled, looking proud of herself. Finally, something positive happening for her. 'Shane crossed over earlier, by the way. He finally talked to his girlfriend.'

I noted she hadn't answered my question about how *she* was, but that was typical Edie. She hated talking about herself. 'She believed you?'

'Eventually,' said Edie.

'I'm glad he got the closure he needed. You could tell how much it ate at him. Any more on your friend with the unusual life essence?'

Edie shifted in her seat. 'I've seen her a couple more times, but I haven't figured out anything else about her yet.'

'As long as she's nice to you, that's all I care about,' I said. 'The rest will happen in time if it's meant to be.'

'Yeah, you're right,' she said. 'She can walk through the wards in the shop, so that's something.'

'You could always try one of the gargoyles outside,' suggested Ben. 'They won't let anything that wants to hurt you through.'

Edie paused for a moment, as if in thought. 'I'll give that a go. Thanks.'

'I've got to go. The static seems to be getting worse.' It was starting to block my view on the camera now.

What was the point in a video call if I couldn't see anything? 'Say hi to Fadil for us.'

'Will do. Be careful, Mum.'

'You too.'

After our catch up with Edie, it was investigation time. Ben and I went in search of who – or what – could be causing my screen issues and people's hot water problems. So far, the cameras hadn't picked up on anything untoward, just ghosts going about their business.

And there was no word from Niall. In fact, I was pretty sure he walked in the opposite direction whenever he saw us.

Ben explored a couple of the more screen-heavy areas, like the cinema, on his own while I went to pools or spas. They might've had fewer screens, but it was almost impossible to relax around them given I was looking for a poltergeist.

That evening, frustratingly empty handed and not wanting to waste our holiday any further, we went to see a water show. It combined synchronised swimming with acrobatics and wire work and all sorts of moves I could only ever dream of being able to do.

Or possibly have nightmares about doing, given the heights they were catapulting themselves from.

Our seats were parallel to the top of the wires the performers jumped from, so it looked slightly more palatable than if we'd been at ground level and looking up, like we'd been with the zip liner. I was still trying to wipe that from my memory. It'd been talk of the cruise ship and the bus to and from Rome. Ben and I had listened in to what the people and ghosts had said, but unfortunately, nobody had said anything useful.

So we'd agreed to try to make the most of the cruise and act like everything was normal while keeping an eye out.

I checked the infrared app on my phone. It didn't work that well, but I tried. My phone wasn't *that* geriatric.

The terrible WiFi signal meant that even if the camera in our room picked up on something, it wouldn't tell us for hours. I'd set up notifications for if it saw anything, although we were so far away we couldn't run back if it did. It kind of felt like our investigation was at a dead end with so many people around and such limited access to investigate.

Without wards for protection, cameras and sound recorders were the best we could do. They wouldn't help us sleep, but they'd at least pick up images or sound if something did happen.

Reassuring.

I checked my phone again, but all I saw was a room in darkness. Ben put his hand on top of mine and lowered my phone into my lap. Leaning into my ear, he said: 'You can still switch off. Isn't that the point of this?'

'But *how*? With everything that we know?'

He squeezed my hand. 'That's all the more reason why we should. If we don't do it now, we don't know when something will happen. So then we won't be rested enough to actually help anyone.'

Why was he always right? Not that that meant I knew how to switch off when a poltergeist could strike at any moment. And said poltergeist clearly knew who we were or they wouldn't have smashed the mirror. Or kept interfering with electronics whenever I was near them.

The music kicked in and the show started. We'd heard the music from it most nights as we'd been walking around when it was on, but we hadn't seen it until now.

The performer's skills took so much trust and physical strength. All things I didn't have and probably never would.

But why couldn't I?

Or at least, why couldn't I be physically stronger?

I was at a make-or-break point with my body. Edie had given me a bit of a reset with her powers, but I doubted that'd last forever. I was still in a forty-one-year-old body. And one that'd dealt with more stress than your average person from a young age.

I had no desire to jump from a wire into a pool, or do synchronised swimming, but there had to be something out there for me, right? A way to exercise that taught me a way to protect everyone and maintained – maybe even enhanced – my physical strength?

I was pulled out of my planning by busier static on the screen behind the performers. It was supposed to be showing close-ups of them, but that image had been taken over by white noise. And so had the music that'd been playing.

I cringed, turning into Ben. This time, I wasn't the only one squirming. Lots of the audience seemed to be able to hear it, too. And, judging from Ben's face, so could he.

'Is that what you've been hearing and seeing?'

'Yeah. Real fun with lots of screens on the ship.'

'I had no idea it was that bad. If I'd known I would've tried to plan you a route to avoid them.'

I kissed his cheek. It was a cute sentiment that I appreciated. Even if it could never happen. 'Pretty sure one doesn't exist. They're impossible to avoid when even the maps are screens. And I kind of got used to it. But this? This is a whole new level.'

The performers continued their performance despite the noise, while a couple of people on the ground level tinkered with the sound system to the side of the stage.

Ben got his phone out, but the infrared app didn't pick up on any ghosts we couldn't already see.

A performer slipped.

He screamed, plunging towards the pool.

Ben reached out, using his powers to slow the guy's fall. We weren't as far away as we'd been from the zip liner, but we weren't close, either. Ben's powers only just reached, so it was more like a gentle breeze that slowed his descent, but it at least meant he hit the water slower than he would've, hopefully doing less damage.

The menacing face I'd become all-too-familiar with seemed to seek me out. It locked eyes with me. This time, I didn't look away.

31

Niamh

Fitful is the best way to describe my sleep after the aqua show. Thankfully, the performer was fine, but the performance had been cut abruptly short since they couldn't get the screens or sound system to work. And everyone was too spooked to keep performing or watching.

Even though the cameras only picked up heat signatures, I felt self-conscious with them watching me. And I felt exposed without wards for protection.

I was finally drifting off to sleep when Ben nudged me. I pulled out my earplugs. The captain's voice echoed through our room. The one piece of tech I couldn't turn off, which turned out to be a good thing.

Someone had fallen overboard.

Had the poltergeist pushed them? Were we at the final stage of a poltergeist: threat to life?

Ben and I hurried out of bed and onto the balcony, where we began to look for the guest. We could hear the guests all around us looking out on their balconies, too. Lights flicked on across the ship, but they didn't do much to illuminate the blackness surrounding us. It was impossible to see more than a few feet away. The only light above the sea came from the ghosts looking for a figure in the open ocean.

'Do you think we'll find them?' I asked Ben as we peered into the black ocean.

'Doubtful, sadly,' said Ben. 'What do you think happened?'

'Maybe they were doing this and just slipped,' I suggested.

'These barriers are pretty high up,' said Ben.

'You make it sound like nobody has ever done anything irresponsible and caused themselves injury or death,' I said.

Ben chuckled. 'Good point.'

'Who are we looking for?'

I jumped so high at the unexpected voice I almost fell overboard myself. Ben grabbed me, pulling me back.

'Oh! I'm so sorry, dears. I didn't mean to make you jump.' In front of us was an older lady with grey and white hair wearing a pink frilly nightdress that looked a lot like what my mother used to wear, never quite having moved on from ugly 1980s fashion. I'd never be able to bleach that style from my mind. Nor would I ever be caught dead wearing anything like it. It seemed to suit the lady in front of me, though.

'Who are you?' asked Ben.

'Delia. I was walking through my room then somehow ended up in yours. I'm so sorry.'

Oh fiddlesticks.

Ben looked at me, his expression suggesting he'd come to the same conclusion as me. Now how to tell Delia…

'What's the last thing you remember?' I asked.

'I just told you: I was walking through my room.'

'Was it towards the balcony?' said Ben.

'It was, actually. Yes. Why do you ask?'

Luca, one of the ghosts who'd helped during the zip liner incident and had since spoken to us a few times, floated to our balcony. He was a blond teenager with 90s-style hair and was haunting his parents. 'I think we found her!' Seeing who we were talking to, he lowered his head. 'Oh…' Well if that didn't confirm our suspicions, nothing would.

'Where is she?' asked Ben.

Luca pointed a few feet away. We couldn't see anything but trusted his judgement – he could float above the water and ghosts glowed, after all – so Ben called Guest Services on our room's phone.

'Did someone fall overboard?' Delia asked me. 'I wonder what they were doing.'

Luca frowned.

'Thanks for letting us know,' I said, hoping he'd take the hint and leave us alone. He saluted, then disappeared out of sight.

I sat on one of the balcony seats, then gestured for Delia to sit on the one on the other side of the table. She tried. But went right through it.

'What the—'

She floated back up, bemused. It seemed cruel, but experience had taught me that evidence was often quicker and more powerful than words to prove to someone that they were dead.

'It was you they found, Delia. I'm so sorry.'

'No. No it wasn't.'

The Poltergeist's Ship

'Then why couldn't you sit on the chair?' Ben asked, resting his hand on the back of my chair and putting his other hand in the pocket of his pyjama trousers. Oh, to have access to so many pockets in clothing. I needed to start stealing his clothes.

She tried to sit on the chair again, but the same thing happened. This time, she disappeared to the deck below and didn't reappear.

'Do you think she'll be all right?' I asked Ben. I felt sorry for her. It must've been horrible to discover she'd died so abruptly. And while on holiday!

He shrugged, sitting in the chair Delia couldn't. 'Maybe she just needs time. Who knows what happened before she fell?'

'Not her right now, by the sounds of it,' I said. 'You don't think…'

'What, you think a poltergeist did this?'

'It's not a huge leap, is it? After everything we've seen so far?'

Ben pursed his lips. 'No, I suppose not.'

Which meant that we'd failed to protect the passengers from the very evil it was our job to protect them from. Bloody brilliant.

32

Edie

Bang bang bang. Bang bang bang. BANG BANG BANG.

What the hell? Who'd knock so loudly so *late*? It was just past midnight and I'd almost been asleep. I needed it after an emotional evening with Shane. So much for that.

Tilly barked, running down the stairs with her tail wagging. It was a friend, not a foe, then. That was something.

I followed her downstairs then checked the peephole. Maggie and Josh. They were in their pyjamas, light coats over the top to keep the chilly breeze off them. Maggie shuffled from foot to foot. Josh cracked his knuckles. Their eyes darted around, as if they thought someone might jump at them from the shadows. What the hell had happened?

I opened the front door and beckoned them inside. Tilly jumped up at them but they were too shaken to even notice. It had to be bad. They always said hi to Tilly. It was an unspoken rule.

They sat on the sofa. Their hands were shaking. Tilly jumped in between them. They reached out and stroked her, clearly needing the comfort. Neither of them looked at her. Their eyes were glossed over; hollow.

Spectre floated in to see what was going on. He settled on his favourite spot on top of the bookcase. Even though Maggie and Josh couldn't see him, I appreciated his presence.

'What happened?' I asked, although I wasn't sure I wanted to know. This was one of those rare occasions where I really wished Mum and Ben were around. But there was no way I was disturbing their holiday.

'Harry found me wearing your mum's amulet,' said Maggie.

'And he ripped the necklace right off her,' finished Josh.

So far, so typical Harry. Not great, but not unexpected. He hated anything with even vague occult connotations. Even after Josh, Maggie, and Abigail's experiences, he still wasn't very tolerant of the concept. He'd just been less vocal in his dismissals.

Maggie's eyes filled with tears as she dug into her pocket and held out the amulet. The amber was cracked. Amber was fragile. But if the amulet was broken, did that mean it wouldn't work anymore?

And what did it mean about Harry?

I passed Maggie the box of tissues from the coffee table. Normally I would've offered them a drink, but getting answers seemed more important than pleasantries. Something big had happened because of Harry and that necklace. But what?

Maggie tore a tissue from the box and blew her nose, resting the amulet on her lap. 'He...he seemed to cringe when he touched it. Like it was painful, but a tolerable level of pain, if you get me? Like a static shock or something.'

Oh no.

That was bad. Really, *really* bad.

I sank on to the floor. If he found it painful to touch a protection amulet, but still could, there were very few possibilities left. Each one was worse than I'd wanted to consider.

'What does it mean?' Josh asked. I really didn't want to answer. But there was no one else who could give them the answers they wanted. Needed. *Deserved*.

They watched me, waiting for me to respond.

'I can't say for definite, but I'd hazard a guess and say that's not the Harry you know and love.'

'Like a shapeshifter?' said Josh. He was still stroking Tilly. She wasn't complaining. She'd rolled on to her side so that he could get another spot and she could fall asleep while he fussed her. At least someone could sleep well.

'Cute, but not a thing. As far as I know.' Anything was possible. 'He's probably more than likely possessed by something. Something bad.'

'How bad are we talking?' Maggie asked, her voice quivering.

I pursed my lips. I hated telling them this stuff. It wasn't like I had much experience in revealing information in a way that wouldn't cause people to freak out, and Mum wasn't exactly a stellar example of how to be tactful. She mostly revealed things with blunt efficiency then spent the rest of the conversation cleaning up her own mess.

The Poltergeist's Ship

'So I want to caveat this by saying that everything I tell you is *in theory*. It's mostly based on what I've read in books.' Fairly extensive books from Ben's library, but I wanted to give them a glimmer of hope that I was wrong.

Maggie and Josh didn't speak, nor did they take their eyes off me. The room was full of an awkward, pregnant silence that even Tilly wasn't trying to fill with her attention seeking. Judging from the way she was watching me instead of napping, even the dog knew I was about to reveal something big.

I took a deep breath. Then, I revealed the last thing they wanted to hear: 'In the same way that a boxer can fight through physical pain to keep fighting, but your average person couldn't because they're not a trained fighter they just know how to throw a punch or two, some forms of evil can fight against protective magic even if it hurts them.' I'd only ever heard about in theory. It was something I'd hoped to never come across. So much for that.

'Judging by the boxing comparison, you're saying that they have to be pretty special to fight through it? Like how some boxers can take a beating while others get knocked out? And others can stay upright even when they've been KOed?' said Josh. He and his dad had watched sports like wrestling and boxing together since he was young. I knew he'd get the analogy.

Slowly, I nodded.

Maggie gasped, covering her face in her hands. Josh pulled her into him and put his arms around her protectively. Tilly shifted so that she was sitting on Josh's lap.

'You're safe here. Both of you. And you can stay as long as you want. Did Abigail stay at her friend's again?'

'Yeah. I dropped some stuff off for her earlier.' Maggie gasped, jumping out of Josh's arms. 'You don't think he'd go to her, do you?'

'I don't see what he'd want from her,' I said. 'But you could ring just in case? Say you had a nightmare or forgot something?'

Maggie nodded and made the call while sitting on the sofa. She apologised profusely to Abigail's friend's parents, then gave them the line about a nightmare and just needing to check in. They said everything was fine. Maggie said if anything happened to call her, which probably sounded ominous to them, but made her feel better. She hung up looking relieved that her youngest was safe.

'I have a feeling Harry has been possessed for longer than we think,' I said.

Josh frowned. 'Why?'

'Do you remember after Goodfellow?' I didn't want to explicitly say *after Goodfellow possessed you and beat you to a pulp*, so I was hoping Josh got what I meant.

'Yes,' he said through gritted teeth. Ah, so he remembered my favourite Victorian doctor.

'The way Harry lashed out in the hospital? Did that not seem…out of character?'

'I thought it was just work stress,' said Maggie. 'But he's always believed in keeping up appearances in public, so that was strange of him. Do you really think it's been going on that long?'

The Poltergeist's Ship

At the time, Mum and I had found it suspicious but dismissed it as work stress, too. Neither of us could sense anything off about him. But if whatever was inside of him was strong enough to touch Mum's amulet, it was likely strong enough to disguise itself, too.

Thomas had disguised his abilities from people for centuries and he was a child. Sort of. The little we knew about whatever had a hold of Harry suggested that it had a plan and was willing to play the long game. This was bad. Really, really bad.

I kicked myself for not visiting their house more. But since Abigail's possession, Harry had been even more uncomfortable with us being there, so Maggie had mostly come to us when she'd hung out with Mum, or we'd met out and about.

And now we knew why Harry had hated our presences even more than usual. We'd dismissed it as him being an overprotective dad. It wouldn't have been the first time. We couldn't have been more wrong.

'How's your marriage been, lately?' I hated to ask Maggie such an invasive question, especially in front of her son, but based on what she'd been implying, I felt like it would provide us with some more insights.

Maggie shifted in her seat. 'I barely see him.'

Josh frowned. 'He's intentionally been staying away from us so that we don't notice the change in him, hasn't he?'

'Seems possible, yes.'

'Oh my god.' Maggie folded herself in half, resting her head in her lap. Josh rubbed her back, his eyes meeting mine. *I'm sorry* I mouthed. *It's not your fault* he mouthed back. Even though he said that, I couldn't shake the feeling that it was, somehow.

'Like I said: you can stay here as long as you like.'

'Thank you, but we can't do that,' said Maggie. 'Abigail is sensitive enough already. If we change her routine any more, she'll know something is up. I don't have it in me to lie to her. She doesn't deserve that. But I don't want to worry her, either.'

'All right. We'll put up as many protections around your house as possible tomorrow. And I'll stay there until Mum and Ben get back the day after. They'll know what to do.'

'Are you sure?' said Maggie.

'Yes. And we'll tell Abigail it's because I'm lonely on my own here. Which is kind of true, to be honest.' I glanced over at Tilly. 'Tilly can sense evil and ghosts, too. She may pick up on something we don't, so it's an extra level of protection for all of us.'

Tilly had never spent much time around Harry. He was one of the few people she didn't seem keen on. She'd tried to get his attention, but he'd always dismissed her and eventually she'd given up and gravitated to anyone else in the room.

'Oh Edie. I'm so sorry for burdening you with all this. You have enough going on with the bookshop, and your exams, and—' Maggie cut herself off as my eyes widened at her mention of my exams. Josh still didn't know about my results.

'Exams are over, though,' said Josh.

'Yes, but finishing college is a period of transition. It takes time to recover,' said Maggie, shooting me an apologetic look. Good cover.

'True,' agreed Josh. 'All right. I can paint the wards in the morning.'

'Unfortunately it has to be me.' Although there was a high chance they would've looked better with his artistic skills. 'I need to paint them as I say the spell. But you could always keep me company,' I added with a hopeful smile.

He smiled back. *He smiled back*! 'Happy to help however I can.'

Had he really just offered to help me? Finc, help his family. But that didn't stop the butterflies in my stomach. Would I always feel this way about him? Or would I be able to move on one day? Would I ever like someone as much as I liked Josh?

Maggie yawned.

Snap out of it, you idiot. Bigger problems.

'We should probably try to get some sleep. We have an airbed in the loft one of you can sleep on if someone can grab it.' I glanced at Josh, hoping he'd take the hint. He was taller, so it'd be easier for him to reach it.

'I can get it.' He looked at his mum, who was shaking with fear. 'Dad stormed out after the necklace thing. We don't know where he went. We didn't want to go after him.'

The subtext was there: they'd been too *scared* to follow him. Who was he now? And what was he capable of? I wasn't sure I wanted to know. But I also didn't think we'd seen the last of him.

33

Niamh

Because of Delia's death, we missed our final stop in Naples. No one was really in the mood for much anyway. There was a sad atmosphere around the ship among passengers and crew. The crew tried to keep things upbeat, but everyone seemed to be struggling.

Ben and I were walking past my favourite coffee shop on the boulevard when my barista friend from the other morning intercepted. 'Is it true? That you found her?'

Ben's grip on my hand tightened. 'Yeah.'

He shook his head. 'I'm sorry. Cruises are meant to be relaxing and all you seem to be doing is dealing with other people's problems.'

I shrugged. I was used to it.

'It's not fair,' he said. 'Captain Ricci said to send you to Guest Services if I see you, by the way. They have orders to take you to see her on the bridge. She wanted to thank you in person.'

'That's really not necessary,' said Ben. 'We don't do this sort of thing for thanks.'

I nudged him. He was implying too much to someone who didn't need to know anything. If the barista noticed my disapproval, he didn't say anything.

'Thanks,' I said. 'We'll go see her in a bit.'

He smiled then returned to coffee making.

'What did you say that for?' I said as we kept on walking.

'It's not like he would've understood what I meant anyway,' said Ben.

'I sure hope you're right.'

*

'Hello, dears.'

Ben jumped, almost hitting the roof of the corridor we were walking down. Thankfully no one else was around.

'Sorry!' said Delia. 'I didn't mean to startle you. Are you all right, dear?'

Ben nodded, adjusting himself so that it looked like he was talking to me, not a ghost. Just in case anyone rounded the corner and thought he'd lost it. 'How are you, Delia? All things considered.'

'I'm all right. It's an adjustment, but I'll be fine. I still wonder why I haven't been able to cross over yet, though.'

'No unfinished business you might've forgotten about before?' Ben asked.

'No,' she said. 'Most of the people I know are already dead.'

'Oh. We're sorry to hear that,' said Ben.

Delia shrugged. 'Such is life when you get to my age. I'd really quite like to join them.'

'Is it possible that your falling overboard was no accident?' I suggested.

'You think I was pushed?'

Or lured. Or tripped. Or something else conducive with murder.

Rather than answer, I simply nodded.

'That's what I was coming to speak to you about, actually,' said Delia. 'You see, I keep seeing this young man around the ship. A ghost man, I mean. I can't see him properly, but he seems to lurk right before something happens – something smashes, someone slips on something invisible, a door flies open, a mirror shatters. From what I can see of him, he's large and has a lot of tattoos.' She shuddered. 'If I never saw that man again, it would be too soon. He's very intimidating.'

Ben and I exchanged glances. Was she stereotyping? Or was this our poltergeist? If he was present at every incident on the ship, it was highly likely he was the latter.

'When you're near him, does the air feel different?' I asked.

Delia wrinkled her thin grey brows. 'Different how?'

'Like all the fun and enjoyment has been sucked out of it. Helpless. Hopeless. Empty,' said Ben.

'Now that you think about it, yes, yes it does. Why, does that mean something?'

It most definitely did.

*

Next stop: visit the captain. I didn't really want to, but she'd asked to see us and I was hoping she'd know something useful that could help us stop the murderous poltergeist. So we went to Guest Services and told them about the message. One of the crew members took us through a maze of corridors and up to the bridge.

We reached a door with a small porthole in the top. The door to the bridge. The staff member knocked, waited for a response, then opened it. 'Good evening, Captain. I believe you wanted to see these two guests?'

She looked up from the table she'd been examining the map on. 'Yes, I did. Thank you.'

A breeze blew through the room, causing the captain's dark brown hair to blow away from her shoulder and on to her back. Most people would've blamed the breeze from the door or one of the open windows that surrounded the room. But we knew better.

The captain stared at the crew member, waiting for her to leave. The crew member stared back. Eventually, she seemed to take the hint, excused herself, and left us alone.

'I'm so sorry about what you went through this morning,' said the captain.

'Could we talk in private, please, Captain?' I asked. We weren't there for her thanks, they were just a convenient way to get an audience with the most powerful person on the ship.

She pursed her lips, glancing around the bridge. Crew members floated around, talking and looking at maps and data and dashboards as we sailed through the open ocean. All seemed calm and well.

'Follow me.' We went into her office. She closed the door that separated it from the bridge and leaned against it. The door directly opposite it, which led into her quarters, was already closed.

Now that it was just the three of us, what did we say? This was always the hardest part because we never knew how someone would respond.

She watched us expectantly. This was not going to be an easy conversation. I was too tired to think of a way to do it tactfully. I nudged Ben, hoping he'd take the lead.

'Do you, um, enjoy being captain?' Ben asked.

That was what how he transitioned the conversation? I resisted the urge to face palm.

The captain smiled. 'Yes.' Her smile turned into a sad expression. 'Or at least, I used to.'

'Used to?' I repeated.

She sighed, pacing the small the room. There wasn't much space to pace, so she mostly walked in a U shape around her desk, which was littered with paperwork.

A large purple vase appeared in her path. She froze, looking around to see where it'd come from. 'Do you see that?'

'Yes,' said Ben.

As quickly as it had appeared, it vanished.

'What the—'

'Apporting,' Ben mumbled.

'Has that happened to you before?' I asked.

'Yes.' She sank into a blue swivel chair. 'Initially, I just felt kind of uneasy. I couldn't shake it but didn't think anything of it. Then it turned into dread and hopelessness. Am I really qualified to be captain? I've never doubted myself like that before. Then things started moving. My phone was in the bath; keys were in the toilet; that sort of thing. Now…objects appear and disappear without warning. I've never had it happen when anyone else is around before.'

'How long has this been happening?' asked Ben.

The captain rested her elbows on the desk. 'About six weeks.' Her hair flopped over her hands, covering her face. 'What's wrong with me?'

'You're being haunted,' I said, no time – or energy – for tiptoeing.

The captain looked up at me, her expression blank as she tried to process what I'd just told her. I could've minced my words, but this had already been going on for weeks. The poltergeist had probably already killed Delia. If we were going to stop them from killing anyone else, we didn't have a lot of time.

'Think about it,' said Ben. 'How else can objects appear and disappear at will? What else could make things move?'

The captain shook her head. 'It's just a prankster.'

'Well, yes, poltergeists can be,' I said.

'*Poltergeists?*' If her expression was anything to go by, at least she believed in ghosts. Even if she was now terrified. Oops.

'Do you believe in ghosts, captain?' Ben asked, seeking confirmation of my suspicions.

'I work in a very superstitious industry,' she said, not quite answering the question. 'I've always wondered, but never seen any evidence.'

'Until now,' I said.

Captain Ricci ran her hand over her face.

'Has anyone else seen anything?' I asked.

'No,' she said. 'Not that anyone has told me, anyway.'

I tapped my fingers against my leg. We'd had older ghosts disturbed and causing issues decades, or even centuries, later. But this didn't fit. I just couldn't work out what did.

She resumed pacing. 'How do you know so much about this?'

Ben smirked, a proud look covering his face. 'It's what we do.'

She studied him. He looked perfectly respectable in his jeans, shirt, glasses, and fluffy brown hair. His expression didn't change as she tried to process this guy telling her he was a ghost hunter.

'You're serious?'

'Yes.' There was no hesitation in his voice.

A ball bearing appeared just in front of Ben and me. It flew at the captain. She ducked. It smashed into the door where her head had been.

I really hoped the ball bearing hadn't been intended for her, but…

A faint figure hovered in the corner where it'd come from, laughing. It was the same laugh I'd heard when the mirror had smashed.

As if sensing we could see them, the poltergeist looked up. They were wearing a hat which disguised most of their face. I couldn't quite place their outfit, but it looked like some sort of uniform. Clearly unhappy that we could see them, they vanished.

Had Delia confused an army uniform for tattoos? Or were we dealing with more than one poltergeist? Oh god. Not two. Please not two.

Had Captain Ricci upset someone back home? Or did a previous captain dislike how she ran the Seraphina?

The ghost having vanished, I could sense the traces of evil it left behind. I shuddered. There was no denying whoever that ghost was, they were responsible for what was happening on the ship.

The office door flew open. 'Captain! Are you all right? What was that?' asked one of the crew members who'd been working on the bridge.

I glanced over at the ball bearing, which lay innocently on the floor.

'I was just annoyed at last night so lost my temper and threw something. I'm sorry if I concerned you.'

The employee frowned, closed the door, and left.

'What the hell just happened?' asked the captain.

Ben walked over to the ball bearing, which was now lying on the floor. He picked it up, throwing it in the air a couple of times. 'Could've done a lot of damage at that speed. You're lucky it didn't break a window.'

'Where did the ghost get it from?'

'Probably worth double checking things downstairs, just in case the ghost has taken anything else,' said Ben.

Her back stiffened. 'Could this get any worse?'

Oh, if only she knew. Poltergeists never slowed down until they were stopped. Things were *definitely* going to get worse.

34
Edie

No one slept that night. The four of us – five, if you counted Spectre – stayed in the living room, the TV mumbling to itself in the background, a small comfort and distraction from what'd happened the night before.

Josh was supposed to be working the lunchtime shift, but he refused to go in, no matter how many times Maggie and I told him to. He wasn't leaving us. I wasn't sure if it was because he wanted to protect his mum or he was as afraid to be alone as Maggie seemed to be.

'So, what now?' Josh asked as the three of us sat around the table, pushing cereal around our bowls but barely eating anything. Tilly stared up at us hopefully, despite having only just eaten her own food.

'We need to protect your house,' I said. 'I can ward it once I've picked up the paint. We can also put the gargoyle back. That will offer an extra layer of protection.' I glanced at Josh. 'And if something *is* wrong, his reaction will tell us everything we need to know.'

Maggie sighed, sipping her tea and shaking her head. Josh reached over and rubbed her arm. This was a lot to take in for anyone. Now, everyone in her family had been affected by the paranormal, even her sceptic husband.

'What if whatever is inside of him *does* something? And Harry gets the blame for it?' said Maggie.

'We'll cross that bridge when we come to it,' I said, not having an actual answer to her question. It was a possibility. Probability, even. We just didn't know what its plans were yet. 'Let's focus on protecting you for now.'

Then, I had to figure out how to exorcise him. To do that, we needed to know where he was.

And since he'd ran off, and we didn't know what was possessing him, we had no idea where he'd go. So all we could do was keep him far away from the people who couldn't protect themselves.

*

After breakfast, I packed a bag for me and one for Tilly. Spectre would have to spend the night on his own, but it wasn't like he'd starve. He'd be fine on his own for a night. If I hadn't needed my powers, I would've tethered him to me.

Abigail would be at her friend's house for a few more hours, then Maggie was talking her out, so that at least bought us some time. We could ward the house without her asking questions.

By the time she got home that evening, I'd have all the wards painted, dried, and covered up. At least then we could avoid her questions and protect her.

But how long could we really hide from her that her dad was possessed? Especially when she'd been possessed herself less than a year ago?

*

I left Fadil to build the replacement bookcase and went to see Tobias. As well as picking up the paint, I wanted to ask him about what'd happened last night.

He'd been right about Goodfellow, and had no reason to steer us wrong here either. Plus, he knew more about the paranormal than anyone else since he'd lived for so long. It was quicker to check with him than anyone else.

I entered his cottage, and said hello to Dave while I waited for Tobias to return from the back room.

'One large tub of warding paint, ready for use.' He placed the tub on the table by the window.

'Thanks,' I said, picking it up to study it. It had an iridescent glow to it. The one Mum and Ben made was matte black. 'What did you do differently?'

He opened the same book from the other day and showed it to me. 'Added a couple of extra ingredients for protection – iron and crushed quartz. I thought, since you don't know what you're up against, we should cover as many possibilities as we can.'

'Thanks,' I said.

'Have you made any more progress on what's possessing him?'

I hesitated, not sure if I should tell him or not. Fadil wasn't there to lecture me or give me the side eye this time. He'd tell me not to say anything. He *always* told me not to say anything to Tobias. But he was our best bet for more information.

'Whatever it was, it could touch an amber protection amulet.'

Tobias sucked in air through his teeth. They were yellow and translucent.

'What? What does that mean? I mean, I know it's bad, but how bad?'

Tobias leaned against the wall by the fireplace. His expression suggested he was either trying to work out what to tell me or how to tell me. Neither was a good sign. 'Have you dealt with demons before?'

I shuddered. 'Once. Yes. You don't think…'

I'd considered a demon, but I'd assumed it wasn't because of how well it had disguised its life essence. How little I really knew.

Tobias pursed his lips. 'I don't know of anything else that could be evil enough to touch a protection amulet. Vampires are strong, but they mostly do what they do to survive. It's not usually with malicious intent. Poltergeists have been tortured either when they were alive or since they died. Demons don't have a reason to be evil. They just are. And that gives them a power far greater.'

I gulped, my voice shaking. 'But we stopped a demon before. We can do it again.' I wasn't sure that my tone conveyed the same level of confidence as my words.

'It's perfectly possibly to stop demons. I'm not saying it isn't. Just be careful. Especially if it's trying to infiltrate your inner circle.'

'Why?'

'Because either that means someone who's willing to cast a powerful summoning spell is out to get you, or worse: an untethered demon is out to get you. Which means they'll stop at nothing until they do.'

*

'You get the paint?' Fadil asked as I walked into the bookshop. All the furniture built, he was stacking the children's book shelves in the corner.

'Yeah.' I thrust the tub on to the counter. It was huge.

'Wow. I didn't expect him to make that much.'

'Me neither. But I'm glad he did.'

Fadil stopped stacking the shelves. 'Why?'

'He thinks it's a demon.'

Fadil didn't move for a moment. It was like he'd turned into a statue. 'And what makes him think that?'

'Because he could touch the amulet but it was painful.'

Fadil pursed his lips. He walked past me, over to the chair by the counter. Another counter sat next to it, the now-fixed coffee machine's permanent home.

He picked up his mummy mug, spun it around a few times, then launched it across the room. It hit the wall, smashing to pieces. 'Haven't we been through enough? Will it ever end? I just…I can't…I…' He started crying, burying his face into his hands.

I put my arms around him, letting him cry into me. 'You're right. It's not fair.'

'Why us? Why is it always us?'

'It sucks,' I said. 'Especially when you consider that the good is tied to the bad. Like Mum wouldn't have Ben without ghosts, and we wouldn't have you, either.'

Fadil snivelled. 'That's what really sucks. Everything in our lives is tainted. It can't just be good, can it?'

'Tilly's good,' I said.

'Tilly can sense demons.' He lifted his head from my shoulder. 'Tilly can *sense* demons. Do you think she could help us work out if he really is possessed?'

'Probably. She'll be with me at Maggie's place tonight anyway, so if something does happen, at least her reaction will give us more information.'

'Are you sure it's wise to stay there? Wouldn't you be better off at Mrs Brightman's? It's not like anyone is using it.'

'We don't want to worry Abigail. She already thinks it's odd she's spent two nights at a friend's house. She's never done that before,' I said.

Fadil frowned.

'And what are the odds he attacks the same place twice? It'd be dumb to. He'd know they'd likely come to me for an extra layer of protection. It wouldn't be worth the risk,' I said.

'I suppose,' said Fadil, his jaw tense. 'Maybe I should stay over too. I can't do much, but the more of us there are, the better our chances are.'

'Are you sure? I don't want to do anything that'll make your pain worse.'

He scoffed. 'It can't *get* much worse. At least this way I'm useful. Maybe one of Abigail's coffee parties will distract me.'

35

Edie

After lunch, we warded the bookshop with the new paint, figuring it was stronger so might give us some extra protection, then decided to do some research into demons at the bookshop. Many of the books Ben had in stock weren't ones we'd come across before, which meant they could contain things we didn't already know.

To protect Fadil and I, or at least, reassure us a little more, we put Ben's pirate gnome outside the bookshop. It gave it a quaint character that got passersby talking and noticing the new addition, despite the only sign it was going to be a bookshop opening soon being a piece of A4 stuck to the front door, since the actual door sign wasn't ready yet.

I still had to paint the wards around Maggie's house, but since Maggie and Josh were at work, I couldn't get in. In hindsight, I should've borrowed a key so that they could've gone home to a protected house. Wasn't hindsight great?

'Where do you want to start researching?' Fadil asked, swinging his legs from the stool by the counter.

'Did someone say research?' Maisie poked her head through the door. 'Sorry for being nosy. I *love* research.'

The Poltergeist's Ship

'You do?' I said, sensing a potential way to speed this process up. I drummed my fingers against the counter.

Maisie leaned against the frame of the newly fitted window and folded her arms. 'Yeah.' She'd walked inside without a problem. That alongside the pirate gargoyle's approval was enough to reassure Fadil and I that she was friend, not foe.

I looked over at Fadil. He shrugged. If we wanted to include her, I had the perfect excuse. It was one that had worked for Mum too many times to count.

Maisie heaved a black tote bag onto the counter. It was full and looked heavy, but she moved like it weighed nothing.

'What's that?' I asked, gesturing to the bag.

'Textbooks. And cake. I wasn't sure what revision stuff you had, so I thought I'd bring all my stuff. I'm a bit of a hoarder. It drives Dad mad. But I figured some of my notes in the margins might help.'

'You write in the margins of books?'

My horror must've been all over my face, because she replied: 'You don't?'

'No! I could never deface a book like that.'

Maisie gave a half-laugh. 'You won't hurt their feelings by writing in them.'

'It's not that, I just like to keep them looking smart.'

She took out a battered copy of *The Beach*. The spine was ridged and white in places where the ink had worn off. The edges were dog-eared and it didn't sit flat. I almost had to grip the counter tighter to steady myself. She opened the book and pointed to a page that was covered in scribbles. 'I know, it looks awful. But all these scribbles helped me better understand the book;

the characters; what the author was trying to say.' She must've sensed my tension, because she added: 'What do you normally write notes on?'

'My laptop.'

'That's fair. That's useful. But it's distant from the text. It's not tangible. Writing by hand can help us process things better. You could use sticky notes instead if it makes you less likely to break out into hives.'

Fadil snorted.

I glared at him. 'I am *not* breaking out into hives.' At least not about defacing books. Even if I hated the idea. I wondered what Ben's stance on it was, with all the books he collected? He had so many I found it hard to believe some of them didn't have scribbles in them. 'I've just got other things on my mind.'

'Can I help?' she offered.

'What about work?' Fadil interjected.

She smirked. 'Beauty of being my own boss. Sort of. My dad won't care. I've done what I need to for the day, and I'm only down the road if he needs me anyway.' I'd never noticed their shop, but then I'd never needed to buy a window before. It turned out that Day and Night Windows had a showroom about a ten-minute walk from town. I'd gone past it dozens of times without even registering it.

Was that my future, too? Co-owning a business with my mum? Out of all the things that looked destined for my adulthood, that looked like one of the better options.

'I'm writing this book,' I explained, 'and I need to do some research.'

'Sounds exciting.'

'If you two want to start here, I can head back to Ben's and see if we missed anything the first time around,' said Fadil.

'As in Ben who owns Ben's Books Ben?' asked Maisie.

'He has a library full of really old books,' Fadil explained for her benefit. He climbed off the stool and lifted the box of cakes from the tote bag. Settling on a Bakewell tart, he picked it out and bit into it, a look of satisfaction spreading across his face.

'Sounds cool. I love an old book.' She glanced at me. 'I don't write in those.' She winked. 'So can I help?'

'I think so. Only one way to find out.' I picked out a brownie.

Maisie chose a chocolate chip cookie. 'All right then. Let's get researching.'

*

'When I agreed to help, I didn't expect to be researching ghosts, demons, and vampires,' said Maisie. She sat by the window, the summer sun bright and hot through the new window, but leaving her unfazed in her cap and trench coat. She flicked through a particularly large and expensive occult textbook.

My grip tightened on the small hardback I'd been flicking through. Was this too much too soon? 'Are you, um, OK with it?' I asked, not sure how to respond. Or what her reaction would be. My back was cramping from hunching over books for so long, but I hadn't found anything useful yet and I needed *something* to confirm or disprove our suspicions.

'Are you kidding? It's super cool!' She seemed fascinated. Phew. 'Like this: *"Demons were once sinful humans. Instead of crossing over when deceased, they enter the Demonic Realm, where they lose their memories and humanity to become demons. This process can take weeks, years, or even centuries depending on the person. The power a demon possesses depends on their strengths and weaknesses when they were human. For example, someone unable to feel emotions may become telepathic or empathic, allowing them to have a deeper understanding of those they wish to torment, but also providing them with further torment through thoughts and emotions they'll never be able to comprehend."*'

'Wow. That's rough.'

Maisie nodded, flicking to the next page. 'There's more.'

More? What else could there be?

'*"Demons can only cross to the Human Realm if summoned or if they escape during a spell to open the portal between worlds. If they're summoned, they're at the behest of their summoner. If they escape, they can do as they wish. All demons must possess a human to survive in this realm, or they suffocate. How long they can survive without a host depends on the strength of the demon."*'

I shuddered. That explained, in part, why Abigail and Harry had been possessed. The demon couldn't stick around without them.

'Does it say anything about getting rid of them?' I asked.

She ran her gloved index finger over the page. 'Exorcisms send them back to the Demonic Realm. But the bit about them perishing without a body…'

'What do you think it means?' I asked.

'It doesn't elaborate, but it reads to me like they'd just cease to exist.' She shuddered. 'Do you think that's it? I can't even imagine. Can you?'

I shook my head as I stood up and stretched my legs. It had been a long day, but it wasn't over yet. 'Thanks for your help. I'd better get going. I need to meet Fadil.' He'd been researching from Ben's and it was time to compare our findings.

Maisie closed the book and returned it to the shelf. 'All right. Give me a shout if you want to do more research. And don't think you're off the hook about revision just because I let you off today,' she said with a wry grin.

I mock groaned.

*

'Did your research say anything about them being able to disguise life essences?' asked Fadil once I'd filled him in.

'No. Did you find anything?'

'No. It might be time to consult the Book of the Dead. If anywhere has something on life essences, it's that,' he said.

I grumbled. He was right, of course. But I really hated trying to translate it. It took forever. But unfortunately, so much of its knowledge didn't exist anywhere else. So I'd have to suck it up.

When I'd practised on Fadil and warded Maggie's house.

'Shall we practise?' I asked Fadil, trying to check something off my to-do list.

'Are you sure you're up to it?' he asked. 'That you're fully recovered from last time?'

'I'll be fine,' I said, not sure if I'd fully recovered or if I just really wanted to be. How long had it taken me last time, when Dominic had made me use my powers? It didn't matter. How I felt wasn't important. I needed to learn how to control my powers. And help Fadil.

I looked down at where he was lying on the sofa. 'And anyway, you need this.'

He grunted, neither agreeing nor denying that he did need my help.

'Ready?' I said.

Fadil nodded.

I zoned in on his life essence. It was weak; fragmented. It had the yellow and brown hues to it that I was used to. I could feel how old he was. I gasped as I absorbed some of his life essence, crouching down as my own limbs became weak. Deep breath in. Long breath out. Focus on Fadil.

I took a little more, but less than I had from Gwendoline. I didn't want him to pass out. Or drain myself.

After checking he was OK – he was lying on his back with his eyes closed, like nothing had happened – I began to return his life essence to him.

Even though I loved Fadil, I was glad to be rid of his life essence. I felt drained just from its presence. No wonder he was exhausted all the time. I gave him a little of mine, too, knowing it would be easier for me to recharge than him, especially if that's what his baseline felt like.

'How do you feel?' I asked, sitting cross-legged on to the floor.

He sat up and stretched his limbs. 'I feel great! Wow!' He looked down at me. 'Are you all right?'

I was pretty terrible, actually. But I didn't want him to know it was because of his life essence. I did, however, need to find a way to convince him to get more tests done because whatever was wrong with him wasn't normal and I doubted it was sustainable.

'Just drained, that's all. I'll be fine.'

36

Niamh

Since we were cruising, we had plenty of time to investigate. Ben saw this as the perfect opportunity to set up the stupid spirit box in our room. We were desperate, so I'd acquiesced despite my hatred for them. This ghost did seem to have a penchant for technology.

The box sat on the side in our cabin, mocking me. Stupid thing. I fidgeted restlessly in the chair as Ben fiddled with it. It hissed to life, letting out a horrible, scratchy sound. I cringed.

Satisfied with his setup, Ben plugged in some headphones. He held them out to me. 'So if you just put these on—'

'Nope.' I crossed my arms, slightly turning away from Ben. There was absolutely no way I was putting on noise-cancelling headphones and a blindfold so that a poltergeist could communicate with me more easily. What I'd seen and heard on a TV screen had been bad enough. I'd hoped he'd use it himself; that was the only reason I'd agreed to it.

The poltergeist had made it hard enough for me to get any peace. I wasn't going to bring them to me.

'But—'

'Nope. Not happening.'

Ben pushed his glasses up his nose. 'We need to figure out what they want.'

'Right. But I can already hear them. So why can't you wear it?'

'It's you they want to talk to, not me. And so far, we haven't been able to get a clear message. The spirit box and headphones will help them channel their energy so we might finally figure out what they want. It also gives us a recording of what they say to play back to the captain.'

An even better idea came to me. 'Or we could get her to put the headphones on.'

*

While I'd been hearing and seeing the ghost – and their aftermath – for the duration of our cruise, I didn't think it was actually about me. I was just intercepting it. The more I thought about it, the more it made sense. Poor Captain Ricci had been seeing objects for weeks and had a ball bearing thrown at her head this morning. She was a far more likely target.

On our way to Guest Services to convince them to let us see her, we ran into Niall.

'Any news on the hot water?' I asked.

He stuffed his hands into his pockets and stared at his black shoes. It was the most subdued I'd seen him. 'They've checked and checked everything, but nothing is coming up. You're not the only passengers having this issue, so even if we put you into a different room there's a possibility it could still happen. How often is it happening?'

'About 50/50,' said Ben.

The Russian Roulette of bathing.

Niall frowned. 'Is there any pattern to it?'

When the poltergeist wanted to torment us?

Ben glanced at me for conformation. I shook my head. 'Not that we've noticed, no.'

Niall crossed his arms. 'I'll keep digging. Let me know if it gets any better or worse.'

'We will, thanks,' I said.

'Before you go,' said Ben, 'Could you take us to see Captain Ricci, please?'

Niall looked taken aback.

He held out a letter the captain had given us. It said to take us to her whenever we asked, no questions asked. It was handwritten on letter-headed paper, with the date and her signature on it.

Niall skimmed the note, shrugged, and took us there. 'Here you go. No questions asked.' He knocked on the door for us then walked off.

Captain Ricci opened the door, looking tired and restless. She forced a polite smile, but it didn't meet her eyes.

'How are you feeling?' I asked as we walked into her quarters. As they were right next to the bridge, and she was always on duty, we'd have to be careful doing an experiment. Given the poltergeist on the ship, though, an interruption from a confused crew member seemed like the least of our problems.

The captain's quarters were bigger than I'd expected. It had two bathrooms, an open-plan living area complete with kitchen, and a dining area. At the far end of the room were floor-to-ceiling windows looking out over the ocean. The view was breathtaking. And at least nobody could see through those windows to notice what we were doing.

She frowned. 'I haven't slept. How can I? My quarters were always my safe place when at sea, but knowing what I know now, I jump at every noise. Every shadow. The crew keep telling me to go back to bed. But how can I tell them I can't sleep because of a ghost and that I'm better off working? They didn't find anything wrong downstairs, so that's something.'

I couldn't even imagine how confused and conflicted she was. There was nothing she could say to her colleagues without looking like she was losing it. And she was probably still processing it herself, so how could she explain it to anyone else?

'We'll get some answers,' said Ben.

'About that…' I explained my plan. She wasn't entirely comfortable with it, but she seemed to want to find answers and a solution, so she reluctantly agreed.

Ben started to unpack the spirit box and its accessories on the coffee table.

'Thank you, Captain.'

'Please, call me Sofia,' she said. 'We're past the point of formal names.'

I gave her a wan smile.

'We'll figure this out,' Ben reassured her.

Sofia took off her navy blue jacket and hung it on a coat hanger by the door, revealing a crisp white shirt. 'Where do you want to do this?'

Ben gestured to the sofa.

She checked her office door was locked so that nobody from the bridge could interrupt, then sat down.

Ben tilted his head, as if listening. There wasn't much to hear beyond the gentle sound of the waves lapping against the ship, mumblings of conversations from the bridge, and the occasional tap, scrape, or bang from one of the upper floors, probably from someone moving something.

'It won't be perfect audio, but I don't think that's going to be possible given our surroundings. Hopefully this will be enough.' Ben plugged the headphones into the spirit box. 'The idea of this is to drown out any possible distractions. So you won't be able to hear what we say. We'll ask questions, then you'll repeat back what – if anything – you hear through the headphones. One of us will tap you on the shoulder when the session is over. Does that make sense?'

'Yes, I think so,' said Sofia. She didn't seem scared, more determined. I liked working with people like her.

'If, at any point, you feel uncomfortable or want to stop, just take the headphones and blindfold off.'

Sofia nodded. 'All right. Let's do it.'

Ben handed Sofia the red silk eye mask I'd been using to block out the lights to try to sleep. She removed her glasses then put it on. After placing her glasses on the table, Ben helped her into the headphones and turned on the spirit box.

Even with Sofia wearing the headphones, I could still hear static. And mumbling voices. I tried to drown them out so that I could focus on note taking.

'Can you hear that?' I asked Ben.

'Hear what?' he replied, walking over to me and away from Sofia so he didn't interfere with the investigation.

'I can hear voices through the static already.' Frustratingly.

That rattled Ben. 'We'd better start the questions.'

'You don't hear anything?'

'No.'

Fiddlesticks.

Ben referred to his phone, where he'd written down the questions we'd agreed to ask. 'Who are you?'

'There are a lot of voices. It's hard for me to separate them all. It feels like they're all fighting it out,' said Sofia.

Ben turned to me, a concerned look on his face: 'Do you sense anyone?'

I shook my head. 'Do you?'

'No.' Ben cleaned his glasses on his shirt, then put them back on.

'Could it be the electricity? Like they're able to tap into the waves and just send stuff through the air or something? Or interference from all the electrical equipment?' I suggested.

'At this point, anything is possible.' He addressed the ghosts: 'Can you speak one at a time, please?'

'It's slowed down a little,' said Sofia.

I concurred. It was still distracting and annoying, but less like everyone was talking over each other. So hopefully it'd help us get closer to answers.

'Can you tell me who you are, please?'

There was a pause. I imagined the ghosts organising themselves into a line so that the right person could speak.

'*Sorella*,' said Sofia, rolling her R.

How many of the Italian guests on the ship had a dead sister? Did Sofia?

I scribbled *sister* in the notebook. With over seven thousand people onboard, that was a lot of potential siblings. We needed to narrow it down further.

'Whose sister are you? Are you the sister of someone on the ship?'

'Sofia,' said Sofia. Her mouth fell open as she realised what she'd repeated. Did she have a sister?

'What's your name?' said Ben, the only one in the room not losing his composure.

'Giorgia.' Sofia removed the headphones and eye mask, then stared at Ben and me. 'Is this some kind of joke?'

'What do you mean?' I said.

'My sister is called Giorgia. We haven't spoken in years.'

'Is it possible that she—'

Before Ben could finish his question, Sofia cut him off. 'No. No. I'd have heard something. You need to go.' She ushered us out of her quarters, clearly freaked out by what had just happened. And to be fair, so was I. It was the first time I'd had anything useful come out of a spirit box. And it had some serious repercussions for the captain. And possibly the ship, too.

*

The Poltergeist's Ship

A few hours later, Ben and I were eating dinner in the steak restaurant when one of the crew members approached us. 'The captain would like to see you in her quarters when you've finished your food.'

'Thank you,' I said.

Having done her job, the staff member nodded, then walked off.

I sliced into my medium steak. It was like slicing through butter. Perfection. 'Do you think it's about earlier?'

'What else could it be about? I guess she's had time to process and now she wants to talk about what we learned. Which is good, because the longer this goes on for, the worse it will get.' Ben cut into his medium rare steak.

We might've been closer to figuring out who the ghost was, but we didn't have anything with us to actually get rid of said ghost. We were helpless.

Was Giorgia the poltergeist, or had she just intercepted the spirit box? If she was the poltergeist, who was the ghost that Delia saw right before something happened? Had she confused what she'd seen? Or was something else going on?

Ever since my nuclear exorcism spell had failed against Goodfellow, I didn't trust it anymore. Especially since it had barely worked on the poltergeist I'd used it on before him. Turned out the one who'd killed Javi hadn't been as powerful as we'd thought.

Ah, the naivety of youth. Sometimes I wished we were still that naive.

Either way, it was too much of a risk to try that exorcism on the ship. Not only could we not guarantee it'd work, but if there were other, friendly ghosts on the ship, it risked taking them out, too. Which didn't seem fair. There were too many unpredictable variables.

I forced myself to finish dinner, then we found Sofia in her quarters. She'd changed out of her uniform and was now wearing grey trackies. Her hair was scruffy and her glasses wonky. Instead of sitting down, she paced up and down the living area.

'My sister was in the army,' said Sofia. 'After you left, I called them. They informed me that she was killed recently and they've been unable to get the message to me.' She scoffed, gesticulating with her hands. 'Seems to me like they didn't try very hard. It's not like modern ships don't have a signal.' She waved her arms in the air as if to gesture to the ship. Given how I struggled to get a signal, that was debatable. But she was at sea *a lot*. And she had said the two of them were estranged, so maybe the contact details her sister had had for her were out of date?

'Giorgia was my only living relative. We last spoke two years ago, I think. She didn't like me.'

'I'm sorry to hear that,' said Ben. 'But I have to ask why?'

Sofia shrugged, her palms out. 'Sibling rivalry, I guess? Do you have siblings?'

'I did,' said Ben. I rubbed his arm. She may have been happy on the Other Side, but it didn't make it any easier for him to talk about her.

'I'm sorry,' she said, noting Ben's use of the past tense. 'Did you get along?'

'Sort of,' said Ben.

Sofia nodded. 'It's a complicated relationship, isn't it?'

'Yeah,' agreed Ben.

'Giorgia was always a prankster. Do you think that's what this is about?' There was a note of hope in Sofia's voice. If it was just her sister playing pranks it was harmless, right?

'It's possible,' said Ben, clearly trying to give her something to cling to. 'We don't know if she just happened to intercept our call, or if she's the poltergeist. But there's definitely a poltergeist who's out to get you.'

'Making it a pretty big coincidence if it's not her,' said Sofia, looking dejected.

'Sadly, yes,' said Ben. 'Which means we need to figure out what she wants and resolve things before they escalate further.'

And figure out who the other ghost that Delia kept seeing was before something happened. Were they working together? Did we have two poltergeists on one ship? Or did she confuse things from a fuzzy distance?

Sofia gulped. 'Could things get any worse?'

Did I really have to answer that?

37

Edie

'Is there anything else I can do?' Josh offered. 'Besides, y'know, moving furniture?'

I crouched down behind the TV in his lounge to paint the next symbol. We'd already done the first one, by the front door. That was the easiest. I still had to do behind the TV, in the dining area, and in a kitchen cupboard. It had to be all four corners of the house or they wouldn't be protected. I was going to do upstairs as well. I wasn't sure if that made a difference or not, but Mum had always done the same, so I figured it wouldn't hurt.

Their snorkelling gargoyle was back by the front door too, in a more prominent place than before. If that threw Harry backwards, that would tell us all we needed to know.

Then we could panic.

I was still exhausted from helping Fadil, but I couldn't sleep yet. How much longer I could keep running on caffeine and adrenaline I didn't know, but I'd drag it out as long as I could.

'Unfortunately not,' I said. In theory, Josh could've helped cast the spell, but since he'd never cast a spell before, I doubted it would work. So it was easier, safer, and quicker for me to do it myself, following the same technique that Ben and I had done for the bookshop and Mrs Brightman's, just using the new (hopefully stronger) paint.

I drew the intricate symbol from the photo on my phone, replicating it as closely as possible. Even though the symbols were in the Book of Shadows, the book never left the house because it was so frail. If we needed something from it away from home we relied on photos.

Once Abigail had gotten back from her friend's house, Maggie had taken her out for the afternoon so that I could ward their house without being bombarded with questions I didn't know how to answer.

'It's actually pretty cool, when you look at it,' said Josh. 'It's a shame we can't put it somewhere more prominent. Make it into a feature.' It had never occurred to me that the artist in him would appreciate the symbols I was painting.

'I mean, we can paint them elsewhere. They just wouldn't offer any protection,' I said.

'At least we know they're here. And they can protect us.' He sat cross-legged on the floor behind me. 'They will protect us, won't they?'

'It was only when your dad removed the wards that...' I trailed off, shifting in my crouched position. I didn't really want to repeat what'd happened to Abigail. But we both knew it was only after Harry had found the wards while redecorating that things had started to go wrong.

Before that, ever since Maggie had found out about ghosts, she'd insisted on getting Mum to ward wherever she lived. She'd even found ways to hide the wards from her parents when she and my parents were teenagers.

'Thanks for doing this, by the way,' said Josh.

I finished painting and put the lid on the tub, and the brush in the tray. It didn't smell like normal paint. It smelled of all the herbs that were inside of it to protect us. Eucalyptus. Rosemary. So many other things I couldn't pinpoint.

I nodded, unsure what to say to him. We'd spoken more in the last few days than we had all year. It didn't feel like we were back to normal, but we were civil, and that was as much as I could ask for.

'What's next after this?' he asked, genuinely seeming interested.

'I'm going to make a potion. Just in case.' I didn't want to tell him what it was for, but of course that's what he wanted to know.

'What kind of potion?'

I stood up, holding on to my painting equipment as a kind of barrier from what I figured would be his negative reaction. 'An exorcism potion.'

Josh frowned. I'd expected him to get defensive, not for him to look defeated. I'd never seen him look that way before. It was unnerving and saddening. 'Do you really think my dad's possessed by a demon? It couldn't be something else?'

I'd reluctantly told him what Tobias suspected when he'd met me after work. Given that he struggled to trust me as it was, honesty felt like the best policy.

I stared at his hands, which he was wringing. I couldn't bring myself to look at his face. 'There's a strong possibility.'

'Meaning yes but you don't want to outright say it.' His lips quirked into a smile.

I shook my head, trying not to smile back. But he was right. Despite everything we'd been through, he still knew me well. 'I think so, yeah. But something is off. It doesn't feel like what I'm used to.'

'What do you mean?'

'I couldn't sense anything when I saw him. Other than what's always been there.' I handed the paint and tray to Josh and he placed them on the floor behind him.

Josh had another suggestion: 'Could when or how you saw him have affected if you sensed anything?'

Was that possible? I hadn't thought of that. 'We were in town and your dad was going on his lunch. It's not impossible but it's unlikely. Everything seemed fine on the surface, but the way he spoke, the way he behaved, it all just seemed off. I can't put my finger on it.'

Josh nodded, helping me over the tangle of wires behind the TV. My hand tingled at the touch of his skin; his proximity when I stumbled and fell into him. 'Sorry,' I mumbled, scurrying to the other side of the room as Josh pushed the TV back into place and started plugging wires back in.

No, feelings for Josh were unacceptable. The skin tingling needed to go away. Stat.

If Josh was fazed by what'd happened, he didn't show it. He continued the conversation we'd been having a moment earlier. 'Yeah, I get that. I've felt the same.' He leaned against the wall. 'At first, I just thought he was stressed. Everyone changes when they're stressed, don't they? I convinced myself that was why he yelled at me at the hospital, in front of everyone. Why else would a guy so obsessed with keeping up appearances cause a scene in public? But then…it was the little things. Forgetting Abigail's birthday and their birthday traditions. Not complimenting Mum's cooking. Barely even touching her. Spending even more hours at work. It was like his whole personality changed. Then the way he behaved last night…'

I still hadn't shaken Maggie and Josh's terrified expressions when they'd ran into my house. They'd looked so scared. Like they'd had nowhere else to go.

Which, to be fair, they hadn't.

'Right, kitchen corner next,' I said.

'Do we really have to paint inside the cupboard? Is there not a way to make it easier for you? And mean we don't have to upset Mum's carefully crafted system?'

'Not if you want it hidden from view.'

'We'd better get on with it, then.'

*

'Edie!' said Abigail, skipping over to where Tilly and I were sitting on the sofa reading one of Ben's books on the history of magic on the off-chance it could tell me something new or useful. So far, so unhelpful.

The Poltergeist's Ship

Josh and I had finished warding the house an hour ago, the paint was dry, and all the furniture was back in place. Abigail would never know. And hopefully neither would Harry.

There'd also been no more awkward interactions between Josh and me. Thankfully.

'Hey you,' I said as she plonked herself on to my lap. 'Guess who's staying over tonight?'

Abigail's face lit up. 'You and Tilly? Please say it's you and Tilly?'

'Might be.'

She put her arms around me and squeezed. 'Can we do a coffee party? *Pleeeeeease.*'

I ruffled her hair. 'Of course. Fadil's joining us too.'

'Why are you all staying over, though? Having the house to yourself sounds amazing,' she said.

This was the question I'd been dreading but needed to answer. I wouldn't quite be lying to her, just not telling her the whole story.

'Promise you won't tell anyone?'

'Uh-huh.' She nodded.

I beckoned her closer, so that I could whisper. 'I've been scared on my own.'

Not a lie – I had been. It was easing the longer I spent on my own, but I hated the nights with just me, a dog, and a ghost cat. Nobody to talk to, nothing to do but worry about my friends and family.

Abigail put her arms around my neck and hugged me. 'Don't worry, we'll protect you!'

If only they could protect themselves.

*

'Are you sure this potion will work on him?' Maggie asked as she, Josh, Fadil, and I sat around her dining table. Abigail was asleep upstairs. We'd considered letting her stay another night at her friend's house since it was the summer holidays, but that would've looked suspicious and we didn't want to give away that anything was wrong.

Based on how tired she was when they got back from the soft play area, I was pretty sure she hadn't slept much. Which worked in our favour, because it meant she could sleep while we planned.

'It's the same potion we used when we exorcised Abigail and Melanie last year,' I said. It was also the only effective way I knew of to exorcise someone.

Mum said that spells worked better when a ghost wasn't possessing someone. So we had to kick them out by making the body inhospitable. Then the spell kicked them back to wherever they came from.

In theory, anyway.

38

Niamh

We had no idea how bad Sofia's sister could get. Just how off the charts a poltergeist went depended on too many factors.

Sofia hadn't spoken to her sister in two years, leaving a lot of unknowns. So we couldn't afford to take any risks. We had to summon Giorgia to see what she wanted and find out what she was capable of. And find a solution that ideally didn't involve exorcising her.

'Are you ready, Sofia?' Ben asked as we stood in her lounge area, all the furniture moved out of the way. I wasn't sure if us summoning a poltergeist when we weren't on solid land was a good idea, but Sofia insisted no ghost could break the glass at the front of her quarters and throw us out to sea.

I daren't tell her what Goodfellow had been capable of.

We'd drawn a salt circle as best we could, but I didn't really trust it. While the boat didn't rock loads, it didn't take much to upset a salt circle. It'd be hard for Sofia to explain it to the cleaner who vacuumed it up after we were done, but that was her problem.

Sofia wrung her age-spotted hands together. They were soaked with sweat. So were mine. 'Can we just get this over with, *per favore*?'

'Of course.' Ben held my hand. We started to chant: 'We call upon the spirits, to commune with us tonight, grant us your presence, come join us in the light.'

A figure flickered in and out of sight for a moment. A tall, chubby, tattooed man appeared before us. I was pretty sure it was his face I'd seen on the TV screens whenever I got too close to them. He matched Delia's description of the ghost who was present every time she'd seen something happen on the ship, too.

He definitely didn't match Sofia's description of her sister. Giorgia had apparently been a petite, muscular brunette.

I clenched my hands into fists. 'Who are you?'

'Sorry fer crashin'. Name's Arne.' He spoke with a thick Cockney accent. There was something comforting about his voice. I liked it. But why had he been tormenting me for our entire holiday? 'That woman you want to summon? She's nuts.'

'What's happening?' asked Sofia.

'Someone else has intercepted,' said Ben. 'It happens sometimes.'

'Who?'

'A man named Arne,' I told her. She frowned, clearly not knowing anyone by that name. I turned back to Arne: 'Who are you, exactly?'

'I've been tryna warn you about the crazy woman,' he said, looking directly at me.

'What do you mean?' I asked.

'The static.'

The Poltergeist's Ship

'That was *you*? I thought someone was trying to torture me!'

Arne looked away, shuffling his feet against the...air. Since he couldn't touch the floor. It was weird the habits ghosts maintained from when they had physical bodies, sometimes. They didn't always make sense. 'I was an electrician, see. Didn't know how else to communicate. If I'd known you could see ghosts I just would've said something. But I noticed you seemed to respond when I tapped into the TV. So I kept tryna get your attention. I couldn't get a clear enough signal, though, and other ghosts kept tryna intercept to talk to their loved ones. Made things fuzzy.'

'We understand,' said Ben. He glanced at me for confirmation. I mostly agreed, although I was still annoyed. But I also didn't want to hurt Arne's feelings as he seemed sweet.

'Sorry if it annoyed you.'

Understatement.

'We sort of got it,' I lied. He looked like he genuinely felt guilty. His reasons had been good, even if his execution had given me a headache that'd lasted most of our holiday.

Arne chuckled. 'No you didn't. You almost shit a brick.'

'Once or twice,' I agreed.

'I'm new to this ghost stuff, so I didn't know what else to do.' He gave a nonchalant shrug. 'I'm only 'ere 'cause me Gran is and she's got no one else, so I wanted to keep an eye on her. Didn't expect to be spending it running around, protecting thousands of people from a madwoman, did I?'

Much as I resented the term 'madwoman' for its sexist connotations, in this case, it did seem fitting.

'Was the mirror you?' I asked.

'No,' said Arne. 'That was her.'

Sofia studied the circle, trying to see something, but for her, I imagined we looked like lunatics talking to thin air.

'What about the hot water?' Ben asked.

'Still her. I keep tryina stop her. She'll give up fer a bit, then start over again.' He rolled his eyes.

'So what were you trying to tell us about Giorgia?' I asked, hoping he could tell us something useful.

'Is that her name?' said Arne.

'Yes,' said Ben.

Arne looked at Sofia for the first time. He did a double take, clearly processing that the captain was an attractive, middle-aged female. Straightening himself up, he addressed her: 'No offence, but yer sister is in a league of 'er own.'

'He said your sister is in a league of her own,' Ben told Sofia.

Sofia pursed her lips. 'What do you mean?'

'I knew a lot of people with vendettas when I were alive, but she could put Inigo Montoya to shame.'

Ben repeated what he'd said to Sofia. She tensed.

'Have you spoken to her? Do you know what she wants?' I asked, fear rising within me. Ben squeezed my hand. It didn't offer as much consolation as I would've liked.

'Can't say for definite – she never stays in one place too long, much as I've tried to pin her down – but revenge seems to play a big role.'

I repeated what he'd said.

Sofia clenched and unclenched her fists. She seemed to be getting increasingly anxious and angry. 'Revenge? For what?'

'Not sure. But I do know it's directed at our captain 'ere.' He nodded at Sofia.

'He says Giorgia has a vendetta against you,' I informed her.

'*Me?*'

That confirmed our theory, at least.

'Dunno what she did to her, but she definitely wants to hurt the captain in any way she can,' said Arne. 'She's angry. Really angry. And I don't think she's going to stop until she gets the captain's head on a platter.'

Ben pushed his glasses up his nose. 'Not to make everyone panic, but if she really does want revenge, she may not target Sofia directly. It's too quick. She'd go after everyone else, first.'

'And without her being able to go too far away from Sofia, a cruise ship is the perfect place for her to easily find victims,' I added.

'Yes,' agreed Ben.

'*Dio santo!*' Sofia let go of my hand and sank on to the wooden floor, tucking her knees into her chest and sobbing.

Ben, Arne, and I exchanged concerned looks.

'I'm sorry I can't help any more, but I think me time's best spent stoppin' Giorgia from causin' any more trouble,' said Arne.

'You're right. Thanks for warning us,' I said.

Arne nodded, fading out of sight to continue what he'd been doing. Leaving us to console Sofia.

Ben and I crouched on either side of her, resting our hands on her back. 'We've done this before. We can help you,' said Ben.

'*Can* you? You said it yourself! She's going to go after *everyone*!'

'We can't guarantee that,' I said, hoping I sounded comforting.

Even though I wasn't massively comforted because having powers meant that Ben and I tended to attract ghosts and other people with powers.

And that included the unhinged ones who wanted to take us down either to steal our powers or show off how powerful they were. Just because those who'd tried had failed, that didn't mean future ones would.

'But now that we know what her goal is, we can put steps in place to protect you.'

'But what about my passengers!' She flung her arms in the air, almost hitting us. We ducked out of the way just in time. 'I should cancel the cruise, send everyone home.'

'Blaming what? No one would believe you.' I said.

'But at least they'd be safe!'

'We can't guarantee that,' I said. 'They're safer here.'

'On a ship? In the middle of the ocean? With a poltergeist? *How*?' She shook her head so hard some of her hair fell out of her loose bun. She tucked it behind her ears.

Ben stood, a determined look on his face. 'Because just like how the passengers can't escape, neither can she. We don't know how far away from you she can go, but it may well be beyond the ship's walls. While we're at sea, we can find her easier and put steps in to keep her from causing more trouble.'

'You really think they'll work?'

'We'll stop her, don't you worry.'

I really wished I shared Ben's optimism. Although, I supposed our track record *was* pretty good. We usually had four of us and a lot more resources, though.

Could Ben and I really track, and stop, a poltergeist with a vendetta all on our own?

39
Edie

We tried to fake that everything was fine for Abigail's sake, but she wasn't stupid. She kept asking us what was wrong. Each time, we deflected her question differently. It was never long until she asked someone else the same thing, hoping for a more honest answer.

But that was the problem: none of us wanted to lie to her.

Nor did we want to tell her the truth.

So Josh, Maggie, Fadil, and I did our best to distract her – and each other – by playing board games and having coffee parties and baking and playing with Tilly.

But we all knew it wouldn't be long until Harry – and whatever was inside of him – tried to re-enter the house. We just had to hope that when he did, Mum and Ben were back from their cruise. And that if he tried before then, the wards would hold up.

Not having Ben's forcefield made us vulnerable. Not having Mum's experience did, too.

Fadil, Josh, Maggie, and I all had vials of the exorcism potion in our pockets. It gave us each a little bit of comfort. And at least Josh and Maggie didn't need powers to use the potion. Assuming – and hoping – it would work on Harry.

The Poltergeist's Ship

When it came to dinnertime, Maggie didn't want to cook. I'd never known her not want to cook. But she looked too exhausted, too drained. So Fadil and I volunteered to make some comfort food to give her family a break. We opted for beans on sourdough toast with some cheese on top. Not the most extravagant food, but it was semi-healthy and filling.

As usual, Tilly inhaled her turkey dinner. But the rest of us ate our beans on toast slowly. No one really seemed to have an appetite. We stared blankly at the TV.

Until the front door handle rattled.

Something smashed outside. The gargoyle? Frazzle.

My hands started shaking. I clenched them into fists, hoping the others wouldn't notice.

The person outside grunted, growling. It wasn't a human noise. It was the sound of an animal in pain. Was Harry trying to break through the wards?

We were in big trouble.

Tilly jumped off the sofa and stood in front of me, ready to pounce. I ushered the others behind me. My powers might've been weakened, but I was still the strongest in the room.

A grunt. A bang. A figure in the doorway.

Josh was still in front of me. Unprotected. Shit.

Harry cracked his neck. 'That's some impressive warding you've done.'

He'd broken through the wards. *He'd broken through the wards!* My stomach plummeted. How powerful *was* whatever was inside of him?

Tilly's back arched. Teeth bared, she growled at Harry. Tilly didn't growl. Not like that. Bark? Sure.

Make weird squeak-like noises? Often. But teeth-baring, threatening growls? She didn't do that. Unless…Tobias was right. Maisie's research had been right.

This was bad. So very, very bad.

I picked Tilly up to try to soothe her, but I doubted it'd help. She'd just be able to feel the rapid beating of my heart. The panic rising inside of me. But at least I could protect her if I was holding her. And get some comfort myself from her proximity.

'What's the matter? Expected your powers to work on me again?' said not-Harry.

'*Again?*' I hadn't intended to say that out loud.

'Oh, yes, *duckie*. You tried that already.' Oh my god. Despite being from Nottinghamshire, Harry had never called anyone 'duck' or 'duckie.' I'd only ever been called duckie in that tone of voice once before. In that very same house.

'The gargoyle hurt the first time, when I studied what you'd done outside your house, but I came prepared this time.'

I bit my lip to suppress my reaction. It *had* been him outside my house the other night. And because of it, he knew all my tricks.

'All it took was a rock and good aim to smash that gargoyle of yours. Wish I'd thought of that the other day.' He rolled his shoulders a few times. 'The paint was new. That was harder. Possibly not yours. But damn. Had a kick to it. Fair play to you. Or whoever created it.'

The Poltergeist's Ship

If even Tobias's paint wasn't strong enough against him, what chance did the rest of us have? What chance did *I* have?

'Your real mistake was coming back here, of course. You humans are so predictable.'

Not-Harry looked behind Maggie to where Abigail was cowering. She may have been young, but she knew something was wrong. She knew that wasn't her dad. He crouched down. 'Hi, Abigail. Lovely to see you again.' He reached out to stroke her cheek. She stood as still as a statue.

I was right. It was the demon who'd possessed her last year. But I thought I'd exorcised it! How had it come back?

'Leave her alone!' said Josh from by the TV. The demon inside of his dad ignored him.

'How's Oscar?' Not-Harry continued addressing a terrified Abigail, using a mocking tone for the next question: '*is he still cute?*'

I had no idea who Oscar was, but I wanted to punch not-Harry. Of course, it wouldn't really hurt the demon inside of him, only Harry. Meh.

Feigning confidence, I said: 'I exorcised you before. I'll do it again.'

Not-Harry snorted. 'Cute, but last time I was in the body of a five-year-old girl. And tethered to that useless necromancer, Dominic.'

I gasped. I was really failing at being stoic.

'You didn't know?' He smirked. I was just handing him all the power in the conversation with my lack of knowledge. Go me! 'Dominic summoned me to help get your powers. After you exorcised me, I managed to sneak out again when Ben and Fadil released your friends from that coma.' So the exorcism *had* worked the first time. Could we do it again? He raised his head at Maggie, gesturing to her. Maggie flinched. 'So I'm in control of where I go this time. I'd like to see you overpower me now.' He sneered, looking down at me. All right, so I wasn't a body builder, but that didn't mean I couldn't take him.

Fine. It probably did. It wasn't the only weapon I had, though.

'It's so refreshing dealing with amateurs again. I've got more years of experience than you could possibly imagine. Well, except you, Fadil.'

Fadil's eyes widened. How old *was* this demon? Did we want to know? Probably not.

Maggie put a protective hand on her daughter's shoulder.

Josh lunged at his dad. Not-Harry pushed him away. It took him so little effort it was scary.

Josh smacked into the wall by Abigail's toybox. I ran to him, Tilly still tucked under my arm. As I reached out, I stopped myself. He still didn't like me touching him. But then he grabbed my hand, staring deep into my eyes as if it was just the two of us for those few seconds: 'I'm OK.'

Phew.

If only it really was just the two of us.

Tilly climbed into Josh's lap. He hugged her to him.

'Harry's having great fun in here, you know. It's impressive how strong his denial is. He thinks he's having a very long nightmare or he's in some sort of coma. Convinced himself he's been in a car crash.'

Maggie let out a strangled sob. 'Leave my husband alone.' Her tone was stern, but masking heartbreak.

Abigail grabbed her mum's hand.

My heart twisted in my chest. Harry and I may not have gotten along, but nobody deserved to be possessed by a demon. All it did was lead to pain.

'Or what?' said not-Harry. 'What are you going to do, hm? Beg me to love you again? To fuck you?' he snarled.

Maggie recoiled, looking fragile and sheepish. The bastard. I curled my hands into fists. What should I do?

The one time I needed backup. But we couldn't stall until Mum and Ben got back. We were on our own.

My powers were our only option. But I was still drained. Would they even work? They hadn't when I'd needed them to protect Josh from Goodfellow. I hadn't even used them for a while, then. And I didn't have Thomas for backup this time.

Gwendoline was around, but she wasn't a necromancer. And I didn't want to risk her getting hurt, especially as I had no idea how powerful this monster was. I needed her to protect everyone else if I didn't make it.

So I did the only thing I could: I started draining his life essence.

I let go of Josh's hand, having only just realised I was still holding on to him. He tried to grab me again, but I shook him off. *Distract him*, I mouthed, trying not to cry so that I could concentrate and exude the confidence and reassurance I knew his family needed from me.

Josh nodded. He addressed not-Harry: 'What did you do to my dad?'

Fadil stepped closer to me, no doubt recognising my expression and what I was trying to do. I shook my head as subtly as I could, hoping he'd take the hint to stay away. He must've done, because he stayed where he was, between Josh and me, and Maggie and Abigail. Their average-sized living room had never felt so small.

'He's just on holiday, that's all,' said not-Harry. 'He's still in here. For now. Every so often he breaks free and tries to talk, but it never lasts.'

'Was it you who got drunk the other night? Or Dad?'

The demon wrinkled his nose. 'Drunk? What are you talking about?'

'We found you. In town, stumbling around in the middle of the night,' said Maggie.

'That wasn't me.'

'Definitely was,' she said.

If the demon had been in control for so long, how didn't it remember stumbling through town the other night?

I lost track of my thoughts and the conversation as I closed my eyes and focused on the life essences coming from Harry. There was a tight lid on one of them. That had to be what I'd been missing. Lids didn't happen very often. That was one thing I had learned from the Book of the Dead. This lid was so tight it reminded me of a jar of honey where the honey had turned into glue. Unfortunately the hot water trick didn't work on life essences.

The last person who'd had lidded powers hadn't noticed when I'd drained them, but she hadn't even been aware that she had any powers. We weren't dealing with an average person here. We were dealing with a demon.

Just how powerful was said demon to be able to disguise its powers for so long? No wonder I hadn't noticed anything unusual. I'd had to really concentrate to find the lid.

I pulled and pulled, trying to maintain my normal breathing so that it didn't look like I was straining. Not being able to take deep breaths to focus my energy made it harder for me to pull the lid off, though.

Josh kept not-Harry talking and distracted. I couldn't tell what they were saying; I was too busy concentrating.

When the lid finally flew off, I shivered. The demon's life essence was the darkest I'd ever felt. Like Goodfellow's and Dominic's combined and then multiplied. I felt sick.

There was a glimmer of another life essence coming from Harry's body. It buzzed nervously and was surprisingly strong. Was it Harry? I'd never paid much attention to his before. But his essence had an intense frequency; a red hue to it. It fascinated me, but this wasn't the time for curiosity. I had to focus. I couldn't give away what I was doing.

So, while I wanted to stand up, to feel more centred, I remained seated, crossing my legs and staying close to Josh but not *too* close.

My body pulsed as I drained the demon's life essence, trying my best not to absorb Harry's, too. My body was trying to reject the demon's life essence before I'd even absorbed enough to do any real damage. It could feel how toxic the energy was and didn't want it. But I had to keep going.

Not-Harry coughed, looking over at me. His eyes widened as he saw me. Did he know what I was doing? I was trying really hard not to give it away in my body language or facial expressions. But I'd never been very good at poker.

Not-Harry coughed again, folding in half. He turned to Maggie: 'Mags, I'm sorry. Please, protect them.' The voice was crackly. Like it took so much energy to speak. It sounded like the Harry I remembered. The one who cared about his family, despite his grumpiness.

Maggie stepped forwards despite Abigail clinging to her arm and trying to hold her back. 'Harry? Is that you?'

Not-Harry cracked his neck again. 'Nice try.' He hit his own face. We all gasped. 'That was unusual,' he said in his demon voice. He turned back to me: 'I see what you were trying there, little necromancer.'

He grabbed my arm and jerked me up. Josh tried to pull me back but wasn't fast enough. I stumbled to my feet, trying to shake my hand free from the demon's vice-like grip. I couldn't. So I did the only other thing I could think of, while still trying to absorb his life essence. Which was totally draining me with how dark it was.

I scratched him.

Taking the opportunity, Josh jumped up, grabbing his dad's arm. I grabbed the other. 'Fadil, the vial!'

Tilly stood in front of Maggie and Abigail protectively as Fadil uncorked the vial from his pocket. Not-Harry wriggled in our grasp. I wasn't sure how much longer we could hold him. Maggie and Abigail watched on helplessly as we tried to save their family. We *had* to save their family.

Fadil tried to force Harry's mouth open. He clenched his teeth. So Fadil prized his lips open and poured the liquid over it. There was so much liquid some of it *had* to go in. But then the demon spat it out over Fadil. He recoiled, the potion having gone in his eyes. Maggie ran to him. Now what?

'What's wrong with your face?' Abigail asked not-Harry. It sounded like a childish insult, but then I noticed his face was turning red where I'd scratched him. No, not just red. It was a *burn*.

'What the hell?' said not-Harry.

Taking a gamble, I placed my left palm on his right cheek. He screamed. So I placed my other hand on his other cheek. He screamed again, pushing me into Maggie and Fadil. I stumbled, righting myself just in time to see crimson burns appearing on his face.

Maggie covered her mouth with her spare hand. Abigail gasped. Josh stepped back from not-Harry. What the hell had I done?

Not-Harry reached out and touched his arms. 'I should've known. Now it all makes sense.'

'*What* all makes sense?' I asked.

Not-Harry smirked. 'Ask your great-grandmother.'

I furrowed my brow. 'My great-grandmother? What does she have to do with anything?' Which side of my family was he even talking about?

Not-Harry shook his head. 'You have no idea who you really are, do you?'

'Sure I do. I'm Edie Hathaway Porter. Teenager. Witch. Necromancer.'

His smirk grew. 'There's more to that list than you think. But that's not my story to tell.'

He turned to leave. I reached out to grab him, forgetting for a moment who he was and that he'd been trying to kill us. I needed answers!

Without even looking at me, he psychokinetically pushed me into the wall. The middle of my back hit it with a thud. Josh crouched beside me, wrapping his arms around me protectively.

'Please, let my husband go,' begged Maggie. I'd never seen her so desperate before. A lump formed in my throat. 'He doesn't deserve any of this.'

Not-Harry chuckled, slowly turning to look at her. 'Oh, sweet, desperate Maggie. That's not how this works.'

He took a step towards her. I dove in between them, using all the power I had to drain him. Quick. Fast. Strong. I'd never done anything like it before. Draining life essence was always a slow(ish) process. This went against everything I'd been taught or tried before. But I had to protect Maggie and Abigail and Josh. I didn't care what the consequences were for me. He wouldn't hurt them any more than he already had.

Not-Harry stumbled back towards the window. His legs buckled but he remained standing. He ran off.

Before I could chase after him, my legs buckled. I blacked out.

40

Niamh

'How the hell are we supposed to get any sleep tonight knowing that she's out there?' I asked as Ben and I lay in bed. The one good thing to come from the seance was that now that Arne had passed on his message, the static was gone. Aside from the lingering ringing in my ears from a near-constant noise for the last few days.

'She doesn't know where our cabin is,' said Ben. 'The ship is huge. What are the odds she'd pick the right one?'

I wrinkled my nose. 'Just because the cameras haven't picked her up, doesn't mean she doesn't know. Not to mention she doesn't need to sleep so has more time to search the ship.'

Ben frowned. 'I'll stay up and use my forcefield.'

'No. You need to sleep as well. There's no way we can stop her if you're falling asleep in your breakfast.'

There had to be something else we could do. We were on a ship full of ghosts. 'I wonder if we could get Gwendoline over to help. We need someone strong, and she's the only ghost we know with powers, now.'

Someone cleared their throat. A minute later, Javi appeared. He bowed. 'At your service, ma'am. How may I help you today?'

Ben sniggered beside me.

I laughed, shaking my head. 'While I appreciate you wanting to help, aren't you meant to stay out of matters for the living?' I reminded him.

He shrugged. 'What are they going to do? I'm already dead.'

I glowered at him. 'We don't know what they could do. That's the point.'

'It's my choice. And I want to help.' He gave me his best puppy-dog face. It worked on me every time. And he was so earnest in his desire to help. 'What do you need?'

Ben didn't seem comfortable either, but at least if Javi was here, we could get some sleep.

So we explained the Giorgia situation to Javi. Before I could even explain what we needed from him, he said: 'Bodyguard duty it is!' He saluted. 'Consider it done.'

'There's another ghost, a guy called Arne. He's been tailing Giorgia to try to stop her from causing trouble,' I explained. 'And Delia. We think Giorgia killed her.'

'How crazy are we thinking Giorgia could be?' Javi asked. 'On a scale of Casper the friendly ghost to Goodfellow the murderous Victorian doctor?'

'We don't think she's as powerful as Goodfellow was, but she seems less…calculated,' said Ben.

'So she's causing trouble because she can, rather than because she has a plan?' said Javi, smirking at his rhyme.

'It seems that way, yeah,' said Ben.

Javi frowned, floating up and down a few times from beside the sofa in our cabin. 'I hate unhinged ghosts.'

'Me too.' That was exactly the kind of poltergeist that'd killed him. And even though it'd been eleven years, that didn't mean I didn't still have regrets. That it didn't still eat me up that we'd been young and irresponsible. It was why I hadn't wanted Ben involved; part of why I was uncomfortable with Javi being there.

But times were different. I had to reflect that in what we did. There had to be meaning behind Javi's death. Otherwise, none of us had learned anything from the past and we weren't the ghost hunters we wanted to be.

Javi looked away, his chin-length hair swishing as he turned his head. 'You two get some sleep. I'll be here.'

'Thank you,' I said, wishing I could hug him so he knew how much I appreciated what he was doing. Even though he claimed to be Team Ben, it still couldn't have been easy for him to see me in bed with another man. And to sacrifice his afterlife to protect us.

Javi flicked off most of the lights, but left one on so that we could see. Which I appreciated, because we all knew that things with a poltergeist could change in a blink.

*

'No. No. *No!*'

Ben and I jumped awake. Hovering above us was Javi, lying his back, pushing a ghost away from our room. Or trying to. She was half in our room, half in the room above us. Her face popped in and out of sight as the two of them fought it out. There was no denying she was Sofia's sister. They looked so alike:

same stern features, same brown hair. She was more muscular than Sofia, and wore an army uniform.

Without saying anything, Ben put his forcefield up then put his glasses on. I hugged my knees.

I knew she'd figure out where we were. I shouldn't have doubted my instincts. Too many ghosts had seen us try to protect people from her. And she had to have noticed who'd intercepted her so many times. We'd been waiting for this moment, and of course it'd come before we'd had the chance to talk to her on our terms. She'd targeted us when we were the most vulnerable. Fiddlesticks.

Why hadn't we summoned her after Arne had left? We'd hoped he could buy us some time while we formulated a plan. But I couldn't even see him now. She couldn't hurt him – he was already dead, after all – but where was he? Was he just too drained to keep stopping her?

'What do we do?' I asked Ben. I was tired and didn't think well on my feet. I was a planner! We did not have a plan for this scenario.

'We need to get hold of Sofia,' said Ben.

'And bring her sister to her? How will that help?' I asked.

Javi continued to push her out of our room. They seemed equally matched. For now, at least. Javi was a necromancer. That made him a lot stronger than an average ghost. But rage also made ghosts strong. That was how poltergeists could interact with the real world. How strong did her rage make her?

'Please come up with a plan sooner rather than later!' said Javi through gritted teeth.

'We're working on it!' I said. 'You're a necromancer! Can't you do something?'

Javi grunted.

Ben scratched his chin. 'Edie mentioned Shane crossed over after talking to his girlfriend. Maybe if Giorgia and Sofia talk…'

'Maybe? *Maybe?*' I said. Maybe didn't give me a lot of hope.

We had limited resources and couldn't get any supplies until we were back in a couple of days. Words were the only weapon we had. It'd helped Shane cross over. It wasn't a huge stretch for Sofia to talk to her sister, was it?

Estranged families were unusual things, as Ben and I knew all too well.

'Maybe is all we've got right now,' said Ben. 'I'm open to other ideas.'

'So how do we get hold of Sofia? It's the middle of the night and we're on the other side of the ship.' I was liking this plan less and less the longer I was awake. Oh, how I wished I was still asleep and dreaming of a never-ending supply of cookies.

'Let's try the phone, first,' said Ben. 'Guest Services are open 24/7. They're our best shot.'

'And if they say no?' shouted Javi. 'Bugger *off!*' He screamed, pushing Giorgia really hard. She seemed to vanish. He floated down to us and towards the bed. He flickered in and out, clearly drained. I guessed it was the ghost equivalent of panting for breath.

'I thought necromancers could control ghosts?' I said.

'Living ones, yeah. I can control the living better than the dead.' He put his hand to his mouth.

'*What* did you just say?'

Ben and I stared at my incredibly powerful dead husband, wide-eyed.

'Forget I said anything. *Please*?'

'Definitely not. Please repeat.'

Javi looked uncomfortable. 'Um…'

I ground my teeth together and glared at him. 'You can control the living?'

He didn't speak, only nodded once. How had he never told me this before? It was kind of an important detail, wasn't it?

Ben lowered his forcefield, running his hand over his face. 'As fascinating as this is, we really don't have time to process this right now.'

'Agreed,' said Javi. 'You need to ring Guest Services.'

Not happy but knowing they were right, I pointed at my dead husband – who could apparently control me if he wanted to – 'We'll talk about this later.'

He looked away, clearly ashamed and uncomfortable.

We needed to focus on the task in front of us, but my brain was also melting at the fact that my dead husband – and Thomas, and my *mother* – could do very, very dangerous things with their powers.

Ben put his hand on my arm. I jumped.

'I'm sorry,' said Javi. And he genuinely looked it. 'Some things it's safer for you not to know.'

'I don't see how not knowing you can control the living is a bad thing. Surely that's something we *should* know so that we can protect ourselves?'

He looked like a kicked puppy. 'Protect yourself from *me?*'

'No you bloody idiot. From bad necromancers!'

'Right. Yes. Of course. Even so. I don't make the rules.'

'So who does?'

'Neevie, you know I can't answer that.'

'This is a joke.' I got out of bed and grabbed the phone from its holder more aggressively than necessary. 'Hello, is this Guest Services?'

'Yes. How can we help you?'

'We need to speak to the captain, please.' I so wasn't in the mood for pleasantries. 'My name is Niamh. She knows me.'

'It's the middle of the night, Niamh. The captain is very busy. She needs to sleep.'

'I'm aware of that, thank you. But this is an emergency.'

'What appears to be the problem? I'm sure we can help.'

I huffed, twisting the phone cord around my fingers. Ben put his hand on me and gestured to the phone. Rolling my eyes, I passed it to him. It was probably better the more patient one explained the situation anyway. I was too angry at Javi. I glared at him. Javi at least looked sheepish. Not that it changed anything. *He could control the living.* Had he done that to us? No. He wouldn't do that. He wasn't that kind of person. But my mother was…would she?

'I would never do it,' said Javi as Ben continued to talk in the background.

'Would anyone else?'

He couldn't meet my eye. 'I don't think so. It's frowned upon. But…' He shrugged. He couldn't speak for everyone. People broke the rules all the time. He was technically doing it by being there.

Ben slammed the phone into the receiver. 'They're not waking her up.'

I grabbed a pair of comfy trackies and a T-shirt, not caring about getting changed in front of them since I was tired, angry, and it wasn't like they hadn't seen me naked before. I hoped they enjoyed the show. 'Then we'll just have to wake her up ourselves.'

41

Niamh

'How does this plan of yours work, exactly?' Ben asked as I marched down the corridor. I think in the right direction. I figured Ben or Javi would correct me if I was wrong.

'We go to the captain's quarters and wake her up,' I said.

'But Guest Services won't let us see her,' he reminded me.

'Details. We'll figure that out when we get there. For all we know, Javi scared Giorgia off. Ugh, this would be so much easier if we could just ring her!' But of course, being out at sea, we had no phone signal and barely any WiFi. And even if we had had a signal, we didn't have her phone number.

'We should really come up with an actual plan before we get there,' said Javi.

I took a deep breath, slowing my march as we went downstairs. 'You're right. But we're short on time. So: options?'

'What if we made up a spell, tailored just to her?' suggested Ben.

'I like it, keep going.'

'It worked with Goodfellow, right?'

'Yeah but that was after Edie had drained him,' I pointed out.

'I don't think we need Edie to do that,' said Javi. 'She's doing it to herself.'

We turned a corner. I stopped. I actually had no idea where we were going and still couldn't navigate the stupid ship.

Ben pointed to the nearby staircase. 'That way.'

'What do you mean?' I asked Javi.

'When I was fighting her, I managed to push her away because she got weak. I think the reason you can't always see her when she does something is because she's preserving energy. She's not the most powerful poltergeist we've ever seen. What makes her dangerous is her unpredictability.'

'Oh my god! Niamh! Ben!' Niall rounded the corner, running up the stairs to us, panting heavily. 'Thank god I found you! The captain…she…she…'

'Let's go,' I said, cutting him off so that he knew he didn't have to explain. We followed him through the ship to the crew area. For the middle of the night, it had a surprising amount of people up and about. Crew members watched with confusion as we ran through the ship and up to the bridge and captain's quarters. Someone screamed inside.

Niall banged on the door frantically. 'I got them! They're here!'

'Thank you,' said Ben. 'You should get somewhere safe.'

'Are you sure? I mean, I don't want to—'

'No, seriously. Go somewhere safe. *Please*,' I said to him. Unfortunately for him, he knew so little that his presence would just be a liability.

'Go to the bridge and keep people out of Sofia's quarters,' said Ben. A solid idea to keep him out of trouble *and* keep other people out of trouble. 'It's really, *really* important that nobody else goes in there. No matter what you hear.'

Sofia flung the door open. She was dressed in black silk pyjamas. Her hair was ruffled and the bags under her eyes were huge. Several pieces of furniture and tchotchke had been flung around the space.

Seeing the carnage, Niall didn't need to be told again. He ran off to do as instructed, clearly not wanting to go through the captain's quarters to get to the bridge. Clever guy.

'Thank god you're here!' Sofia ushered us inside as a vase flew at our heads. Javi intercepted it, throwing it back. It shattered against the closed curtains that blocked the darkness of the nighttime ocean.

'What was that?' said Sofia.

'Complicated,' said Ben.

'We have, uh…our version of Casper here,' I said, wanting to give her something without overcomplicating the situation and giving her more questions than answers.

Javi seemed happy with my description as he grinned, straightening up a little. I laughed.

Arne floated in and out of sight in the room, clearly trying to intercept what Giorgia was doing, but not fast enough or strong enough. He looked exhausted. 'I'm sorry. I tried,' he said, dejected.

'We understand,' said Ben.

'How long has she been here?' I asked.

'About fifteen minutes. I thought she was going to kill me,' said Sofia.

Ben put up his forcefield. Its faint white iridescent hue glowed in the overhead lights.

'What is *that*?' Sofia reached out to touch it, but changed her mind and retracted her hand.

Giorgia picked up a photo of Sofia with a friend and threw it at us. It hit the forcefield, bounced off it, and fell to the ground.

Sofia gasped. Well, that answered her question.

While we could see Giorgia's wrath, we couldn't see *her*. The best indication we had was wherever Arne was, but since he was getting fainter, it wouldn't give us much for long.

'We need to get her to make herself visible,' I said.

'You can't. There's no way to do that if a ghost doesn't want to appear,' said Javi.

'There has to be a way!' I said.

Sofia looked confused at me talking to air, but stayed silent, cowering behind Ben and me.

'Yes. It involves a necromancer. A live one.'

I rolled my eyes. Of course it did.

'Could we write something?' I suggested. 'I mean, Ben and I have some of the genes, right? And you… well you're complicated and annoying, but in theory we could channel you to make it work.'

Javi stuck his tongue out at me. But he didn't deny that he was annoying.

'Worth a go,' agreed Ben.

All right. Time to write on the fly. I'd done it before. I could do it again. Think Niamh. Think. 'Repeat after me: We call upon the spirit Giorgia, to be visible to everyone tonight, grant us your visibility, join us in the light.' It wasn't my best, but I was hoping the repetition of what we wanted would help manifest it.

Giorgia flickered in and out of sight. She looked around, clearly confused as she materialised in front of us. Sofia grabbed my hand. 'What the hell is this?'

'You can see her?' said Ben.

'On and off, yes. What is going on?'

'Damn, I didn't expect it to work that well,' I said, chuffed with myself.

'Nice work,' said Ben, giving me a playful squeeze.

'Why thank you.'

'What did you do!' said Giorgia. Javi was right: she really wasn't that powerful. Even though she was visible to all of us, she was pretty translucent. That would work in our favour – her being visible when she's interacted with so much would drain her energy faster.

And the way I'd worded the spell meant that she'd stay in that state until we said otherwise. Or we exorcised her or she crossed over on her own. Whichever came first.

Arne hovered in the background, still flickering in and out, watching the drama unfold.

Feeling safe in the forcefield, Sofia stepped closer to her sister: 'Giorgia, *perché?*' She gestured to the destroyed room around us. It looked like a drunken rock band had been let loose.

Giorgia floated to her sister, getting as close as she could. Her scowl was intense. '*Tu.*'

'What did I *do*? I don't understand.' Sofia seemed genuinely confused. The poor woman. It was bad enough to get haunted by a poltergeist, but for said poltergeist to be your sister who'd died with a vendetta against you? I couldn't even begin to imagine how she felt.

'You never will,' said Giorgia. She went to grab another photo to throw at her sister, but Javi grabbed her wrist.

'That's enough, now,' said Javi. 'Stop it.'

She tried to wriggle in his grip, but she couldn't get out of it. 'Who *are* you? What are you doing here?'

'Casper the friendly necromancer,' he said, smirking.

Arne floated over to them, clearly knackered. And a little confused about what was going on. Poor guy.

'Who is she talking to?' said Sofia.

'Oh. Right.' Javi must've made himself visible to Sofia, because she jumped.

'Meet Casper,' I said, pointing to Javi. 'My dead husband.'

42

Niamh

Sofia let out a low whistle.

'Yeah. It's complicated,' I said.

She glanced at Ben. 'It sounds it.'

'It's fine, we're fine,' said Javi, gesturing to Ben. 'I'm Team Ben. I'm dead, after all.'

'Can we stay on topic, *please*?' I begged. This was so not the time to discuss my love life with strangers.

'Good idea,' said Ben. 'Giorgia, you have to stop terrorising your sister.'

'No.'

Of course she'd be stubborn. I was so done with her drama. 'Or we can play it your way and we can exorcise you and you can get a one-way ticket to the Demonic Realm. Your choice.'

'You're lying,' said Giorgia. But she looked terrified. Javi still held on to her so that she couldn't run off or cause any more trouble.

Arne steeled himself, ready to pounce if she tried anything, but he looked too weak to actually do anything. A week of tailing a poltergeist could do that to a ghost, no matter how good their intentions. Your average ghost just wasn't as powerful as a poltergeist.

'Nope. Definitely not. Never been there myself, but it's not somewhere I really want to go. Never heard good things about it. Have either of you?'

'Nope,' said Ben.

'Me neither,' said Javi.

'When a poltergeist is exorcised, they spend the rest of their lives there, tortured by demons,' explained Ben. 'Some people have the privilege of going there straight after they've died. Over time, they get turned into demons. If they ever come back to the land of the living, it's usually to do the bidding of the person that summons them. They're prisoners, basically. It's not fun.'

'I don't believe you.'

'Your prerogative. But is it worth the risk? Or would you rather go to the nicer place – where I assume is the nice place – with people like this guy?' I gestured to Javi.

He smiled, bringing out his cheeky, boyish good looks. 'I'd say it's pretty nice, yeah. Fewer politicians.'

Ben, Arne, I sniggered. Sofia was too freaked out to show any emotion, and Giorgia just kept looking more and more horrified.

'So, shall we get this exorcism going? Or are we ready to talk things out? Cause I'm tired and this holiday has been far more stressful than I'd planned,' I said. If our plan to talk Giorgia around didn't work, we were in trouble. We didn't actually have an exorcism potion with us. So if we had to exorcise her, I had no idea what we'd do. All we could do was try to ensure it didn't get to that. 'Did I mention it's demonic torture for *eternity*?' The thicker we laid it on, the more likely we were to win her over. In theory.

'Please, Giorgia,' said Sofia, her tone pleading. 'Talk to me. I'm begging you. If not for me or yourself, then for our parents.'

'Our parents? What use were they?' she snarled.

Ah. We were getting somewhere.

'What do you mean?' asked Sofia.

'They never cared about me. It was always about you. Sofia this, Sofia that. Sofia the overachiever.'

Ben tensed beside me. This was a serious case of sibling rivalry. I was definitely out of my depth. Something told me he'd be able to help with this.

'Do you think your parents played favourites?' Ben asked.

'*Favourites?*' echoed Giorgia. 'I was practically invisible! They valued academic intelligence, but that wasn't me. I was the sporty one. But they never came to any of my football games. Not one.'

Sofia wiped a tear from her eye. 'But they…they…' She obviously didn't know what to say. It sounded like she'd had no idea what her parents had been doing. One thing I'd learned from Ben was that two children could have very different experiences of the same parents. One might've had a healthy upbringing, the other a toxic one.

'I was never good enough,' said Giorgia. 'It didn't matter what I did. All the trophies I won, they didn't mean a thing. But if you managed to even catch a ball during any sport you got taken out for gelato or given extra allowance. I could score the winning goal and they wouldn't even notice.' Giorgia began to shake, as if she was crying. Were we getting through to her?

Arne opened his arms to her. Javi let go and she curled into a total stranger who'd been fighting her just minutes before. And trying to stop her from causing havoc for most of the week. She seemed to take comfort in his embrace.

'No. They wouldn't do that,' insisted Sofia. 'They were good people.'

'No one is inherently good or bad,' I said. 'Different people bring out different sides of us.'

Ben and Javi nodded in agreement.

Sofia wiped at her face with her fist, tears streaming down her cheeks. 'So—so—you hate me because of them?'

Giorgia nodded, her face covered by Arne's broad chest.

'But you can't blame your sister for what your parents did,' said Ben. 'It isn't her fault. She did her best to please them, just like you did. But they had different values and priorities to you. That doesn't make either of you right, it makes them wrong.'

The sisters turned to look at Ben.

'My family valued my younger sister over me. And it hurt me for a really long time. Still does, sometimes. When my sister died suddenly, they blamed me for not protecting her. I struggled to accept that it wasn't my fault. None of it was.' Ben sniffed. I reached out and put my arms around him. He leaned into me. 'My sister didn't always see how they treated me, but she knew we came from a matriarchal family that valued women and their powers first and foremost. And since my power was defensive not offensive, they saw it as less valuable. It took me a long time to realise that my forcefield is just as useful as anything else.'

'It's a pretty awesome power,' said Javi. 'Your parents are idiots. No offence.'

'Thanks. None taken.' Ben took a shaky breath. 'My point is, you can let your parents drive a wedge between you because of their priorities, or you can accept that your differences are your strengths. And while their treatment of you sucked, Giorgia, I see from the badges on your uniform that you worked your way up to a pretty high rank in the military. Could their treatment of you have given you the drive to work harder than most people your age?'

Sofia was full-on bawling, now. There were no tissues in sight, so I slipped out of Ben's forcefield, ran into the bathroom, grabbed a loo roll, and passed it to her. *'Grazie,'* she said before blowing her nose so loudly it could've been a fog horn.

Giorgia hadn't spoken since Ben had addressed her, but judging from her body language, she was processing what he'd said. She let go of Arne and paced in a small circle. She seemed to have calmed enough that she wasn't a threat to us, but Ben kept his forcefield up just in case.

Ben, Javi, and I watched her, waiting for her to say something. Sofia continued sobbing. Were we getting somewhere?

'Are you all right, love?' said a disembodied voice. A moment later, Delia appeared. She hovered in front of the circle, watching Giorgia.

Giorgia's eyes went wide. 'You…you…'

'Yes. Hello.'

'I'm…you shouldn't be here,' stuttered Giorgia.

Delia smiled. 'Where should I be? Sunbathing by the pool?'

Giorgia's mouth fell into an O. She clearly hadn't expected the lady she'd murdered to show up, let alone to have so much sass.

'I could've had twenty more years, you know. But I'll never know because you took that from me.' Delia didn't speak with malice. Instead, her tone was matter-of-fact. 'I could hold that against you, but actually, I quite like being a ghost. It's fun.' She floated up and down a couple of times, as if to prove her point. 'Am I mad at you? Yes. But you shouldn't be mad at your sister for something that wasn't her fault.'

'Yes it was! She could've said something to them!' said Giorgia.

'What difference would that have made?' asked Delia. 'Do you think they'd have listened?'

Giorgia lowered her head. 'No.'

'What's going on?' asked Sofia.

'Giorgia is talking to another ghost,' said Ben.

'Another ghost who didn't treat her daughters equally, either.' She shook her head. 'I had one daughter who was academic and one who was creative. I never fully valued her creativity. Even when she opened her first photography show, it didn't mean as much to me as my academic daughter getting an office job.' She lowered her shoulders, staring at a piece of debris on the floor. 'It's silly when I think about it now. I should've loved them both equally, helped them lean into their strengths. Who was I to tell them they weren't good enough?' She turned back to Giorgia: 'Who were your parents to tell you that *you* weren't good enough?'

I flinched. That one hit a nerve. Ben rubbed my back. We knew the sting well.

'She's right,' I said, unable to not say something. 'My mum never valued me, either. I was never powerful enough for her. Couldn't continue the family legacy, so I was useless to her. But I'm not defined by how she sees me. I don't have to live my life constantly seeking her approval. I have to accept that no matter what I do, she'll never approve of it. So instead, I have to live my life how I want.'

'But I can't do that now,' said Giorgia.

'No,' agreed Ben, 'but you can let go.'

'I don't know how.'

'It takes time. But it starts with not blaming your sister,' said Delia.

Giorgia stepped to the part of the forcefield closest to Sofia. 'I never understood until now. It wasn't your fault. I want you to live a long, happy life doing what you love. You deserve it.'

Sofia smiled, her eyes bloodshot from crying. 'Thank you. I'm sorry we didn't get to spend more time together.' She wiped at her face with a wad of loo roll.

'Me too,' said Giorgia.

A glowing white light appeared behind her. It looked both close and far away. It was her time. And it looked like she was going to the not-so-bad place, after all.

'Is that…is that for me?' asked Giorgia.

'Looks like it,' said Ben.

'But how do I know where I'm going?'

'If you were going to the other place you'd be gone by now,' I said.

Giorgia gave her sister one last smile. Sofia smiled back at her. 'Go. I'll see you again one day.'

'It better not be for a long, long time,' Giorgia said to her sister. She turned to the rest of us: '*Grazie*. All of you.' She faded into the light. It didn't go away.

'Do you think that's for us?' Arne asked Delia.

'It's our time. We've done our bit,' she confirmed. 'Look after each other,' she said to us. She hooked her arm into Arne's, then the two of them faded away, too.

The light remained. 'My turn to go home,' said Javi. He saluted, then faded away.

'I'm so confused,' said Sofia. 'What just happened?'

43

Edie

Mlem. Mlem mlem. What the—

Tilly. Tilly was licking my cheek. I giggled, pushing her away slightly to stop the westie face wash. 'All right, Tills. I'm awake. Thank you.' She licked my face one last time, then backed off but continued to watch me with her beady brown eyes. She'd always been good at telling when something was wrong.

Where was I?

I turned my head to the side, noticing the Morgans's fireplace to my right. I was lying on their sofa, Tilly on guard beside me.

Josh, who'd been drawing in the armchair by the window, noticed I was awake and handed me a sports drink. 'Here. I remembered you used these after someone had been possessed, so thought it might help with this, too.' He helped me sit upright, using some cushions to prop up my back. It stung where I'd hit the wall. I inhaled through my teeth.

Tilly adjusted herself so that she was sitting on my lap, then lay down once she was satisfied I was comfy.

'How's your back?' I asked.

He rubbed where he'd hit the wall but didn't flinch. 'I'll be fine.' Not a straight answer. Not that I was surprised.

I sipped the sports drink, the fizzy orange tickling my tastebuds as it went down. I wasn't sure if it'd help after what'd happened, but it was a physically draining process, just like sports, just like possession, and I was thirsty.

Voices echoed in from the kitchen. Maggie and Fadil. Where was Abigail?

'How long was I out for?'

'About twelve hours, give or take. Doc checked you over and said you need to rest. Alanis said she sensed your life essence was weak and had been darkened. You could handle it, but need time to recover. She said that'd make sense to you and to call if we need her.'

I squeezed my eyes shut, taking a moment to process all of that. My life essence was weak but dark? Could that have been from the demon? It had to be, right? Was it worse because I'd been practising? Would the darkness go away? How long would it last?

Alanis had told them I'd be fine, so I used that to reassure myself. I didn't have the energy to be worried about anything. Could I go back to sleep?

I took another large gulp of the sports drink. Yeah, I really needed it. I tried to take another, but it was empty.

Josh laughed, taking the empty bottle from me and handing me a glass of water from on top of the fireplace.

'Thanks.' Hopefully the electrolytes in the sports drink would allow me to absorb the water better.

'Thanks for saving my mum and Abigail. I don't know what I would've done if something had happened to them.' He smiled.

My insides tied themselves in knots. It didn't mean anything. It was just because I'd helped him and his family. Shut up, brain.

I stroked a half-asleep Tilly. 'How's Abigail?'

He frowned. 'Pretty shaken up. She hasn't said much since, and you know how talkative she usually is. I tried encouraging her to draw to see if it'd help her work through things. So now the dining table is covered in crayons and paper and drawings, but at least she's doing something.'

'It'll take time,' I said.

'Sadly,' he said, looking heartbroken at how little he could do to take away her pain. 'Sometimes she'll get really into a drawing, then she'll get annoyed and scribble it out. I'd rather she take her anger out on that than bottle it up though, you know?'

'Yeah, definitely. If she's not talking, at least she's doing something to express her emotions.'

He ran his hand over his hair. 'Exactly. Mum's tried talking to her but she's not ready yet. Alanis suggested she go over tomorrow, when she's calmed down a bit and we've all gotten some sleep.'

'If nothing else, seeing Alanis will give her some cute cats to fuss and take her mind off things,' I said. 'How much sleep did you all get?'

'None of us have slept. How could we? We had no idea if he'd be back, or really what even just happened.' Josh sat on the floor beside me and crossed his legs. 'I've never seen anything like it. Not even with Goodfellow.'

I forced a laugh. 'You did technically miss out on most of that due to being, you know, possessed.'

'And then passed out,' he finished.

'Yeah. Well. None of that was your fault,' I told him, my hand still touching his.

'It wasn't yours, either.' He met my gaze. It was the first time he'd looked at me with genuine compassion since his coma. If my heart twisted any more it was going to implode.

'I meant what I said, after Goodfellow. I'll always help you if I can,' I said.

'I hope you do it out of more than just obligation.'

My insides twisted again. Had he just said that?

The kitchen door opened. Fadil walked in. Damn him. Could he have timed that worse? 'I thought I heard voices.'

Maggie poked her head through the door. 'How are you feeling? Do you want some food?'

'I feel weak. And confused. How are you?'

Maggie shrugged. She didn't need to answer: the tiredness and worry were written all over her face. Fadil looked as drained as he had before I'd practised my powers on him. And through the door, I could see Abigail hunched over a sketchpad, scribbling with a red crayon.

'Do you know why the demon mention my great-grandmother?' I asked Maggie.

'To torture you?' suggested Fadil.

'It is what they do,' said Josh, scorn in his voice.

I reached out and squeezed his hand. 'But he wouldn't have said it if there wasn't something to it, right? Why say it otherwise?'

Silence.

'Do we know which grandmother he was referring to?'

I was met with more silence.

'So we don't even know who he was referring to, let alone why.' Wasn't that just great? 'Do you have any idea? Any possibility at all?' I pleaded with Maggie, desperate for there to be some memory at the back of her mind that could give me some insights.

'I only ever met your dad's adoptive grandparents, and even that was only once. Your best bet is to ask him or your mum. They might know something we don't,' said Maggie.

I grunted. I hadn't wanted to tell Mum and Ben what'd happened. And if I told Dad, he'd inevitably tell Mum. So either way, she'd find out.

Maggie frowned. 'We've got to tell them. They need to know, especially with him still out there.'

Josh and Fadil nodded. They weren't supposed to take the same side.

'It's safest for everyone. We both know it,' said Fadil.

Ugh. I was going back to sleep.

44

Niamh

'This is what I pictured when I booked a cruise.' I leaned back on my lounger and looked up through the glass ceiling above us. Cloudless skies and a golden sun shone down on us as we cruised back to Barcelona. It was over. Giorgia was gone, Sofia could sleep again, and we could finally relax on holiday. Even if it was our final day. 'Although I'm never going on a cruise again.'

Ben sat up. 'Why not?'

As if on cue, a ghost floated past us.

I stared at him, deadpan.

'You can find them anywhere,' said Ben.

'At least anywhere else I can escape them. It's hard to escape them when you're in the middle of the ocean.'

'But at least Sofia and Giorgia got the closure they needed.' Ben rummaged in the beach bag I'd brought with us, switching his normal glasses for sunglasses.

'Who'd have thought you could cross over a poltergeist by helping them confront their emotional trauma?' I said. 'Have you ever come across anything like that before?'

'No, never. But until I met you I mostly just investigated. I didn't really solve anything,' he said.

'Really?'

'Yeah. I saw my passive power as useless and didn't have anyone to back me up after Lindsay died. Most of my ghost-hunting friends can't see ghosts, and the one who could, Goodfellow killed. She didn't like conflict so preferred not to solve anything in case things turned nasty.'

'I'm sorry,' I said.

He frowned. 'She's at peace now, at least.'

We sat in silence for a few moments. I looked back up at the bright blue sky, taking it in while I could. I doubted England would look quite so brilliantly blue. Maybe a brilliant grey with a rainbow, if I was lucky. The heatwave they'd been dealing with was due to end when we got back, and from then on it was forecast rain for a fortnight. Fun times.

'There's still something that's bugging me,' I said, sitting up.

'What?' Ben sipped the tea that was sitting on the table between us.

'The stuff Javi said. What he could do. It totally changes how I see him. And I've known him longer than almost anyone else.'

A couple walked in front of us and headed into the pool. As we were in the adults-only area, it was quieter than many of the other parts. Which, given how my senses had been assailed all week, felt like heaven.

Sofia had given us free access to anywhere and anything we wanted as a thank you for everything we'd done, and instructed the staff to get us anything we needed. Which meant they came to check on us about every half an hour. Worked for me. Extra free drinks and cookies.

'But you said it yourself: you don't think he'd ever use that against you,' said Ben.

'No, but it means my mother can do it, too. And maybe Edie one day. Doesn't that freak you out?'

'A little, but he said it's frowned on when they do it, right?'

'Yeah, but since when does that stop people?'

Or, more specifically, if Dominic ever came back as a ghost and had his active powers, would that mean he'd use them against *us*? Did he even know that dead necromancers could control the living? It didn't seem to be common knowledge. It needed to stay that way.

Not to mention Dominic was comatose in a sarcophagus somewhere in the UK. The odds of someone breaking him out were pretty slim. Even just lifting the lid on the sarcophagus would take several people unless the person wanting to resurrect him had telekinetic powers.

That didn't make it impossible, though.

Why was I letting Dominic ruin the last day of my holiday?

He'd taken enough from us already. We deserved a break.

Niall appeared with a glass jar filled with cookies. 'I don't know what the two of you did last night, but we just wanted to say thank you.'

'With cookies?' said Ben, his face lighting up.

'All the cookies,' said Niall. 'The captain's been really on edge lately, and ever since you did…whatever you did, she's literally singing. She's also really tired, but who wouldn't be when they'd been up all night with… whatever happened.' The way he spoke suggested he didn't want to know, and we sure weren't going to tell him.

'Tell the captain thank you,' I said, taking the jar from Niall and placing it on the small table between Ben and me.

'She also wanted me to invite you to dinner with her tonight.'

Ben opened the jar and took out a cookie. 'She doesn't have to do that.' He bit into the cookie and grinned.

'Whatever you did, she's like a different person. We're all grateful.'

'Of course. She's welcome to give us a call if she ever needs help with something like this. The crew are, too,' said Ben. Were they now? I gave him the side eye, but I wasn't sure he saw it. If he did, he didn't react.

'I'm sure everyone will be pleased to hear it,' said Niall. 'We're not entirely sure what happened, but most of us don't want to know. Can I get you anything else while I'm here?'

'A jug of water to share would be great,' I said.

'And a pot of tea to go with these cookies.' Ben raised his half-eaten cookie. He finished off the tea sitting beside him, then Niall collected the empty cups and teapot.

'Coming right up.' Niall saluted then headed back to the buffet area.

'Give us a call if any of the crew need help with anything like this again, huh?' I shook my head, taking a cookie from the jar as well.

Ben smiled, looking a little sheepish. 'It's what we do though, right?'

Whether I liked it or not, it most definitely was.

*

After a relaxing day on the cruise, we headed to Sofia's quarters. Being back there after what'd happened eighteen hours ago was disorientating. The debris had been cleared up, but the memories remained.

A new photo stood on the cabinet under the TV. One of Sofia and Giorgia. Sofia noticed me looking and picked it up. 'We took this a few years ago, when we were on holiday together. It wasn't long after that we stopped speaking.'

'What happened?' Ben asked, joining us and looking over my shoulder.

'Is it bad that I don't really remember? It all feels so stupid now.'

'It's not stupid,' Ben reassured her. 'We don't always remember what happened, but we remember how we felt. And that's what haunts us.'

'You can say that again.' She put the photo down. 'Do you think she'll be all right?' She looked through the window at the sunset. The orange sun glowed over the glistening water as it marked the end of a stressful week. There couldn't have been a better place to watch the sunset.

'I have it on good authority it's pretty nice on the Other Side,' I said, thinking of how happy Javi always seemed. He wasn't allowed to tell me what it was like, but he'd implied enough.

She smiled, then gestured for us to sit at the table between the living area and kitchen area. Menus sat in front of each place setting.

'She didn't have a proper funeral because they couldn't find a living relative,' said Sofia. A tear trickled down her cheek. She pulled her glasses away from her face and patted under her eyes with her finger.

'I'm so sorry,' I said. How awful, to know that your only relative had died alone and you hadn't even been contacted for the funeral.

'It's not your fault. It's no one's fault. She deserves more than that, though. I'm going to organise a memorial for her when I'm back in Italy. I've found some of her old school friends online, and they're going to get in touch with other people she used to know and help find a suitable venue.'

Ben smiled. 'That sounds lovely.'

'Yeah. I think she'd approve.'

45

Niamh

With our remaining few hours on the ship, we went to the spa and had a couple's foot massage. I was pretty sure we both fell asleep. If Ben's snoring was anything to go by, anyway. I definitely did because when the masseuse said she was done I practically hit the ceiling.

Anyway.

We'd done our bit to help four people directly, and the rest of the ship and future visitors, too. We hadn't even had to get into fisticuffs with a ghost for once, which was refreshing. And now I was glad to be leaving.

'So, what did you think to your first cruise?' I asked Ben as we locked up our room and headed back to the atrium ready to disembark.

'It was eventful, I'd say. Wouldn't you?'

I gave a small laugh. 'Yeah. That's one way to put it.'

'What do you think to Sofia's offer of a free cruise whenever we want?' he asked. 'Did it win you over?'

'No. Definitely not. Never again. You couldn't pay me to go on a cruise ever again.'

'But we missed our last stop!' said Ben.

'And one day we'll visit it,' I replied. 'Just not on a cruise.'

He chuckled. 'You know, I quite enjoyed it.'

Of course he bloody did.

We rounded the corner to head down the stairs. My phone buzzed. It was a text from Maggie. 'That's odd.'

'What's wrong?' said Ben.

'Maggie's asking if we can get a taxi home, says she's got to babysit.' Since when did someone refer to looking after their own child as 'babysitting'? Maggie never had. The hairs on the back of my neck priced up.

'That's fine, right?'

'I get if she can't pick us up, but something feels off. She never calls looking after Abigail "babysitting".' My legs locked into place. 'Oh my god. Did something happen to Edie?' My finger reached for the icon to call Maggie.

Ben put his hands on mine. 'Let Maggie do her job. She hasn't asked for help. Edie can protect herself, Fadil, and the Morgans better than we can.'

'Speak for yourself, Mr Forcefield.' It was still my job to protect my daughter, even if she *was* more powerful than me.

'Even so. She's a good problem solver and a strong necromancer and witch. Let's not catastrophise. It'll make travelling home harder.'

He was right. Of course he was right. But for the rest of the journey home, I couldn't shake my growing sense of dread.

*

As soon as we walked through my front door, suitcases in tow, Fadil took our suitcases, put them in the living room, then turned us around to head out again. Hello to you too?

'Er, hi?' I said.

'We've got to go.'

Spectre watched from the top of the stairs, his expression as unreadable as ever. I waved at him. He didn't respond.

'Please explain. It's been a long week,' I said as Fadil pushed us out the front door. 'Where are Edie and Tilly? Why aren't we getting beaten up for leaving for a week?' There was no way Tilly was going to let us off without a couple of bruises on our legs, not when we'd left her for so long.

'I will,' said Fadil. 'Let's go see Edie and Maggie and we can explain together.'

*

Maggie let Ben, Fadil, and myself into her house. Her eyes were swollen and bloodshot, her hair tied into a messy bun. The house was the quietest I'd ever seen it. What the hell had happened?

'Josh and Abigail are asleep upstairs.' Her voice was low, so as not to disturb them. She jerked her head into the lounge. 'Edie and Tilly are on the sofa.'

The energy in the house was wrong. Dark.

No.

No no no.

Something was not allowed to happen while we were away.

The Poltergeist's Ship

The one week I left!

Tilly ran up to me, jumping up and pawing my legs. I stroked her head, then crouched down beside Edie, tucking her dark brown hair away from her face. She twitched her nose, then yawned. Opening her eyes, she realised it was me. 'Mum. Hi,' she said sleepily.

Tilly jumped on to the sofa, flitting between Edie and me. We both stroked her while we talked.

'What happened?'

Something had to have happened. The atmosphere. How tired Edie was. How quiet Maggie's house was. The *darkness*.

Maggie sighed. 'Come on. Let's talk in the kitchen.'

Edie rolled over, facing the back of the sofa and wrapping her arm around Tilly, who happily snuggled into her. At least some things never changed.

We closed the kitchen door behind us. Ben, Fadil, and I settled into chairs around the dining table as Maggie made us each a cup of tea. She didn't offer us any snacks. She *always* offered guests snacks.

When she'd said she couldn't pick us up from the airport, I'd known something was wrong, but I hadn't expected it to be on this scale. I'd spent the flight trying to convince myself Abigail had the chickenpox or something.

I tried to get Maggie to tell us what'd happened a few times, but she ignored me as she made our drinks. She *never* ignored me.

Fadil, meanwhile, looked more exhausted than ever. Something told me it wasn't just lack of sleep that was responsible.

As Maggie was taking the teabags out of the mugs, I walked over to her and put my hands on her arms. 'Mags, if you don't tell me I'm going to wake Edie up.'

'She needs to rest,' said Josh, walking in and closing the door.

Maggie looked like a deer in headlights as she turned to see her oldest standing there.

'It's OK, Mum. You need to rest, too,' said Josh.

'I'm fine, honestly.'

'You're not fine, Mum. You haven't stopped since he left.'

'Since he *left*?' I echoed. Had Harry left them? Oh my god. Talk about the worst-timed holiday ever.

But why would Harry leaving make the house feel so dark?

Josh sighed, gesturing to the dining table. All five of us sat round it, then Josh filled us in on what'd happened: Harry's strange behaviour, Edie's suspicions, the warding, their confrontation. That explained the debris on their front drive: it was the remains of their gargoyle.

Maggie slid my amber amulet across the table to me. It was cracked. It'd never failed me before, but now I doubted it'd ever work again.

'We don't know where he went or what he wants. All we know is that when Edie touched him, it burned his skin. And he mentioned Edie's great-grandmother,' said Josh.

'Why? Which grandmother?' I asked.

'He implied there was more to Edie's powers than we knew but didn't say any more than that,' he replied.

What else could there possibly be?

The Poltergeist's Ship

'Do you think your mum might know?' asked Maggie.

I grumbled. 'Who knows with her? She plays more games than a professional chess player. Even if she did know, I doubt she'd tell us.'

Fadil was practically asleep at the table, his head lolling forwards towards his cup of tea. I moved it away so that he wouldn't fall into it and could get the rest he needed.

'It's probably still worth consulting her on something like this,' said Ben.

I tightened my jaw. She'd just *love* me to go crawling back to her after refusing to speak to her for months. Although I supposed for her it wouldn't feel like that long. 'It's probably on Javi's side.'

'Even so, Nika is the only lead we have. It's worth exploring,' said Ben.

'I think that's a problem for another day, to be honest,' said Josh. 'I'm more worried about Edie. She really drained herself last night. And she was talking in her sleep about Dominic and Goodfellow, and how they were small fry.'

'Small fry to what?' said Maggie. 'Why didn't you wake me?'

'You were napping with Abigail. I didn't want to disturb you,' he said. 'And I really didn't want Abigail to hear what Edie was saying. Not with how freaked out she's been.'

'How is Abigail?' I asked.

'She's only spoken to ask for something to eat,' said Maggie. 'It's not like her. We're going to see Alanis later, but I'm not sure what good it will do with him still out there.' She sipped her tea, looking dejected. 'Do you think Edie was saying that the demon inside of Harry is worse than Goodfellow or Dominic?'

'That was the impression I got, yeah,' said a solemn-looking Josh.

Ben and I exchanged worried glances. Worse than Dominic? Than Goodfellow? We'd only just survived taking them down. Could we really handle a demon who'd broken free and was now without restraints?

I was proud of how Edie had stood up for the people she cared about on her own, but I was terrified, too.

If the demon that had possessed Abigail was still out there, and it was now inside of Harry – a fully grown man with a comfortable pay cheque and who blended in with his average looks (sorry, Harry) – what was its plan? What would it do next?

If it'd been possessing Harry for eight months before the reveal – and it'd really only happened because Edie had figured out that something was wrong – that meant it was willing to play the long game. The demon could be back tomorrow, in six months' time, or when Edie had a family of her own.

I had no doubt that it was her the demon wanted, though. She'd exorcised it last time when new to her powers. None of us had known what she could do back then, or the toll using her powers had on her. The demon had been caught off guard then, too. I doubted it would be again.

The Ghost Hunter's Haunting

Being able to see ghosts is one thing. Being tormented by them at school? Doesn't exactly make it easy to pay attention in class.

And right now, a ghost I don't even know really wants my attention. Why now? If only I knew. More importantly, what does he want? And how the bloody hell can I get rid of him without my entire school finding out?

Meet teenage Niamh, Javi, and Maggie in *The Ghost Hunter's Haunting*, a companion prequel to the *Afterlife Calls* series. Available exclusively to mailing list subscribers.

Get your free copy today: https://www.kristinaadamsauthor.com/the-ghost-hunters-haunting/

NB: This book was previously called *The Mother's Lesson*, so you may still see it called that in some places.

The Dead Man's Blood

The seventh *Afterlife Calls* adventure is coming soon. Make sure you're on my mailing list and/or following me on social media to be the first to find out more.

I haven't written the blurb yet, so I'll leave you with this: we finally meet some vampires.

Acknowledgements

This book. Where do I even begin?

When I started the *Afterlife Calls* series, the plan was to stretch myself as a writer with each book. Well, with this, *The Mean Girl's Murder*, *The Witch's Sacrifice*, and *Hollywood Heartbreak*, I have definitely done that. Over and over and over again. (And it's not over yet.)

A big thank you to Chelle, without whom I'm not sure I'd have finished this or *Hollywood Romance*. Your notes have been invaluable. And I'd just like to apologise in advance for the slew of stupid questions coming your way for *The Dead Man's Blood*.

Also thank you to Chelle's mum, Trish, for answering my cruise-related questions. And to Emma Cruises on YouTube, who helped me picture what a cruise ship would be like, since I've never been on one. And had no desire to go on one until I started writing this book.

Thanks to Susan and Carol in my Facebook readers' group for sharing their cruise ship stories, and Julia and Ciera for naming Shane and Luca.

Thank you to Alexa, for always listening and helping bounce ideas around.

Thanks to Charlotte and Cassie for beta reading this and being amazing sounding boards. And to Nicole and Jodie for spotting things that I missed from having read it far too many times!

And thanks to Lauren, for keeping me in food, acting as my therapist, and hosting a lovely book reading last Halloween.

Also by K.C.Adams

Afterlife Calls
The Ghost Hunter's Haunting
The Ghost's Call
The Mummy's Curse
The Necromancer's Secret
The Mean Girl's Murder
The Poltergeist's Ship
The Dead Man's Blood

Writing as Kristina Adams

What Happens in Hollywood Universe

What Happens in…
What Happens in New York
What Happens in London
Return to New York
What Happens in Barcelona
What Happens in Paphos

Hollywood Gossip
    Hollywood Gossip
    Hollywood Parents
    Hollywood Drama
    Hollywood Destiny

    Hollywood Heartbreak
    Hollywood Romance

Standalones
    Behind the Spotlight
    Hollywood Nightmare

Boxsets
    Welcome to the Spotlight
    What Happens in… books 1 and 2
    What Happens in… books 3 - 5
    What Happens in… the Complete Collection
    Hollywood Gossip books 1 - 3

Nonfiction
    How to Write Believable Characters
    Writing Myths
    Productivity for Writers

Poetry
    Revenge of the Redhead

Milton Keynes UK
Ingram Content Group UK Ltd.
UKHW030820010824
446082UK00003B/55